GENES, DOTS, & SPIES

A NOVEL

By David Bradford Welsh

For Ahlene

my wife

For your patience and support during the
many hours I spent working on this book

I thank you

ISBN-13   978-0615864792
ISBN-10   0615864791
LCCN   2013917380

CreateSpace Independent Publishing Platform
North Charleston, SC

Acknowledgements

I would like to first thank my wife Ahlene,
our sons Joe, Terry, Terry's wife, Clara,
and Professor John Ferling for reviewing
the drafts and making numerous suggestions.

I would also like to commend my colleagues
in the Claremont Writers Group and the
Cambria Writers Workshop who also
reviewed parts of the book and graciously
provided many criticisms and suggestions.

About the Author

David B. Welsh, a vascular surgeon and native of Massachusetts, graduated from Iowa State University. He received his MD degree from Tufts University School of Medicine and served with the Air Force in Japan for three years. After completing residency he joined the Southern California Permanente Medical Group at the Kaiser Hospital in Fontana, California.

Since retiring, Dave has written three novels. He and his wife Ahlene, a metalsmith and weaver, divide their time between Claremont and Cambria, California.

Genes, Dots, and Spies

Chapter 1

Ames, Iowa

Kate Summers let out a big sigh as she dropped her last final exam in the box on the proctor's desk. Carrying two courses and two labs along with her research had been grueling, but from this moment on class work was a thing of the past and she'd be free to concentrate on the research project and writing her dissertation. Another a year and a half at most and that PhD would finally be hers.

She spotted Jenkins, the other grad student with whom she shared a cubbyhole office in the Dawson Science Complex, come bouncing down the stairs to the lobby.

He called over, "You coming to the party tonight?"

Kate shook her head. "Wish I could, Dewey, but I promised the folks I'd drive out for a visit this weekend. I haven't seen them since semester break."

"You'll be missing a good time," he said. Jenkins was aware she'd recently broken up with her on-again off-again boyfriend and thought maybe he ought to ask her out sometime.

"I know," Kate replied, "but there are some things a girl just has to do. Remember, they still pay most of the bills, and my lab assistant stipend sure doesn't cover everything."

"Tell me about it." He laughed and kept going.

Summers continued up to her office to gather a few articles on gene sequencing she planned to read over the weekend and check her e-mails, then stepped out into the sweltering spring afternoon. She stopped at the house she shared with three other grad students only long enough to gulp down a glass of orange juice, toss her dirty clothes in a laundry bag, and then got back on Highway 30 heading west into a blazing sun.

When she passed by the shuttered old Mapleton high school she was surprised to find that one of the town's two drugstores had closed. Even the old pool hall where many of the locals used to hang out had a for rent sign in the window. She spotted Todd, her old boyfriend, in front of Colbert's Food Market with his arm around a girl she didn't recognize. For a second it made her feel a little melancholy but she knew Todd would never match her drive and that was what precipitated the break-up.

Kate's father worked the four hundred and fifty acres alone except at harvest time when he hired extra hands on a temporary basis, sometimes migrant workers from as far away as Mexico. He'd given up raising hogs some years earlier but still fed a small herd of Black Angus cattle. Kate's mother had made him promise to get rid of those in another year or two and stick to grain crops. Kate highly approved of that plan, believing that her folks deserved to get away once in a while, maybe even buy or rent a condo in Arizona to spend a few weeks during the long Iowa winters.

She glanced at her watch as she pulled into the driveway. *"Six-thirty, and I know just what she's going to say.*

Her mother came hurrying out and gave her a hug then asked, "You look so thin. Did you have anything to eat on the way?"

"No, didn't have time," she replied. Tired after finals and the long drive, Kate wanted only to lie down for a few minutes, but when it came to food she found it impossible to argue with her mother. She smiled and dug into the bowl of warmed-up stew and a salad while she began answering the same old questions about school, her friends, and if she were seeing anyone special.

Fortunately, living on a farm, her parents were early to bed people. They bade her good-night and went upstairs at nine-thirty. Kate pulled out one of the articles she'd brought, but when the clock over the mantle chimed ten she turned on the TV, slouched back on the couch, and closed her eyes for a minute. She didn't wake until a little after midnight with an annoying crick in her neck and the idiot box still blaring away.

Ames, Iowa

O'Leary groaned as he reminded the young student in the left seat to request clearance to land. They'd done five somewhat shaky touch and go landings already and it was time to head for the barn. As they banked to turn on final he noted the plane was drifting left and their rate of descent was a hair fast. "Tony, bring the nose up a little and keep an eye on your air speed. Remember the stall speed for this aircraft is fifty-five knots so nudge it back up to around sixty or so." He glanced around to make sure no other aircraft were in the vicinity. "The wind is out of the northwest so give it a little left rudder to stay lined up."

A couple of minutes later the Cessna 172 touched down with a little bump and they taxied to the tie-down area. As they headed for the parking lot O'Leary gave him an encouraging pat on the back. "That last one was probably your best landing so far. A little more practice and it won't be too much longer before you're ready to solo."

"Thanks, Brian. You have any lesson time next week?"

"No, but we can set something up for the week after if that's okay with you." O'Leary filled out the log and headed for his battered old Toyota Corolla. He smiled at the numerous deep indentations that resembled craters on the moon which always reminded him of that late summer day when it all happened in less than five minutes. The sky had suddenly turned a dirty grayish hue and the wind picked up making him wonder if there was a tornado coming. He'd pulled over to the side and hail stones, some larger than golf balls, had suddenly poured out of the murky sky. It was all over in a few minutes but it always prompted a little shudder when he recalled how scared he'd been.

As he turned into the parking lot behind the computer engineering building his cell phone buzzed. It was Mrs. Stoddard.

"I'm glad you have your phone on, Brian. The professor wants to see you in his office at two o'clock."

O'Leary wondered if he was about to be chewed out for something he'd either done or hadn't done. "Do you know what it's about?" he asked tentatively.

"Sorry, all I know is he wants you to meet someone, or more specifically someone wants to meet you. That's all I can tell you at the moment."

When he hit the 'End' button he wondered if that last sentence meant she didn't know or that she wasn't about to tell him. He glanced at his watch and decided he had time to run over to the Union and grab a quick lunch.

When he returned to Professor Evans' office a little before two, Mrs. Stoddard smiled and told him to take a seat. "He has someone with him I think you'll enjoy meeting, Brian. I think they'll be ready for you before long." She was the grandmotherly type and knew most of the computer engineering graduate students by their first names.

A few minutes later the intercom buzzed and she motioned for him to go in. The professor and a tall, well-tanned, gray haired man O'Leary didn't recognize were sitting in chairs flanking a low coffee table in one corner. Evans smiled and said, "Brian, I'd like you to meet Doctor Ted McGregor."

McGregor stood and held out his hand. "It's nice to meet you, Brian. Professor Evans was one of my teachers some years back and he's been telling me some things about you."

O'Leary suddenly realized that this was the Theodore McGregor, the founder and CEO of McGregor Industries, the outfit that made some of the world's most advanced supercomputers and was a major supporter of the university. "It's an honor to meet you, sir."

"Tell me a little more about yourself," McGregor said looking down at his notes. "I see here you applied for a summer internship with our company a couple of years ago but unfortunately we had to turn you down. I did happen to look over your proposal at the time and thought it had merit but back then the topic wasn't one of our priorities. Professor Evans tells me you're originally from Boston. What made you come out to the Midwest for college and grad school?"

"Well, sir, mostly because I wanted to see a different part of the country," O'Leary replied. "When I first came out to Iowa my plans were to go back East for grad school, but I liked it here so I stayed on to work on a PhD in computer engineering." He wondered where all this was going.

"I understand your father's a police officer."

"Yes, sir, he's a captain in the Boston Police Department."

"And Professor Evans tells me you've finished all your course work and are ready to begin writing your thesis."

"Yes, sir, that's correct."

"Tell me about it."

"Well, I've been doing research on quantum computing, trying to see if such a device might ever be workable. I've read a number of articles that seem to demonstrate the concept is at least feasible."

"I see," McGregor said with a smile, "and you've taken courses with Professors Howland, Hernandez, and Dalton. Sal mentioned your interest in that field and also that you've taken a couple of high level physics courses. They all speak highly of you by the way."

Even with his perpetual sunburn O'Leary was sure his blush must be obvious. *What the hell's this all about?* He looked over at Evans who was smiling, and then back at McGregor. "Thank you," he stammered.

"Brian, if I were to offer you a chance to work with those same professors I just mentioned on a project related to your own proposed research, even if it meant it might take an extra six months or possibly even a year or more to complete your PhD, is that something that might interest you?"

O'Leary glanced over at Professor Evans again who merely gave him a cryptic smile and then looked up at the ceiling. He turned back to McGregor and blurted, "Yes, sir, of course I'd be interested."

McGregor turned serious. "Before we go any further you must understand that whatever you learn or produce while on this project will be the sole property of McGregor Industries and that you must not divulge anything about what we're doing here to anyone without my express permission. Is that clear?"

O'Leary nodded. "Yes, sir, I understand."

"And you'll be required to sign a statement to that effect?"

This was happening fast and O'Leary already had plans for the summer. He hesitated for a millisecond but then grinned, "Yes, sir. Whatever this project is, I'm game."

McGregor glanced at Evans. "Okay with you, Professor?"

Evans merely nodded.

McGregor continued, "What we're doing is cutting edge and will require some travel. I'm sure you'll find it very interesting and you'll learn a great deal over the next few months. One more thing, I've also invited one of your colleagues, Harry Hickman, to sign on. Rather than telling you any more about what's involved I'll wait and let the principal investigators explain things to you. For the next three months or so you'll be dividing your time between here and Ontario, California. That's where some of the research is being done. Your first assignment will be to spend a few days there for orientation."

"Aren't your company's research facilities mostly in San Jose?" O'Leary asked.

"For this project I've decided to use outside people and facilities for the time being."

"I see," O'Leary replied, wondering why McGregor would go outside on something this big. Then he ventured, "I take it this project must have either a large profit potential or possibly security concerns."

"Very astute, and it indeed has both, young man." He glanced over Evans. "Professor, you have anything else before we wrap up?"

"No, Ted, I think you covered everything he needs to know for now."

McGregor reached in his jacket, pulled out an envelope addressed to O'Leary. "Ewen Howland wants you in Ontario on Tuesday. Here are your plane tickets and an advance to cover expenses. There's also an agreement to sign. You can read it over and leave it with Mrs. Stoddard. You'll also find a map that shows how to find the building we're renting. Welcome aboard."

On that note the meeting ended, and a very surprised and puzzled O'Leary took his leave. He now had a pretty good idea what the new two-story structure sequestered by tall, canvas-covered fences a couple of blocks north of the Durham Center might be for.

Once outside, O'Leary realized there was no way he'd be able to concentrate on the articles he'd planned to read that afternoon. Instead he drove back to the old house he rented along with several other grad students. It was a typical farmhouse dating back to the forties. Most of the farm had been sold off and houses constructed on sizable lots with plenty of separation. The house itself and its' associated out-buildings were surrounded on three sides by low fencing and rows of mature pine trees. The house had a porch across the front and a mudroom off the back. The downstairs had a large kitchen, living room, dining area, a small den, a bath, and two bedrooms. There were three more bedrooms and a bath upstairs. None of his housemates were in so he walked out past the garage to the old shed the group had converted into a workout room. It was outfitted with a large mat in the center and various weights and exercise machines scattered along the walls. He got on the treadmill for twenty minutes and then did a few bench presses and curls, all the while pondering what he'd just gotten himself into.

After his workout O'Leary showered and drove back into town where he pulled into the lot behind the China Moon. With most of the students gone, the place wasn't very busy. Tommy Lee, the proprietor, glanced up from the chess game. "Don't say a word, I think I've got him this time," he muttered, pointing at Hickman who was leaning back in his chair with a cryptic smile. "Help yourself to a beer, Brian. It's on the house this time," Lee said without taking his eyes off the board.

O'Leary popped open a Sam Adams and called over, "Thanks, Tommy, but no way will you ever beat Harry, not even in your wildest dreams." He pulled up a chair, looked over the board for a minute, and smiled.

Five moves later Lee scowled, turned over his king, stamped his feet, and let out a long string of Chinese expletives.

O'Leary really didn't know Hickman all that well but he'd heard the perpetual grad student had double majored in physics and philosophy as an undergraduate, had written a popular video game which he'd sold to one of the large Silicon Valley outfits, held a couple of computer software patents, and that he occasionally drove a blue Ferrari instead of the weathered brown Volkswagen Thing he used most of the time. "So, Harry, did you sign on?"

"Certainly did, and you?"

"Yeah, me too. The thing is that I really don't know what the hell it's all about. You get a ticket to California also?"

"Yes, but I still have a project going on so I won't make it out there for at least a couple of weeks. So, McGregor didn't give you any hint on what it's all about or what we'll be doing?"

"No details, but I have a pretty good idea."

"If you're thinking what I'm thinking, those things aren't supposed to exist for a long time, maybe never."

Mapleton, Iowa

Kate didn't sleep well that first night home. As much as she enjoyed visiting her folks, the family farm wasn't really her place anymore. She tossed off the covers around five, put on a pot of coffee and stuck a slice of bread in the toaster, then began reading several articles about a piece of automated equipment she was working on at the university that could read short lengths of DNA at a rate of five nucleotides per second with an error rate of about one percent. This meant at least two more runs on the same sample were needed for confirmation. Alternatively she was trying out an automated hybridization process where an unknown DNA sequence could be paired with several known DNA fragments on a chip, thus aiding in identification of the unknown portions. This could also be useful in detecting differences in DNA between individual subjects. Her initial idea of using mass spectroscopy so far didn't seem very workable.

Her hope was to leapfrog these methods by using high-resolution 3-D real time imaging of tagged DNA and mRNA. This idea wasn't unique, but thus far some of the techniques and necessary equipment weren't available. She believed that some of the schemes she'd bounced off her colleagues might lead to a better answer. O'Leary had come up with some suggestions on the computer end of things but so far didn't think there was anything powerful enough to support her requirements. She realized that if such a machine were built it would be nearly impossible for a grad student to secure time on it anyway. She wondered if Oldenberg might be able to help put together a proper grant proposal. In the end it would be up to her to come up with the means to stabilize the extremely fragile material to allow scanning without destroying the codons she hoped to identify.

At six-thirty her mother came down, kissed her daughter, and naturally made a full breakfast of bacon, eggs, and buttermilk pancakes. Kate had to admit it tasted much better than her usual morning fare in spite of all the cholesterol. She knew she'd have to work out more than usual over the next week to compensate for all the food she was bound to consume during her days at home.

Tokyo, Japan

Dan Oldenberg spent most of the day flying, first from Des Moines to Minneapolis and then on to San Francisco where he caught an ANA evening flight to Narita, the main Tokyo area airport located about thirty kilometers north of the city. He managed to sleep during much of the eleven hour flight, waking only for meals and visits to the head. When they touched down he could see many 747s parked by the terminals and waiting on the pad. After clearing customs, he shouldered his duffle and made his way to the train station. From Narita-eki he took a Keisei Honsen Express train to Ueno and from there the Ginza line to Tameike. A ten minute walk brought him to the embassy in Asakasa.

The young marine at the gate stared hard at the tall sandy-haired man in rumpled khakis and a navy-blue blazer with a backpack and lugging a duffel bag slung over one shoulder, somehow finding it difficult to believe he was truly the son of the ambassador. He asked for an ID and studied Oldenberg's passport before making a phone call.

A few minutes later Nakamura-san came out and shook his hand. "Konnichi-wa, Oldenberg-san. We've been expecting you. You should have let me know when you planned to arrive and someone would have met you at the airport."

"Konnichi-wa, Nakamura-san. I didn't want anyone to go to all that trouble. Besides, I know my way around the area pretty well."

Nakamura shrugged. "Your parents are at a reception right now but should be back shortly. I understand you plan to spend a few weeks down in Kyushu. How long do you plan to stay with us before you have to be there?"

"Ueda-sensei expects me in Dazaifu the beginning of next week."

On their way to the ambassador's quarters, Nakamura said, "If there's anything you'd care to see in and around Tokyo I can ask one of the staff to make arrangements for you. There's a nice young woman from Tokyo University who's spending a few weeks with us. She's studying for her doctorate in political science and wants to learn more about the relationship between the government and private industry in America. Perhaps I can ask her. Her name is Yukiko Kawakami and her father is a physician."

They ran into each other in the canteen later that afternoon, and when he saw her name badge he introduced himself. She asked what he was doing and he told her he'd come to Japan partly to visit his parents but primarily to study karate at a martial arts institute located in the small town of Dazaifu just south of Fukuoka. She seemed surprised to hear him speak rather fluent Japanese and asked where he'd learned the language.

"I was born in Japan. My father was in the service and stationed at Yokota. I started picking it up as a baby and later when he was stationed here again I went to a Japanese school for a year. When I was in high school I spent my junior year in Kyoto courtesy of the American Field Service. Later, in college, I studied it again so I wouldn't lose it completely."

"Are you still in school?"

"I'm working on a PhD in Foreign Relations at Iowa State University. I understand you're doing a similar thing."

"Yes, I am. Nakamura-san told me a little about you and asked if I'd show you around. He's asked me to do that with several visitors thinking that would give me some firsthand exposure to American thinking about your country's economics." She giggled softly and covered her mouth. "Of course the first place most of them want to go is Akihabara."

Oldenberg laughed, "Akihabara is where my parents bought my sister and me our first computer. I think it had all of two hundred and fifty kilobytes memory. We spent many pleasant hours with that little toy, so I can understand about the Akihabara attraction. I think I may still have it tucked away somewhere, but back to the city. Actually I know my way around pretty well but I'd certainly appreciate it if you'd point out any places you think I should see." He noticed she wasn't wearing a ring.

They ended up talking for over an hour and he invited her to have dinner with him that evening. It turned out to be the first of many evenings they spent together over the following week.

Ontario, California

O'Leary arrived in Ontario a little after two o'clock, rented a car, and asked the woman at the desk how to find the address he sought. It turned out to be in one of the many industrial complexes just east of the airport. He was surprised there wasn't a sign for McGregor Industries on the drab gray concrete structure, and that it differed from its neighbors only by the presence of a guard at the entrance. "My name is Brian O'Leary. I'm here to see Doctor Howland."

The portly, red-faced guard glanced at his list, examined O'Leary's driver's license, and looked closely at his face before nodding. "Okay, I'll buzz you in," he grunted.

O'Leary spotted two cameras on swivel mounts just below the roofline. *Damn, there's a lot of security here.* He pushed open the heavy door and felt the welcoming cool of the air conditioning.

The pretty young woman behind a desk smiled and extended her hand "We've been expecting you, Mr. O'Leary. I'm Cindy Murray. Doctor Howland is out running some errands and asked me to help get you settled in. I've reserved a room for you at the Marriot. It's only a mile from here and right near the airport."

Her smile was warm, her thick light brown hair pulled back in a ponytail, and her blue eyes seemed to sparkle. He figured she was in her early to mid- twenties and thought she was gorgeous. "Hey, just call me Brian. How long have you been working here?"

"Actually only a few days. Last summer I worked in the San Diego office but since I finished school in LA they asked me to fill in up here for a couple of months."

"What school?"

"UCLA law school, I graduated about ten days ago."

"This doesn't seem like the ideal job for a lawyer," O'Leary observed.

"Of course not, my father is a lawyer and does a lot of work for McGregor Industries. He knows Doctor McGregor personally and that's how I got this job. When we close up here I'll be moving to Ames where you go to school. I'm supposed to work mostly on contracts and handle legal problems regarding this project. I admit I'm a little nervous about it." She smiled, "You know, Doctor Howland has said some nice things about you."

O'Leary grinned. "Cindy, you just made my day. He'd never say anything like that to my face. Howland's a pretty hard taskmaster. Let me buy you a cup of coffee."

Cindy let out a laugh. "Some offer. C'mon, I'll show you where the coffee pot is. It's always on, and the one who empties it has to refill it."

Ewen Howland, the oldest of the three engineers working on McGregor's newest computer under development in Ames, found them in the break room. "Brian, looks like you found the place all right. Has Cindy showed you the lab?"

"Not yet. I arrived only a few minutes ago and she's been telling me about the area and how to find the hotel where I'm supposed to stay."

"Well, I hate to break up this little party but it's time to get down to business. I'll give you the dime tour."

The lab, although spacious, was cluttered with all types of equipment scattered on workbenches and desks and piled on shelves. O'Leary's eyes immediately settled on something against the far wall.

"Is that a prototype of McGregor's new supercomputer over there, the one they're calling the Super G?"

"That it is."

"So what's all the other gear for?"

"What do you think it's for?"

"I'm not sure, but Hickman and I wonder if you're looking at trying to build a quantum computer."

"Good guess. Hernandez and Dalton and I needed a couple of grad students to help and I mentioned your names to Professor

Evans and McGregor. He had you checked out. We're doing some of the research here until the new building in Ames is finished."

Howland spent the next two hours explaining what they were doing in much greater detail. Finally he stood up, stretched, and glanced at his watch. "My wife and I are renting a small apartment in Rancho Cucamonga. We usually start around eight o'clock but we often work pretty late. See you two in the morning."

Cindy was still at her desk trying to sort through some of the paperwork when Howland left. "Are there any restaurants close by you'd recommend?" O'Leary asked.

"Lots of 'em. The one at your hotel is supposed to be okay but I've never eaten there."

O'Leary smiled, "Say, if you don't have any plans for dinner why don't you join me? It'll be my treat."

She looked closely at him for a second then smiled back. "Sure, I tried the Macaroni Grill over in Rancho Cucamonga recently and it was pretty good. That okay with you?"

"Sounds fine to me. It's almost seven. Want to go now?"

"Sure, but since you don't know your way around the area yet, why don't you let me drive?"

Cindy's car was an ancient Buick Riviera, and O'Leary whistled when he saw it. "How long have you had that thing? Rivs were one of the first cars to have a computer screen."

"Since I started college. My older brother had it before me and my mother drove it for at least a dozen years before that. It's always breaking down now and it's hard to find parts anymore. I guess it's almost ready for the junkyard. I'll try to sell this one on E-Bay when we close up here and get a new one when I move to Ames. I tried out a Toyota Camry the other day and I was impressed with the room and how easy it was to drive and the better mileage."

"Nice. I have this old beat-up Corolla that's hard to start, especially in the Iowa winters."

The Macaroni Grill was located in a shopping center on Foothill in Rancho Cucamonga, and had become a popular place among the locals both for the good food and entertainment that varied nightly. This evening they had a singer who was actually a music professor at one of the area's many universities. He played the piano and sang mostly popular songs and oldies, but every once in a while someone would ask him to sing something else. Cindy raised her hand and asked if he'd do something from an opera.

He waved back and gave her a smile, then sang something she recognized from La Boheme. When he'd finished he came over to their table and sat down for a minute.

O'Leary asked if he sang here often and if it was common for someone to request opera.

"No, I don't get a chance to perform very often due to my teaching load, and no, almost no one requests opera. I sing here once in a while mostly because I enjoy it. Besides, my wife and I like the extra money. Teaching for the state university system has its good points, but a huge salary isn't one of them. Most of us in the department supplement our incomes by giving private lessons or doing a gig here and there."

When he'd left O'Leary asked, "Where did you learn about opera, Cindy? I've never been to one."

"My folks both like it a lot. They had it on either the radio or the stereo all the time when I was growing up. I just sort of learned to enjoy it by osmosis. Now I listen to it when I'm reading. I've been to the LA Opera a couple of times when someone in my parents' group couldn't go and there was a free ticket."

"Mostly the people I hang around with like to go to the local pub and hear one of the contemporary groups," admitted O'Leary, "but I really enjoyed listening to him."

"I like almost all kinds of music," Cindy replied. "A lot of the modern composers and lyricists have been influenced by older music styles, like opera. You ever take any music courses or play an instrument, Brian?"

"Oh yeah, my folks made me take trumpet lessons when I was a kid. They had me practice a half-hour a day. I had to go down in the basement and practice quietly with the mute on and the door closed."

"Poor baby! That's no way to learn to enjoy music," Cindy laughed. "That must have been a real turn-off."

"It was, but don't blame my parents. They thought they were doing the right thing by exposing me to a little culture." O'Leary was now a bit on the defensive. It was okay for him to blame his folks for something, but not someone else.

Cindy couldn't help noticing his reaction. "My parents did sort of the same thing with me about sports. They made me play soccer and take swimming lessons and skiing lessons when I was real little. That turned me off for a long time, but eventually I started doing those things on my own and found that I really liked them."

The remainder of O'Leary's two weeks in California flew by with long days spent learning about the new computer and the many evenings he spent doing things with Cindy. Finally it was his last day in Ontario before he was due to fly back to Iowa and Cindy had a suggestion. "I know of a Japanese restaurant only a mile away that's good, want to give it a try tonight?"

They pulled into a crowded parking lot just off the 10 freeway and made their way to the entrance.

"Irashaimasu!" rang out the traditional welcoming greeting from the diminutive Japanese hostess as they entered. They ducked under the decorative green piece of cloth hanging from the door frame. When he asked what it was for she told him it was a common tradition in Japanese restaurants and it was called a *noren*. They were shown to a table near the back where they could see into the kitchen and scanned the menu with some difficulty due to the low lighting.

"What do you think about this sukiyaki for two in the upper right hand corner?" O'Leary asked.

"I'm game. Shall we go whole hog and try the sake instead of beer or a coke?"

"I've never tried sake," O'Leary said. "That's rice wine, isn't it?"

"I think so; I've never tried it either," Cindy admitted.

"To understand this kind of food we need Oldenberg. He and I rent a house along with two girls who are also graduate students. Dan's spending time studying karate in Japan this summer."

"Sounds like an interesting guy."

"He is. You'll meet him when you get to Ames."

A waitress took their order and soon brought a small ceramic bottle and two thimble size cups. She poured a bit of the warm liquid from the bottle into each of their cups and said, "Be careful, just a little goes a long way." She also asked if they wanted forks.

"No thanks," Cindy replied, "we'll use chopsticks.

O'Leary tried the sake first, and made a slight grimace. "Taste's different, but not bad. I'm not used to warm drinks unless it's tea or coffee."

Cindy tried hers, but sipped more slowly. "Maybe I could get used to this. It tastes strong, and there's got to be more alcohol in this than in regular wine."

"There sure must be," he said as he refilled their cups.

The first course was miso soup. "You drink it from the bowl and pick up those white cubes with chopsticks," Cindy told him. "They're called tofu, a type of bean curd."

A small salad came next. The waitress noticed O'Leary was having difficulty with the chopsticks and showed him how to use them properly.

"What are they called in Japan?' he asked.

"They're called *hashi*." She poured what Cindy told him was cooking oil in the wok and lit the gas, then began adding vegetables and thinly sliced meat using a pair of long chopsticks. When it began to sizzle she deftly placed first the vegetables and then the meat on their plates. "Enjoy," she said with a smile. "I'll check back with you in a few minutes."

When their waitress returned with the bill, she asked, "How did you like it?"

"I liked it a lot, better even than when I tried it before" Cindy replied.

"It was really good," O'Leary added, patting his stomach and smiling.

The next morning he said good-bye to Howland, kissed Cindy, and turned in his rental car. During the flight back to Des Moines he tried to concentrate on some papers Howland had given him to read but his mind kept drifting back to Cindy and how much he missed her already.

Dazaifu, Japan

Oldenberg's first day at Udea-sensei's institute in Dazaifu began before dawn with an hour of mediation followed by a typical Japanese breakfast consisting of miso soup, grilled bonito, rice, a sweetened rolled omelet with vegetable and tiny bits of meat called *tamagoyaki*, seaweed pressed into thin sheets used to pick up the rice and *tamagoyaki,* and of course *oocha*. After the meal, the twelve novices for the summer session knelt on tatami mats facing the master. There was one other American and the rest were all Japanese. Ueda-*sensei* had each pupil tell the group their name and where they were from. Next he asked everyone to describe their previous martial arts training, which in each case was quite extensive.

After the introductions, everyone assembled in the *dojo* and the training began in earnest, beginning with the customary stretching exercises followed by having them pair off to practice various basic moves under the watchful eye of an instructor. By the end of the day Oldenberg was sore all over. After a long soak in the steaming *ofuro* the novices ate supper together in the dining hall which this evening consisted of rice, vegetables, and a small portion of fish.

After the meal Oldenberg had a chance to talk with Cruz Lopez, the other American. Lopez turned out to be from Washington DC, and proved to be very interesting. He was considerably older than the rest of the group, a short, stocky man sporting a beard tinged with gray. When Oldenberg asked what he did in the States, Lopez told him he'd started out in the seminary with the intention to become a priest but became disillusioned and dropped out. Soon after that he joined the navy and when his tour was up returned to college. After graduating, he worked as an engineer for IBM in Poughkeepsie and now ran his own karate *dojo* in DC.

Oldenberg asked if he was married.

Lopez frowned. "Once, it was back when we were in college. I was beginning to grow up but she wasn't about to do that. She was the quintessential flower child. Anyway, it was after that when I became interested in religion again. I ended up getting a mail order license on the internet that said I was now a minister. I've actually married several friends and performed a couple of funeral services. For an extra ten dollars I could have been a bishop but figured that was a bit presumptuous."

"What made you come here to the institute?"

"I felt I needed to learn more, you know, explore the spiritual side of karate and the other disciplines. What about you, how did you end up here?"

"I've spent time in Japan on several occasions because my parents were stationed over here," Oldenberg replied. "I began karate lessons when I was in grammar school and came to enjoy it. It's the way I stay in shape. What did you think about today's session?"

"Man, I thought I was in good shape but now I not so sure anymore." Lopez massaged his sore knee and smiled. "I hope this old body can hold up for the duration."

"I'm pretty sore myself. I hear he really pushes everyone pretty hard."

"That's what I heard from a friend who spent a couple of months here three years ago. He was the one who suggested I give it a try."

Chapter 2

Tokyo, Japan

It was late on a Friday night when Oldenberg eased out of his seat on the Shinkansen, shouldered his duffle, and headed for the east exit of Tokyo station where he found a taxi. The trip had taken over seven hours counting the local train from Dazaifu to Hakata where he'd boarded the Hikari bullet train. When he finally arrived at the embassy he found his father still at his desk catching up on the never-ending pile of paperwork.

Oldenberg senior peered over his glasses and exclaimed, "You look awful, Dan. Is it really worth it?"

"All the others in our group look just as bad if not worse, but the important thing is I've learned a lot from Ueda-sensei and his two assistants." He managed a weak smile. "Our days begin at dawn and aren't over until after dark. Anyway he let us have a long weekend so I decided to come back for a couple of days."

"Well, your mother's already turned in so you'd better go get some sleep yourself. You can tell us all about it in the morning."

When Dan sat down to an American breakfast of cereal, eggs, and toast for a change, his mother studied his face. "What have they been doing to you? You've got a black eye and a big welt on your neck."

"It's okay, they're fading. Have you seen Yukiko?"

She smiled, "Ah, so that's why you made the long trip up here?" She glanced at her husband. "Oh, to be young again, right dear?"

The ambassador nodded. "Yukiko is a very nice young woman and all the staff says good things about her. Since it's Saturday and she won't be in, are you going to call her?"

Dan nodded. "I e-mailed her that I was coming and told her I'd call when I got in but it was late and I was exhausted. I even took a cab over here. I'll call her after breakfast."

"You must have been really beat to take a cab," his mother said. "You almost always use the subway."

"You're right, but I feel better now and my eye isn't quite so ugly this morning."

That afternoon Oldenberg met Yukiko and Junichiro, her brother and a junior at Tokyo University, at the entrance to the park that surrounded the famous Meiji Shrine, the home of many Japanese treasures.

"What happened to you?" she asked, involuntarily bringing her hand to her mouth. "What did they do to you at that place?"

"It's not as bad as it looks. None of us have any real serious injuries but we did get banged up some."

"Those bruises, they must hurt a lot."

"Some, but we're all getting used to it. At least the food is good and there's plenty of it."

"But you're thinner, like you've lost weight. Are you sure you get enough to eat?"

"I'm sure. You're right though, we've all lost some. I'm down to about ninety kilos. What have you been up to?" he asked, trying to get off the subject of how awful he looked.

The temple itself, situated at the northern end of the vast property, was crowded with visitors as usual. At the entrance, Dan watched as Yukiko and her brother each dropped a few coins in a box, bowed, and clapped their hands twice. He did the same and noticed their smiles.

"Have you been here before, Dan-san?" Junichiro asked.

"To this particular shrine? I think so but it was long time ago and I hardly remember it."

The weather was overcast, hot, and humid, and they were all eager to move inside the *Homotsuden*, an air-conditioned building holding ancient artifacts and displays collected from all over Japan. After spending an hour there Dan decided they should visit the *Shiseikan*, a more modern structure a couple hundred meters away that was devoted to the martial arts. Similar to Ueda-sensei's facility in Kyushu, this institution espoused *Budo*, a lifestyle that aims to seek one's niche or way of life through a combination of mental and physical training.

Yukiko's brother soon left to return to his dorm to work on a paper that was due. Dan and Yukiko found a *kissaten* just outside the grounds to escape the heat. He asked if she'd considered his suggestion that she spend a semester or two in the States given her interest in American politics and economics.

"I've been thinking about it quite a bit and I've looked on line. I really only need two or three more courses and I should be ready to begin my thesis"

"They've got some strong humanities departments at my school."

"I've sent for a catalogue and yesterday I emailed a professor from Japan who teaches there now."

"Good for you. I'm sure you'd like it," he said, squeezing her hand.

Monday morning, on the train back to Kyushu, all Oldenberg could think about was in three more weeks there'd be another long weekend and he'd see her again.

Ontario, California

Ray Brown greeted Hernandez and O'Leary at the Ames Municipal Airport as they boarded the McGregor Industries sleek Gulfstream IV. "I hear you're a flight instructor," he said to O'Leary.

"Yeah, with the university's flying club for about four years now, but I've never even been inside one of these babies," O'Leary exclaimed as he peered over Brown's shoulder into the cockpit, hoping for an invitation.

Brown knew exactly what the young man was thinking and smiled. "Well, feel free to take the right seat and ask all the questions you want. The weather looks good all the way out to Ontario. I hear you're closing up shop there pretty soon."

Hernandez said, "Right, and it's about time. Thanks for swinging by to give us a lift."

"No problem. I was heading to San Diego anyway to ferry a couple of board members up to San Jose for a meeting."

O'Leary lowered his six-two frame into the seat and slipped on the head phones. He looked over the instruments while listening to

Brown talk to the tower. He was amazed at the rapid acceleration and short rollout before the nose lifted off the runway.

Once they'd reached altitude, Brown quizzed O'Leary about his flying experience and ratings. Since it was a calm, clear day he let O'Leary take control of the plane for an hour or so as they passed over Nebraska and the southeastern corner of Wyoming. Brown took over when the air got a little choppy over the Rockies and on the approach into Ontario he gave a running commentary on the landing procedure.

O'Leary grinned and thanked Brown profusely once they'd touched down and taxied to the private area on the south side. "Ray, I can't tell you how much I appreciated the opportunity to actually fly a jet, and I can't wait to tell Cindy about it. She's been working here in Ontario and will be joining us in Ames in a few weeks."

"I enjoyed it too. Sometimes these trips get boring and it's nice to have someone to talk to. You seem to have a good touch and did very well by the way."

Dazaifu, Japan

Oldenberg sat on the *tatami* at the low table across from Ueda-sensei, only the third time he'd spoken to the master one-on-one.

Oldenberg-san, please tell me what you expect to take away from your time here with us?"

"Over the last few days I've reflected on the many things I've learned during my training, sensei. My karate skills have certainly improved, but it's more than that. I believe I can see things going on around me much more clearly and don't seem bothered by little annoyances the way I used to. I'm not sure I understand why that is, but it happened here. Have any of the others experienced similar feelings?"

"Most certainly, Oldenberg-san. This is precisely the lesson you were meant to take away from your brief time at the institute. I hope each of my students develops more confidence in himself or herself, and equally important a heightened tolerance for others." The sensei smiled. "As your own abilities increase so does your obligation to do good work for others. I hope you always remember that. I have great expectations for your particular group." On that note Oldenberg was excused.

Tokyo, Japan

Oldenberg, finished with his stint at Ueda-san's institute, had almost two weeks before he was due back in the States. He'd made two brief weekend trips back to Tokyo mostly to visit Yukiko, and had encouraged her to consider going to the States to complete her PhD. Upon arriving at the embassy his first stop was at her desk where he found her bent over a book.

"*Konnichi wa*", he murmured.

Startled, she looked up and smiled. "*Konnichi wa*. I was hoping you'd stop by." She stood up as he came around the desk to give her a hug. He would have kissed her but the others girls in the room were watching. He could just picture them averting their eyes, covering their mouths, giggling, and later teasing her unmercifully.

"I was hoping I'd find you here."

"Have you seen your parents yet?"

"Not yet, do you have any plans for tonight? If not, how about going to out to eat and taking a walk maybe? "

"Sure, I'd like that." She reached over on the desk and held up what she'd been studying. It was a catalog,

"Ah, so you're really thinking about doing it. It's a great school and Ames is a nice little city."

"I sent in an application but I understand it takes quite a while to process. Even if they were to accept me I probably couldn't start until the second semester."

Oldenberg had a thought. "Would you be able to start this next semester if that could be arranged?"

"Probably, but I'd really have to rush things here."

"I'd be happy to make some phone calls, or better yet I could ask my father to do it. An inquiry from him would carry more weight."

A few days later Yukiko received an e-mail saying that she'd been accepted for the fall term and would receive credit for the courses she'd asked about.

"What about living arrangements in Ames, Dan," she asked.

"They have grad student housing but most people prefer to rent an apartment. They usually share it with one or two other people. I'd be happy to look for a place for you."

"My parents said they'd help with the cost. I'll probably try to get an assistantship for the second semester."

Oldenberg was invited to have dinner at Yukiko's parent's home the following evening. They'd been extremely cordial during his prior visits and he was impressed by how well her father spoke English. While Yukiko was in the kitchen helping her mother, her father inquired about living arrangements. He particularly wanted to know what Ames and the university were like and if they were safe places for his daughter to live.

"Ames is a fairly small city but the student population itself is nearly thirty thousand. There's very little crime, nothing like you read about in larger places like New York or Chicago or Los Angeles," Dan replied.

That seemed to satisfy Doctor Kawakami who smiled back at him.

Oldenberg was aware that in general Japanese people often looked askance at someone dating a foreigner, and he felt the family probably suspected that he and Yukiko were becoming more than just casual friends. The fact that he spoke Japanese quite well had seemed to mollify them somewhat.

This time Yukiko's whole family was there, her sister, Tamiko, age twenty-one and a senior in college, along with Junichiro. Of course they'd heard quite a bit about him, and Tamiko wanted to know why an American would go all the way to Kyushu to study karate. After he explained that he'd practiced karate for years she talked him into demonstrating a few moves.

After they'd finished dinner Doctor Kawakami guided him into the study and asked, "After you complete your studies will you join the Foreign Service like your father?"

Oldenberg hesitated for a moment. "I've always thought that I'd follow in my parent's footsteps because they've enjoyed nearly all their assignments. I believe they've made a positive difference wherever they've been. I'd like to carry on the family tradition but I haven't ruled out teaching in a university."

Meanwhile in the kitchen, Yukiko parried her mother's attempts to learn how serious things were.

Around ten o'clock Dan took his leave and walked back to the embassy. He fell asleep dreaming of Yukiko.

Yukiko's dreams were more disquieting. What would her parents think if she were ever to marry a *gaijin*? How could she even be thinking like that when they'd known each other such a short time and seen so little of each other?

The day before Oldenberg was to leave for the States his mother took him aside. "You've been spending a lot of time with Yukiko. Your father and I think she's very nice. Are you two becoming serious?"

"C'mon, mother, we've only know each other for only a couple of months." He smiled and put his arm around her shoulder, "You're right though, I do like her a lot."

"Well, your father and I like her a lot too. She's a very nice young lady, and from what he tells me, she's done an excellent job here at the embassy this summer. He said she could have a job here anytime."

Ames, Iowa

Kate and Sheila Lawrence, the other person sharing the house, were busy in the kitchen fixing a welcome back dinner for Oldenberg. O'Leary and Hickman were supposed to join them but one never knew about those two. "What courses do you have this semester?" Kate asked.

Sheila, in her last year of Vet Med, replied, "It's all clinical now. I start off with the equine clinic and next it's other large animals before I can get to small animals which, as you know, has been my aim all along."

"Are you still planning to join your boyfriend in Massachusetts when you graduate?"

"That's the plan. Right now we hardly ever get to see each other. This long distance romance business is for the birds."

"You sure he's the one?"

"Pretty sure," she said with a little smile. "You've been seeing a lot of Harry the past few weeks. Are you two becoming a thing?"

"Oh, I don't know. He's fun to talk to once you get to know him. We'll see."

"I'm happy for you. You've definitely been looking a hell of a lot more upbeat lately. What's he really like?"

"Well, I think he might be the smartest person I've ever met. He does have a serious side. I've asked why he hasn't finished his PhD yet and he told me it's because he simply likes taking courses. He owns a really nice house north of town and has a cat named Socks. He's definitely not your struggling grad student."

"I've heard he owns a fancy sports car."

"He does, a Ferrari, but I've only ridden in it once."

"Where does he get his money?"

"He said he has an inheritance. He also told me he has some patents that pay good royalties but didn't explain what they were about. Guess I'll have to ask him."

Ames, Iowa

Oldenberg burst through the door whistling. He dropped his duffle on the floor, headed straight for the refrigerator, pulled out a beer, and plopped down in his usual chair. Then he noticed their smiles. "And what have you two been gossiping about?"

"Oh nothing, just girl talk. Now give us the scoop on this Yukiko. What's she like?"

"You'll see for yourselves in a few days. I emailed you that she's coming here for grad school. Her flight gets into Des Moines around three in the afternoon on Wednesday. I'll pick her up at the airport."

"Does she have a place to stay yet?" Sheila asked.

"I'll have to check with student housing tomorrow and also start looking for an apartment for her. I might have to reserve a motel room or something for the time being."

Kate shook her head. "No need for that. She could stay here in the spare bedroom until she finds a place, unless of course you'd prefer more intimate accommodations," she said with a coy smile.

Thy watched his face turn red and couldn't help laughing.

"Hey you two, I've only known her for a couple of months. Give me a break here."

A short time later O'Leary showed up. Shelia proceeded to grill him about Cindy Murray and what she was like, not for the first time.

"She's really nice, a lawyer and works for McGregor Industries, a lot of fun to be with and good-looking too. I'm sure you'll get along with her just fine."

Des Moines, Iowa

The Des Moines airport was quite small and Oldenberg spotted her immediately. He swept her up and gave her a kiss. "I've missed you. How was the flight?"

"Boring, but I slept some and read a lot. The customs line in Los Angeles took forever to get through."

He grabbed her carry-on and led her to baggage claim. "We'll need to get you registered tomorrow or the next day and I want to take you to look at a couple of apartment possibilities, but those things can wait for now." He kissed her again. "If it's okay with you the people I share the house with suggested you can take the spare bedroom until we find you an apartment."

"That's very nice of them. I didn't want to have to stay in a hotel if I could help it."

On the way back to Ames they told each other what they'd done over the past few days. He drove around the campus and pointed out places of interest before they went to the house.

Ames, Iowa

No one happened to be home when they pulled into the gravel drive shaded by a row of tall trees. Dan carried her bags up to the room and showed her around.

Sheila came in a few minutes later and found them in the kitchen looking over a map of Ames. "Hi there, you must be Yukiko. I'm Sheila Lawrence, one of Dan's housemates. He's told us all about you and we've been anxious to meet you. Welcome."

Yukiko reached out and grasped her hand, "Thank you so much for letting me stay with you while I search for an apartment. Dan's told me all about you and the others too, and he showed me your pictures. He said this will be your last year of school and you're going to be a veterinarian."

"That's right. We've planned a welcome dinner for you tomorrow at a place we go to in town. We figured you'd probably be too tired after the flights to do it today."

"I appreciate that. I did get some rest on the way but I was much too excited about coming here to sleep very long. What should I wear?"

"Nothing fancy, the joint is a combination bar and restaurant across the street from campus."

The next morning Dan helped her open a checking account and then they looked at apartments. She settled on one the first one they visited. It was located on Turnberry Court only a mile south of town. "You can bike to classes from there, but it gets awful cold in the winter for that. There are shuttle buses which I'll show you later."

"My father told me he'd send money for me to buy a second-hand car once I get an Iowa license." She squeezed his hand. "Do you think you can take me to where they give the tests?"

"Sure. First they give you a booklet to study before you actually take the test. They may want to see you drive but they may just accept your Japanese license for that part."

Later Dan drove her to campus to register and showed her around and then took her shopping. They returned in the late afternoon and Kate prepared a light snack for everyone before they were to leave for the welcoming celebration. Dan and Yukiko left for the party about twenty minutes after the others.

"Well, look what the cat drug in!" O'Leary exclaimed as Oldenberg and Yukiko wormed their way toward the China Moon's bar. "Listen up, everybody say 'hi' to Yukiko Kawakami. She arrived here from Japan yesterday to work on a PhD in International Relations. Yukiko, we've all heard a lot about you from Dan, and I assure you it's all been very good."

O'Leary whispered something to Kate, pointed at Oldenberg, and turned back to Yukiko. "This tall guy next to you never says much of anything, but you already know that. Even if he did want to say something, Kate and Sheila wouldn't let him get a word in so it probably doesn't make any difference."

"Just don't you believe a word he says," countered Sheila. "We have to put up with Brian all the time. We've learned not to listen a long time ago."

"Right," added Kate. "Anyway, all he ever talks about are computers. Boring!"

The banter went on until Tommy Lee whistled, waved his arm, and banged a pan on the bar. "All you regulars know the tradition. We welcome a new friend by ringing the bell and demanding a speech. Dan, has she prepared anything?"

Oldenberg shook his head.

"Ah….Daniel, then why don't you stand up and introduce your friend to the rest of our patrons," cajoled Lee. "I could go ring the gong."

"You do, Tommy, and I'll show you some new tricks I learned in Japan this summer. You really don't want to see those tricks, believe me on that."

"What do the rest of you think?" Lee called out loudly, looking around at the rest of the faces. Suddenly the restaurant became silent. Some nodded vigorously and others clapped. "Should I ring the gong? Will you guys protect me?"

"Sure, we'll protect you, Tommy. Go ahead, hit the damn thing," cried Sheila.

The gong was a large bell hanging over the bar. A tradition of the restaurant was that a patron might ring it if he or she had an announcement to make, or was celebrating something special.

"This qualifies, Tommy," encouraged Kate, "it's a special occasion."

That was all the impetus Lee needed. He grabbed the cloth bound wooden mallet from behind the bar and gave the bell a resounding blow. All the chatter stopped instantly. Most had been here many times, and were familiar with the meaning. Tommy hurried back to their table and hoisted Yukiko to an upright position. "Speech!"

"Tommy. I'm going to get you for this. Yukiko, don't be embarrassed. This is what passes for normal for this crazy place. Let me introduce you."

Turning to face the restaurant at large, Dan called out, "Listen up everyone. I want to introduce our very special guest for this evening. This is Miss Yukiko Kawakami. She comes to us by way of Tokyo, Japan, as part of our graduate student community and she'll be studying International Relations. We only hope she'll not be so embarrassed by the long-standing customs in this mediocre hole-in-the-wall that she'll refuse to return to partake of the watered down fare that Tommy regularly serves. She also requests an opportunity to beat him at chess."

Yukiko interrupted, "I'm not embarrassed, Dan. When I first arrived I felt like a small face in a big crowd. Even with you and all the people around, I felt a little lonely. Suddenly all this attention feels good, and I'm so happy to be here tonight that it makes me feel like singing."

"Oh boy," moaned Sheila, "all of you know what that means. Yukiko, I have to tell you a little something about another tradition in this place. Tommy Lee has a karaoke night. If someone says they feel like singing, they have to go up there to the bar, pick up the mike and sing." She grabbed Yukiko by the arm and whispered in her ear, "I'm sure you have a good voice because I heard Kate say she heard you singing in the bathroom while we were getting ready to come over here."

Lee stood up on a chair and clapped his hands for attention. Again the place quieted a bit. "Listen up all you Chinese food-lovers; we've got a hot one here. Yukiko, to whom you were just introduced, wants to sing a song for us. C'mon, Yukiko! Everybody give a hand for Yukiko Kawakami!"

With that the restaurant patrons broke into cheers and clapping and foot stomping. Tommy grabbed Yukiko by the arm and half dragged her up to the bar and thrust a mike in her hand. "We've got any song you can think of on tape or disc. Pick your poison, m'lady."

Dan was just a half step behind. "Yukiko, you don't need to do this if you don't want to. You didn't know the house rules. Nobody will be upset if you don't want to sing."

Yukiko took a breath and looked around, then looked back at Dan defiantly, "But I do want to sing. Tommy, there's an Irish song that's usually sung by a male tenor, but I learned it in Japan. Do you have it? It's called 'Danny Boy'?"

"I don't have it for karaoke, but I do have it on disc with voice as well as background if that would be okay?"

"Please play it, Tommy. I'll try my best."

One could have heard a pin drop in the usually raucous bar as Yukiko launched into a unique female version of the tune. It was silent in the room for a full minute after she finished, and then the applause began and went on for at least two or three minutes. The housemates were stunned. They congratulated Yukiko and asked where she learned to sing like that.

Back at the farmhouse Sheila again asked Yukiko about her singing.

"I've been taking singing lessons since I was a little girl. I once thought that I'd like to sing opera and dreamed I'd be the perfect "Madam Butterfly' and all that. Even after I went to college, I took lessons occasionally. I guess it's like what the rest of you do with the karate. It relaxes me. In Japan, American and European songs are very popular, even old ones like what I sang tonight. Dan, I guess I never told you about my singing, did I?"

"No, but it was beautiful, Yukiko, just like you are," beamed Dan. Now it was Yukiko's turn to blush.

Shortly after the group returned to the house, Yukiko said she was tired and went upstairs to turn in. Sheila and Kate immediately buttonholed Dan in the kitchen. "Yukiko is very nice, but not at all what I expected. I thought Japanese girls were all giggly and demure and walked in little mincing steps. I was amazed when she stepped up and did that song. Good voice too. She was a damn good sport"

Ames, Iowa

The spacious windowless room designated for the Super G machine was located on the ground floor the new two-story building designed specifically for the two computers. Large racks holding power supplies, memory banks, and servers dominated one side of the room. In the center were three work stations. Cabinets and desks and floor-to-ceiling shelves sat against another wall. This area had its own temperature and humidity controls, much like a modern operating room. The front half of the first level across the hall from the computer lab contained offices with windows for the principal investigators, a conference room, and a break room. On the second floor were offices for the junior staff and secretaries, storage space, and a larger conference room. The heavily reinforced and shielded below-ground level was to be the home of the quantum computer they'd recently begun building. That portion of the structure was connected to the upper levels by many feet of color-coded cabling that lay hidden in the space between floors and in the walls.

There were already signs of personalization in the new quarters. Hernandez had stuck a printout over his workstation that read *Illegitimus non carborundum est,* and his chair was ergonomically designed for maximum comfort. It was here that O'Leary found Sam Dalton, Salvatore Hernandez and Ewen Howland loudly bickering over which radio station to listen to. Some things never changed. He and Hickman were still learning about the computer and testing the interface while the principal investigators worked mostly on building the QD itself. Dalton often managed to spend an hour here or there with the newbies explaining how they envisioned the new machine would work and had them reading countless obscure articles relating to quantum computing.

Getting the Super G computer up and running correctly kept everyone there most evenings until at least eight o'clock. O'Leary nevertheless made it a point to roll out of bed around six to go for a brief run or pump a little iron before showering, then ride his bike to the lab. Entry into the building required inserting a card into readers by the doors and punching in a personal code which irritated him a little. When he mentioned that to Howland, the man merely nodded and told him to get used to it, that it was a McGregor dictum.

One thing he and Hickman particularly liked about their new location was the chance to get to know their professors better.

They were surprised to learn that Howland's background was not in computer engineering. He'd majored in materials science in undergraduate school, gotten his PhD in Electrical Engineering, and only later drifted into computers where he'd made a major breakthrough in the fabrication of a special type of semiconductor.

Sal Hernandez, the consummate tinkerer despite his three degrees in computer engineering, all from UCLA, had grown up partly in East LA, partly in migrant farm labor camps, and partly in Mexico. One of eight children in a household poor in financial terms but rich in the quest for knowledge, he knew his father's goal had always been at least a college education for each child. While Hernandez's friends hung out on the corner and talked about one day owning their own low-rider, Hernandez either had his nose in a book or was working at some boring, menial job that nobody else wanted to help pay his expenses. His parents' constant pressure and encouragement had produced a most remarkable group of siblings including professors, lawyers, physicians, a businesswoman, and an accountant. Hernandez senior somehow had the foresight to make sure that each child was born in the United States, and hence entitled to become a US citizen. On three occasions this had required hiring a coyote to facilitate making it across the border. Like most of his siblings, Hernandez had obtained his education in the UC system, aided by scholarships, loans, and work-study jobs, one of which had been with McGregor Industries and ultimately led to his current position. Despite all the success he'd attained, Hernandez still preferred beer over wine and mowed his own lawn. He prayed his children would have that same impetus to excel, but it disquieted him to think that living with a roof which didn't leak and plumbing that actually worked might dampen their motivation. He hoped not.

McGregor had brought the two together specifically for this project, and now his insight and faith might be on the verge of paying dividends. Quantum computing had long been thought impossible or at the least highly improbable. The concept itself was not the problem, only the nuts and bolts of actually putting one together that would work. Quantum mechanics recognized that the very smallest bits of matter were constantly in motion. Its equations predicted the likelihood that a given bit of matter would be at a particular location at a given time by means of probability theory.

One afternoon Howland gave Hickman and O'Leary his version of things. "Quantum computing relies on the ability of certain materials to confine a small bit of matter, in this case an electron, in fewer than three dimensions, and on the particular properties of matter so confined. This confinement can be visualized in two dimensions by imagining a very thin semiconductor sandwiched between two layers of a different type of semiconductor material, each only a few nanometers thick. An electron in the middle layer would be trapped in two dimensions in a device called a quantum well. If one next imagined slicing the plane that made up the quantum well into many very thin strips this could then be called a quantum wire, a one-dimensional device. If one next cuts the quantum wire into multiple short segments these can be viewed as zero-dimensional quantum dots. The power of a quantum computing device lies in the various energy states that an individual electron can have at any given point in time. In some instances this might be two, and thus visualized as an on-off switch like an ordinary transistor. The key to the power inherent in a quantum device is the ability, or more correctly the
probability that your electron can exist in two, three, four, or more different states, the computing power rising logarithmically with the number of possible energy levels. Howland had made a major breakthrough in the fabrication of various semiconductors that could be made to so confine something as miniscule an individual electron.

Hickman and O'Leary had read numerous articles that went over what they'd just heard, but each time they revisited the basics it sharpened their insight. It irked O'Leary that they weren't allowed to take any articles or papers that related to quantum computing out of the lab, especially not anyplace where someone not connected with the project might see them and ask questions.

Ames, Iowa

Summers' assistantship required her to teach a lab section of the introductory undergraduate genetics course, the same class that had stimulated her to pursue a career in biophysics and molecular biology. Her ambition was to find a better way to read the human genetic code, something faster, cheaper, and more accurately than current methods allowed.

On this hot humid first afternoon Kate began by calling the roll and trying to associate each name with a face, not one of her strong points. She briefly reviewed how the genetic code resides within the forty-six chromosomes that determine each individual's characteristics, things like height and eye color, and how they carry information from one generation to the next in the form of DNA. She spoke of how in 1953 Watson and Crick had elucidated DNA's two stranded double helical structure comprised of a series of base pairs called nucleotides, each attached to the five carbon sugar ribose and a phosphate group all held together by hydrogen bonds.

She went on to discuss how in order to create new cells within an organism, each DNA molecule must first separate into two separate stands by breaking the bonds that kept them intertwined in a double helix. "The single strands then serve as scaffolding for the formation of proteins in a process called transcription. Groups of three contiguous nucleotides consisting of adenine, thymidine, guanine, and cytosine are called codons. They determine which of the twenty different amino acids combine in the proper sequence to make up a given protein."

After Kate handed out the lab syllabus she spent the remainder of the time answering questions, impressed with how much these young students knew already, and worried her introduction had probably been far too basic. It seemed to her that high school biology classes must have improved in the few short years since she'd graduated.

As soon as class was over Kate returned to the office and found Jenkins busy preparing materials for the introductory biophysics lab course he was scheduled to run. "How's it coming along?" she asked.

"Okay, but it takes a lot of time away from the thesis project. I'm not sure I can finish it this year."

"Me either. I'm still toying with that spooling technique I told you about. DNA is so fragile I'm not sure I can get long enough sequences to make it worthwhile. I'm going to talk with Gary Wong about it again."

"Didn't I see you at the China Moon the other night talking to Hickman?"

"Yeah, he and Brian were there and I sat down with them for a few minutes."

"He's one strange dude."

"I always thought so, but now I'm not sure. He seems like a pretty regular guy since I've gotten to know him better."

"He's been around here a long time. How old do you think he is?"

"Twenty-seven, only three years older than I am."

Ames, Iowa

O'Leary heard the distinctive ring of his cell phone and his mood immediately brightened.

"Hey there, you miss me?" she asked in greeting.

"You know it, babe. Where are you?"

"At a Ramada Inn in Kearney. Last night I stayed with a college friend in Denver and was late getting away so I ended up stopping here. I can't believe how fast people drive out here. I thought we were bad in California but these Nebraskans are something else. Besides, I'm exhausted from all these monotonous straight roads that stretch for a hundred miles."

"I can believe that. You should be able to make it to Ames by mid-afternoon if you get an early start in the morning. I can't wait to see you."

"Did you make a reservation for me?"

"We have an extra room at the house so you can stay there until you find an apartment. Everyone here's been looking forward to meeting you."

"That'll be great. I don't have any furniture so it'll have to come furnished."

"That might be difficult but we'll work something out."

"How are you and Harry getting along with the honchos?"

"No big problems. The hours are pretty terrible but we're learning a hell of a lot and they're good at explaining things. Well, Hernandez gets a little impatient sometimes, but he's a damn good teacher."

"Yeah, he can come across that way. Well, I'd better turn in. Sweet dreams, kiddo."

"You betcha. Can't wait to see you."

O'Leary pulled out her picture and starred at it for a minute thinking how much he missed this perky brunette with the cute smile and infectious laugh. Finally he sighed and turned his attention back to perusing the manual about coding instructions for the Super G.

Late the following afternoon O'Leary managed to get out of work early and took Cindy to look at apartments before they drove to the house.

She liked the second one they visited, a two bedroom townhouse with 1280 square feet of living space on Prairie View West Drive, only a short walk from the new building. "It's only eight hundred and twenty a month!" she exclaimed. "You can't rent a room in a private house for that most places in Southern California."

He tested the faucets, peeked in all the cupboards and drawers, and checked the heating and air conditioning, before finally pronouncing it satisfactory. "I think you ought to take it. I'm surprised it's still available with all the students back."

"The agent told me someone who was supposed to rent it backed out of the deal. As you can see, it's unfurnished but she told me where I can lease some things. It comes with all the major appliances and there's a washing machine and dryer available."

O'Leary took her for a walk around the area and showed her the stops for Cy Ride, the campus shuttle bus, before going back to his place for a late supper and to let her get acquainted with his housemates.

They decided she'd look for furniture in the morning and stock the kitchen a little. He'd pick her up at seven that evening to go for dinner at Aunt Maude's, a nice restaurant in downtown

Ames. Iowa

The weeks had flown by for the occupants of the old farmhouse west of town. Hickman was seeing Kate Summers on a regular basis. Yukiko and Dan shared a class together and usually studied at her place several evenings a week. Brian and Cindy would see each other whenever he wasn't stuck late in the new computer building, but those nights were becoming less frequent all the time as Howland was determined to speed up progress on the QD.

Despite their crowded schedules Oldenberg had pestered the others into working out in the old shed they'd converted into a gym. He was teaching them basic karate moves one or two evenings a week. Everyone seemed to enjoy the sessions despite the bruises and mat burns. They even talked Hickman into participating. Once or twice Hickman showed Kate and Sheila how to make fancier dishes than most of them were used to. Each of the little cadre seemed happy in spite of their hectic workload.

"So, Harry, how's this project coming along that you can't tell me anything about?" Kate asked, not the first time she'd brought the subject up.

Hickman shook his head. "Look, Kate, I made a promise. What we're working on is really something special, but it's the only thing I can't talk about, even to you. You don't speak with the people you work with about all your ideas."

"I talk with you about them."

"That's different."

"How's it different?"

"For starters you didn't have to sign a confidentiality agreement like Brian and I did."

Kate nodded. "I guess you've got me there, but I still don't see why you can't say anything. It isn't like the university is doing secret military research or anything."

"Nope, it's nothing like that at all. Let's drop it, huh?" He knew she was disappointed and gave her a hug. "Someday it'll all become public knowledge, but not for at least a couple of years or more."

Boston, Massachusetts

Christmas fell on a Thursday. Most of the staff in the new computer building had been scheduled to take only Christmas Eve and Christmas Day off, but Professor Evans told Brian and Cindy they could have Wednesday through Sunday to spend the holiday with O'Leary's parents. They flew from Des Moines to Chicago and then into Boston where O'Leary's father picked them up at the airport. Captain Thomas O'Leary, almost as tall as his son and a good twenty-five or thirty pounds heavier with a thick shock of gray hair, embraced Brian, then turned to Cindy with a grin, shook her hand and gave her a hug too. "You're even more beautiful than the pictures this big lug sent us," he said in his heavy Boston accent.

The family home was an older two-story like all the others on Eliot Street and only a couple of blocks from Jamaica Pond. O'Leary kissed his mother and Meagan, his younger sister. His mother latched on to Cindy again and kissed her on the cheek. "I'm so glad both of you could come out," she said. "We've been dying to meet you. You're all he ever talks about when he calls. Can I get you something to eat?"

"I've been anxious to meet you too, Mrs. O'Leary. Brian has all kinds of stories about growing up here. And no, we had something on the plane, such as it was."

"Just call me Mary, child. Brian told us you're a lawyer. You look so young."

Cindy laughed. "I'm twenty-four. I'm sure he told you that I graduated from law school last spring."

"That he did, and about how he helped find you the apartment and get settled in. Do you like your job?"

"I like it very much. Everyone I work with is extremely bright and hardworking. They're all bright and fun people to be around."

The brief holiday passed all too quickly. The couple attended Midnight Mass with the rest of the family, one of the few occasions either of them had been inside a church in several years. On Christmas they all took a walk around Jamaica Pond. Brian and Cindy, along with Meagan, spent Friday ambling through Boston Common and looking around the downtown area. Later they took the T over to Harvard Square where they had dinner at The Grafton Street Pub and Grill. That evening the trio watched the Boston Bruins lose a close one to the New York Rangers.

It was nearly eleven when they made it back to Jamaica Plain. Brian's mother discreetly probed for where things stood but didn't get a straight answer from either of them. Early Saturday afternoon they had to catch their return flight.

On the airplane Cindy said, "I liked your parents a lot. They're real down-to-earth people. Your dad told me that he used to jog with you and your sister and one day he raced you in the mile. Do you remember that?"

"I sure do," O'Leary said with a laugh. "It was when we were in high school. We both lapped him in the mile. The next day he went out and bought a set of golf clubs and hasn't run since. That's a true story by the way."

"Are you going to look like him when you're his age?"

"I guess I probably will."

"She put a finger to her lips and then smiled. "That wouldn't be bad at all. I think he's quite handsome. Do you know you even talk like him sometimes?"

"Whenever I'm back here for more than a couple of days the old accent comes back. I wasn't even aware of that until Megan pointed it out a couple of years ago."

Tokyo, Japan

Yukiko and Dan flew back to Tokyo to spend the holidays with their families. Dan's sister Liz also had come from DC where she was perusing a master's degree also in political science at Georgetown University. The ambassador and his wife invited Yukiko's parents to join them for Christmas dinner. As tradition required, Mrs. Kawakami presented Dan's mother with a gift, for this occasion a small *furoshiki* wrapped wooden box containing a pair of exquisite *Arita-yaki* tea cups. Mrs. Oldenberg took one out and politely examined it. "These are lovely, Kawakami-san. Thank you very much. Several years ago my husband and I visited the kiln where these were made," she said.

Dinner was served in the small dining room reserved for special guests within the family residence. After coffee and dessert they retired to the living room where the ambassador asked Doctor Kawakami, "What do you see as the major differences between the medical care systems of our two countries?"

Yukiko's father maintained that medical care itself was very similar, but methods of financing contrasted markedly. The discussion went on for almost thirty minutes with the others relegated to listening. Finally Mrs. Oldenberg suggested they let the young people give their views on the two country's education systems.

Everyone seemed to have a good time. Doctor Kawakami and his wife took their leave around nine o'clock. Dan, Liz, and Yukiko played a game of Trivial Pursuit before Yukiko had to leave.

Liz and Dan met Yukiko and her brother, Junichiro, at Ueno Kooen on Monday. Despite the frigid, cloudy weather, they took a long walk through the beautiful park covered by a sprinkling of fresh snow. They stopped for lunch at a tiny restaurant for bowls of *udon*, thick white noodles in a steaming salty broth, and of course, *oocha*, and also to warm up. Junichiro complained about how busy he was at the university. Yukiko admonished him that this would all seem easy if he went on to med school like his father. She told him he'd better get used to it, for although most Japanese students regarded college as a time for fun after enduring the traditional grueling high school years, those planning to apply for medical or graduate school were forced to continue the intense studying necessary to do well in the entrance exams. That afternoon they browsed the art shops and bookstores just to the south of the famous park.

Before leaving for the States, they again all had dinner with Yukiko's parents at their home. When Liz later questioned her brother about Yukiko, he confided that things were getting serious but admonished her to remain quiet. "We'll tell them when we know for sure," was all he'd say.

Mapleton, Iowa

Hickman drove out to Mapleton on the twenty-fourth to spend Christmas with Kate and her folks. The next morning they all attended a service at the Lutheran church. When they returned to the house Kate and her dad gave Harry a tour of the farm. While Kate and her mother were fixing lunch, her father spent time talking with Harry. He showed him around the farm and was impressed when he let Harry try backing up a four-wheel wagon. "Where'd you learn how to do that?" he asked.

"This is my first time, never driven one before today."

"I'll be damned. I don't think I've ever seen anyone catch on so quickly. You're not pulling my leg, are you?"

"No, it was easy and I have driven a tractor a few times."

That evening, when they had a moment alone, her father quizzed Kate about why Harry was taking so long to finish his PhD.

"He says he's in no rush to graduate, claims he enjoys taking courses in many different disciplines. He's extremely bright," Kate replied with a big smile.

"You like him a lot, don't you?"

"Yes, I think I do. He's fun to be around."

Hickman returned to Ames the following afternoon while Kate remained at the farm for an additional day.

Tokyo, Japan

Hidehiko Takayama, a thirty-four year old mid-level project manager at Yokohama Industries Limited, awoke disoriented and drenched in sweat. It was the same miserable nightmare he'd been having every night for the last two weeks and it showed no signs of letting up. He tossed off the quilt and rose from the futon, stumbled into the tiny kitchen and put on the kettle to heat water for tea. He stared out the window and for a moment thought he saw her face looking in causing him to almost break down.

They'd been very happy. Fumiko was pregnant with their first child, and they both looked forward to more. They had a decent apartment less than two kilometers from his office and fairly close to her parents. One night toward the end of her sixth month she woke him, "Something's wrong. I'm having cramps and I feel sick to my stomach. I think the baby's coming."

He'd rushed her to the hospital. The baby was born prematurely at twenty-seven weeks gestation with hyaline membrane disease, a scrawny infant weighing less than a kilogram. They named him Junichiro, but he survived only a few hours. He and Fumiko were disconsolate.

Ten days later the unthinkable happened. Fumiko's leg, swollen during the last two weeks of the pregnancy, was the problem. A massive blood clot had broken off and traveled to her lungs. She died almost immediately.

For several weeks Takayama felt utterly alone and numb and was unable to work. Simple everyday tasks like tying his shoes seemed to require a superhuman effort. For a while he contemplated suicide but gave up that notion because his elderly parents would eventually be dependent on him. Matsumoto-san and his co-workers were supportive and concerned, but he knew that couldn't last indefinitely.

One morning Matsumoto's office called and asked him to come in. Matsumoto poured two cups of *oocha*, handed one to Takayama, and cleared his throat. "Takayama-san, you have been an excellent manager ever since you joined the company, but after this terrible tragedy I think a change would do you good. Because of your fluency in English I've decided to offer you a position in the States.

You'd become our eyes and ears over there. Your task will be to visit large companies and universities to learn as much as possible about new technologies and products that might be of interest to Yokohama Industries. Would you be agreeable to this plan?"

"I'm not sure, sir. How long would it be for?"

"At least a few months, possibly a year or two. That will depend on whether you are able to make enough contacts that might provide information we can't acquire here, information that might prove valuable."

"May I have some time to think it over, Matsuda-sama?"

"Of course, but I'd like your answer next week."

Takayama took the train to Mashiko, a town north of Tokyo famous for its pottery, to visit his parents for a couple days. When he returned to Tokyo he visited the graves of his wife and their child and purchased prayer cards from one of the monks. He spoke by phone with several of his co-workers about the new position.

The following Monday he told Matsumoto he'd accept the offer.

Ames, Iowa

Tuesday morning Cindy Murray coped with falling snow and slush on her way to Des Moines to register for a course in patent law at Drake University. McGregor had indicated a couple of months earlier that he wanted her to take the exam so she could file patent applications. It would mean at least two trips a week to the city, but she wasn't all that busy in the office and thought she might enjoy learning something new.

That evening O'Leary went over to her apartment for dinner. After polishing off a warmed-up stir-fry, they moved into the living room and turned on the TV. As they sipped coffee he asked her to read what he'd written so far on his thesis. He watched over her shoulder as she scribbled a few notes in the margins and highlighted several punctuation errors.

"It looks good, but I really don't understand much of it. This quantum business is still like Greek to me."

"I have to admit this stuff is way out there. I still have trouble grasping some of the concepts myself. They told Harry and me that we can use it for our theses, but the hooker is they won't let us publish it for a long time. Howland, Hernandez and Dalton will serve as our committee so no one except the project members will ever see it for quite a while."

She seemed surprised. "That's unusual, isn't it?"

"Professor Evans told us it's been done before, but only rarely. He said he was involved with a similar situation several years ago."

Cindy, a little tired after a long day, set the papers on the coffee table and snuggled up to him. "Enough about our work," she said.

He leaned down and gave her a kiss, then murmured in her ear. "You know what?"

"What?"

"I love you, Cindy Murray." He felt her slight shudder.

She pulled back and looked up at him and starred in his eyes for a second, and then hugged him tight, "And I love you too, Brian

O'Leary, even if you are a nerd sometimes," she whispered. "I can't tell you how I've waited for you to say those three little words."

Chapter 3

New York

The JAL Boeing 747 touched down precisely on time at JFK after the thirteen hour flight. Takayama had a comfortable seat in business class and managed to catch several hours of dream-free sleep. He pulled his carry-on from the overhead bin and followed the long line of passengers to customs and immigration.

He took a shuttle into mid-town Manhattan where he had a reservation at the ExecuStay on 50th Street, a Marriott facility catering to business people. This one-bedroom unit would be his base of operations during his stay in America.

That afternoon he walked around the neighborhood for a couple of hours taking in the sights and smells and looking at the people who always seemed to be in a hurry. That evening Takayama studied the list of persons he was supposed to contact over the next few weeks and shook his head. He was sure he'd be traveling a lot and actually thought he might like that.

Fort Meade, Maryland

William Timmons, the Deputy Director of the National Security Agency, underlined a section in the morning brief covering the previous day's take and shook his head.

"Sir, you have a call from the White House on line two," Rita, his secretary, announced over the intercom. "It's a Mr. Whitman."

He smiled and wondered what his former protégé wanted this time. "Go ahead and put him through."

Timmons picked up the phone. "Hi, Brad, how are things over there?"

"I'm beginning to get used to the new job. It's interesting of course, but there's a great deal of pressure to make things happen yesterday."

"Ain't that always the way? What's on your mind?"

"I was at a meeting with Senator Slocum yesterday and I could use some advice. He's got a bug up his ass about industrial espionage. Seems he's getting a lot of flak from some big companies about the problem. He says there's a lot more pirating of proprietary secrets going on than I was aware of. Some comes from disgruntled employees trying to make a buck, but a lot, especially the more dangerous ones, come from overseas hackers. Anyway I got tasked to look into the problem. I've learned that both the FBI and CIA share some jurisdiction and responsibility in this area but neither of them has picked up the ball. Slocum wants the administration to set up a task force, one that includes personnel from both agencies, to evaluate things further and move everything along."

Timmons, remembering all the requests when he was an Air Force two-star before taking his current post at NSA, tapped his pencil on the desk as he considered the implications. "That sounds reasonable, Brad, but the problem I foresee is that since the directors of those two agencies don't get along there might be quite a turf war. How can I help?"

"You know both of 'em and you carry a lot more weight than I do. Could you possibly come to a meeting with me and the deputy directors?"

Timmons smiled. "You mean to be a referee and maybe twist arms a little?"

"Exactly"

"Okay, when?" he sighed.

"Will a week from Tuesday at ten o'clock work for you? That's when the good senator can make it, and could you come early so we can go over things?"

Timmons glanced at his calendar and wondered how much time this would require. "That works for me," he finally replied without much enthusiasm. "E-mail me a copy of the memo and send whatever else you have so far."

After he hung up Timmons leaned back in his chair and mused about how fast Whitman had moved up the ladder. The young man had spent a year and a half working for him at Fort Meade. Timmons thought the kid had a bright future in government service given an undergraduate education in engineering at MIT and then law school at Yale. Of course having a father who'd been a six-term congressman from Missouri didn't hurt either. Well, Timmons knew

the directors and assistant directors of both agencies and figured he might be able to encourage them to cooperate.
Washington, DC

Timmons fought traffic all the way into DC. He found Whitman at his small office in the EOB. "Who else is coming?" he asked.

"Senator Slocum, also Vance from the Bureau and Casper from CIA. They faxed me the names of possible candidates to take the lead." He handed over their several page resumes and evaluations. Timmons slipped on his half-frames and spent a few minutes going over them.

"This Sean Harrington is only thirty-five. I see he graduated from Boston College with a degree in business and served in the Marines. The FBI guy, Dougherty, is from Rhode Island and a former Air Force pilot with a master's from George Washington. He's thirty-six. They've both moved up pretty fast. You have any qualms about either of them?"

"No, but I'm having them vetted. You think they might be a little young?"

Timmons couldn't help laughing. "Hell, Brad, they're older than you are by a few years. Will either of them be at this meeting?"

"No, but if we decide go ahead with them could you to talk to 'em about starting up, you know, maybe give them some advice. Neither one has had much admin responsibility."

"I suppose I could do that," Timmons said after a slight pause, hoping that helping Whitman wouldn't take too much more of his time. "Probably be interesting actually, but before selecting the people you need to have a good idea of what you want this group to do."

"That's what bothers me. What Slocum's told me so far is all very vague."

It would be a few minutes before the others were due to arrive. Timmons pushed his chair back and glanced around. It was a small space and the furniture looked old. The walls were bare save for a couple of non-descript watercolors hung crookedly. "You'd better get your wife in here to spiff this cubbyhole up a little, Brad."

When the other participants arrived they moved to a small conference room just down the hall from Whitman's office. Henry Casper, the Deputy Director of the CIA, short and nearly bald, had a firm handshake and a good reputation. He'd spent his time on the intelligence end. Timmons had met him on several occasions and found him easy to deal with. On the other hand, Clarence Vance, the FBI's Deputy Director for Intelligence, was considerably overweight with a florid face and dour expression. Timmons had met him a few times and heard he was a tyrant to work for.

Senator Slocum had yet to arrive, but Whitman was anxious to get started. "Thank you for coming over today, gentlemen. I asked Director Timmons to join us since NSA also has an interest in this problem."

Casper and Vance glanced at each other and nodded to Timmons. Vance immediately brought up the subject of budgets. "Where's the money for this going to come from?" he asked. "The FBI is already stretched tight."

Whitman smiled. "The CIA and FBI will need to share funding responsibility equally. Senator Slocum was adamant about that."

Thomas Slocum, the crusty three-term senator from Maine and Chairman of the Senate Oversight Committee, showed up twenty minutes later and immediately took charge. "As I'm sure you're all aware, we're making things much too easy for foreign competitors to cash in on discoveries made here in America by our own scientists and business people. It's a terrible shame that despite all the laws congress has enacted to deal with this pirating of new technologies the problem persists, and indeed it's growing. Allowing this to go on and on the way we have, coupled with the current administration's determination not to piss off our so-called friends and allies, causes many of our best discoveries to wind up in the hands of these overseas crooks. Young Whitman here is supposed to outline the administration's plan to deal with this horrible menace to our national security. Son, you have the floor."

Whitman took a small sip of water, cleared his throat, and nodded to the senator. "Thank you, Senator Slocum. Gentlemen, this problem of industrial espionage is as old as American history itself, and I must admit that we've certainly done our own share of it ever since the time of the Revolution. But the tables have long since turned on us. We're the victims more often now, not the looters. Both my boss and the President himself have decided that change in the way we safeguard America's business interests is necessary and long overdue. It is our duty to protect that which is rightfully America's, and we need your help."

He continued, "We've had some preliminary discussions about how best to respond and the administration has concluded that it will require both teamwork and a coordinated approach on the part of several of our agencies. The administration agrees with Senator Slocum that an interagency task force should be created to deal exclusively with this problem. This effort must have the joint backing of the Senate, the Congress, and the White House as well as your individual agencies. Since much of the threat originates offshore but is largely carried out within our borders, it is logical that close cooperation between the Bureau and the CIA be the cornerstone of any overall strategy."

Slocum took over. "Gentlemen, I've discussed this with many of my colleagues on both sides of the aisle. Most are in agreement with this approach. Can I count on you to work with Mr. Whitman to make this happen?" He stared hard at Vance and Casper.

Neither responded verbally but both nodded in the affirmative. In reality they were given no choice but to agree since neither dared make an enemy of this powerful senator.

"What did you think, Bill?" Whitman asked once they were alone.

So it's Bill now, not Sir or Director Timmons anymore. "I think it went reasonably well, very pro forma."

"I'd really appreciate you giving me some advice about getting this thing off the ground the way you did at NSA."

"The first thing you need to do is to talk to your boss and be sure you have his support. You know it won't be one of his priorities despite the clout Slocum has. There are many more pressing problems facing the administration right now. Begin by putting down on paper exactly what you think this task force should do, how big it should be, what sort of budget it should have, where it should be based. Try to keep it clear and concise. Once you have all that worked out fax it to me and I'll go over it with you."

Langley, Virginia

Sean Harrington sipped his first cup of coffee as he perused the many messages that had accumulated during his time off. He and his wife and their three kids had made the drive up to Boston to visit the relatives. Vacations were almost always much too short, but spending the whole time with his extended family made him almost glad to be back at work. He'd had all he could take of Peg's brother who'd just been kicked out by his second wife. The kids missed their friends from school and were bored a good part of the time. There'd been a bunch of chores to get done around Peg's parents' old house. All in all it hadn't been very restful and a flat tire on the way back had topped it off. Even worse, he'd managed to get grease on a new pair of pants changing the damn thing. He punched up his schedule and muttered, "What the hell is this three o'clock meeting with Casper all about? This was supposed to be a catch-up day!"

Ruthie entered with a coffee refill and said, "The boss wants to see you tomorrow, something about a new assignment.

That certainly got his attention. Most of the work lately had been routine. Harrington, now a seven-year veteran with the CIA, was regarded as one of the bright young agents at the Farm.

She pointed to his in-basket. "A memo and something to read."

He leaned back, adjusted the light, and opened the book. The other memos on the desk would have to wait.

By noon he was more than halfway through the book and was finding it very interesting.

Washington, DC

James Dougherty entered the FBI Building and headed up the stairway to his office several floors above. He climbed the stairs now whenever he had the chance, in part to pacify his better half. She used the Stairmaster fifteen minutes a day religiously and was always after him to get more exercise and lay off the junk food. He couldn't argue since his waistline was two or three inches larger than the day they got married, but that had more to do with Claire's cooking than his lunches, at least in his mind.

Panting heavily as he pushed open the door to the fifth floor, he made his way to the office. The first thing he noticed was a manila folder and a book on his desk next to the photos of Claire, his two kids, and the one of himself sitting in the cockpit of an F-16. After finishing at UMass, where he been in the ROTC, he'd joined the Air Force and was sent to flight school. Four years later when Congress decided to cut back on flight billets he'd been given the opportunity to go to grad school at Uncle Sam's expense and obtained a master's in history at George Washington. When his tour was up he'd been recruited by the FBI. After his initial training he'd been sent to the Detroit office for a year and a half and then to Boston for a couple of years before being transferred down to DC.

The memo in the folder directed him to read the enclosed book in preparation for a meeting with someone named Whitman at the Senate Office Building later that same day. The book, by John Fialka, chronicled the history of industrial espionage in America. Despite his background in history, the subject matter wasn't something he was familiar with. He sat down and began to read.

Around two-thirty he leaned back, rubbed his eyes, and set the book down. He had just enough time to catch up on a little paper work before the meeting. He rang Claire and told her not to wait on him for dinner.

Ames, Iowa

Hidehiko Takayama spent a good part of the morning walking around the Iowa State University campus and wishing he'd packed better for cold weather. A few weeks earlier he'd heard that a prototype of the new McGregor Super G supercomputer was being installed for testing at Iowa State. It was rumored to be ten times more powerful than any machine currently in use but little hard data was available regarding its specifications and capabilities. His superiors in Japan wanted to know more, hence this visit to the frigid Midwest.

As he strolled around the northern part of the campus where the engineering and science complex was located he came upon a building that looked new and asked someone what it was for. The man told him he'd heard it was for a new computer.

Takayama mentioned that he was visiting from Japan and asked if anyone could go inside for a peek.

"I don't think so," the man replied shaking his head slightly. "I think they're still setting things up."

Washington, DC

Harrington, Whitman, and Timmons sat around an antique table in a small conference room adjacent to Slocum's office chatting while they waited for Dougherty to arrive. The senator hadn't made his appearance yet so Whitman explained what the meeting was about. "You've both been recommended by your agencies to lead a new task force whose charge will be to deal with our nation's industrial espionage problem. I was assigned to be the liaison between this task force, the congress, and the administration. I had no idea how bad some of our companies are being hit by this thing until I read up on it." He went on to discuss the scope of what would be expected of them, and his view of how it should be constituted and function should they accept the assignment.

"Aren't there already groups working on this same thing?" asked Harrington.

"Yes, but nobody accepts it as a primary responsibility."

The questions went on for another twenty minutes before Senator Slocum, a lean, white-haired man in his seventies, strode in and set down nodding at the other participants.

"Gentlemen, I assume you know why we're here. Industrial espionage is costing the United States billions of dollars every damn year, and the problem is that probably over half of the companies that have been ripped off never own up to that fact because they don't want their stockholders to know how loosely they guard the family jewels." He looked sternly at each participant in turn, especially the two candidates.

"Begging your pardon, sir," Harrington said, breaking the silence, "but is that the only reason those companies that have been compromised don't seek help, or is it because they have no confidence that anyone can or will do anything about the problem?"

"A bit of both things, unfortunately," replied Slocum, somewhat annoyed that he was called upon to answer a question. He was here to make pronouncements, not to give reasons or make apologies for what had been done before.

Dougherty asked "What is it about this task force that will be any different than what the FBI and CIA and Justice Department are already doing?"

Slocum replied emphatically, "That's the problem, people. There's no single agency in our government that's been willing or forced to take charge. We need some group, a task force if you will, that will take this on as their sole function. If you accept this opportunity, the project will become your mission in life for the next few years. How well you perform will determine not only how high you eventually climb in your respective agencies, gentlemen, but it just might determine how nice your retirements will be. Our good old Social Security and even our private pensions may not be worth all that much if we keep giving away the store. That's why I expect this effort to be different than some of the lip-service programs that have preceded it."

A few minutes later Senator Slocum glanced at his watch, stood up, and headed for the door. The formal part of the meeting was over. Whitman called for a break after Slocum and his aide departed. Harrington and Dougherty called their wives to inform them they'd be late again. Another aide brought in chocolate chip cookies and soft drinks. The meeting went on for another hour and both men decided they wanted to speak with their spouses before agreeing to take on the new assignment. They promised Whitman they'd let him know within a day or two.

"They're a little young for this sort of responsibility," Whitman observed after they'd left.

"You mentioned that before, Brad, and I reminded you they're a few years older than you are," Timmons chuckled. "Both of 'em asked pertinent questions and their credentials are good and their directors recommended them. I think you should go along with their choices."

"I suppose you're right."

"You understand that this is your baby now, and you'll need to stay involved."

"Yeah, I know that, just one more thing I'm stuck with. I'm not complaining, mind you, but they want everything done yesterday. Anyway thanks for coming down and giving me your input."

"Anytime, Brad."

Ames, Iowa

While they worked hunched over in the space between the first floor and basement level of the new building that would house the QD computer, O'Leary mumbled, "You know what bugs me about this gig?" He and Hickman were busy checking the labels on the dozens of heavy fiber optic cables that snaked down to the basement level. These would serve to connect the Super G to the experimental machine now in the process of construction.

Hickman, used to O'Leary's bitching, sighed. "What this time?"

"Everyone else can talk to their friends about what they're doing, about their research, about how their thesis is coming along, things like that. You and I aren't allowed to say shit about what we do here to anybody."

"Hell, I don't like it either, but that's the price we pay to be a part of this. Remember, we both agreed to it before we signed on."

"I know, and I haven't said anything. Of course Cindy knows some of it because she works with us, but the others keep asking and I have to keep shining them on. We can't talk about qubits or superposition or entanglement or almost anything to do with computers."

Hickman grinned. "Suck it up and live with it, man."

Laurel, Maryland

At Whitman's request, Timmons, the Deputy Director of the National Security Agency agreed to meet with Sean Harrington and James Dougherty for advice about how to build the new task force.

It was a Saturday morning and Timmons had invited them to his home in Laurel, Maryland. They sat in the study admiring the wood paneled room lined with bookshelves holding mementos of the Timmons' time in Japan as well as dozens of books and folders. Martha Timmons brought in coffee and warm muffins with butter and jam and left the men to their own devices. Timmons began by bemoaning how HUMINT had been gradually usurped by ELINT in the spy business. It didn't take long for both men to realize their prior training and experience had ill-equipped them to deal with this new project and they'd need to learn a lot more about computer security in a hurry.

"We had someone at CIA in mind to be our computer expert but the boss didn't want to let her go," Harrington asked if Timmons knew of anyone he might suggest.

"There are quite a number of capable people out there. Some of them make a very good living as consultants, and you don't absolutely need to select someone from inside the government. One person I can think of, and who we've actually used on occasion, doesn't need to make a living at it. He claims to do it for fun, but only if the problem interests him. Mind you, he doesn't do it for free; it's just that his main motivation is the sheer challenge of a project. In fact the prices he charges when he does take on a job are out of sight."

"Who is this guy, and how do we get hold of him?" queried Harrington.

"Well, the Firm knows him as Robert Smith. I call him John Foster."

"Never heard of him. And what's with the double identity?"

"It's part of the game," Timmons replied. "I'm sure you wouldn't have heard of him. At NSA only the Director and I have access. We've called on him a couple of times. The one problem I used him for was a particularly difficult code-breaking project and he got a huge kick out of showing up our in-house experts."

"Who is he really?" Dougherty asked. "And how do we get in touch with him? Would he be interested in dealing with a small agency like ours?"

"I'll try to answer the last question first. If your concept for the mission of your team breaks new ground it's possible he might help you. As for getting in touch with him, you don't. I can see if he wants to get in touch with you."

Harrington looking skeptical, said, "Whitman wants to know who we talk to about this. What do we tell him about this guy? We don't even have a real name, or do we?"

Timmons glanced out the window and laughed. "I'll contact him and let you know. Now let's move on to the staffing and budget issues you asked about. Do you envision manning a hot line, or do you want to be low key and deal only with cases involving particularly egregious security threats?"

"We think we should concentrate primarily on major problems," Dougherty replied. "The budget we're allowed is too small for anything else. We're thinking at most about maybe fifteen to twenty people or so."

"I agree with him, Jim," said Harrington. "We're supposed to meet with the good senator and our bosses along with Whitman in a couple of days so we need to have something concrete on personnel by then.

The discussion went on for another hour before Dougherty saw Timmons glance at his watch. He took this as indicating they'd taken up enough of his time for one day. "I'm sorry, sir, but we'd better be running along. Our wives are ready to shoot us because of all these late nights and weekends. Thank you so much for making the time to help educate us.

"Happy to oblige. I'll let you know about that staffing matter we discussed."

Ames, Iowa

It was eight o'clock as Hickman walked in the kitchen door. The gray cat with small patches of white fur on his chest and paws purred and rubbed his head against his master's ankle. As usual, Harry bent down to give Socks a good scratch before filling the white dish by the stove. Socks immediately began nibbling on his evening feast. Hickman was looking over the mail when he heard the distinctive ring of a cell phone emanating from a locked drawer in the desk. He fumbled for the key and pulled out the green one. "Yes?"

"General Timmons, Harry. How've you been?"

Hickman was stunned. This dedicated phone was programmed to accept calls only from half a dozen people to whom he given the number. "How did you learn my real name?"

Timmons chuckled. "Harry, you of all people should know better than to be surprised. Just because we needed your help once or twice doesn't mean we're totally inept. The reason for the call is that some friends of mine are stuck setting up a new joint task force and could use someone with your talents to teach them a few things about computer security and how it relates to industrial espionage."

Despite his shock over the name, Hickman was pleased Timmons had thought to call him. "Sir, thank you for thinking of me, but for the next year or two my time is totally committed. I'm sorry."

Timmons paused for a moment. "That's unfortunate. You'll be missing out on something very interesting. Is there anyone else you might recommend?"

"Well, there is this fellow I know out in Vegas. You have a pencil and paper?"

Timmons jotted down the information and asked. "By the way, are you going to be at DEFCON this year?"

Hickman wondered how Timmons knew about that little slice of his life and managed to mutter, "I'm not sure I'll be able to make it this time."

"Sorry to hear that. Thanks for the name."

Hickman glanced at his watch and thought for a minute wondering if Andriani was really the best choice. Finally he picked up one of the prepaid cell phones. "Hi, Gus, how are things out in Vegas?"

"Not bad, Zeus. How about you?

"Can't complain. You interested in a gig?"

"Depends. You got details?"

"Write down this number. It's a secure line belonging to William Timmons, the Deputy Director at NSA. He can explain what he wants. I told him you'd be in touch."

Bethesda, Maryland

It was almost ten o'clock on this rainy morning in Bethesda. They were using the small study in Dougherty's home to conduct interviews since they didn't have office space yet. The next candidate on their schedule was Gustavo Andriani, the one Whitman had doubts about. Dougherty met him at the door. "Come in, Mr. Andriani."

Andriani was a tall, lanky, youngish looking man with long black hair tied back in a ponytail who grinned as he extended his hand. Dougherty introduced Harrington and asked him to take a seat.

Harrington shook his hand and began the interview. "Please tell us a little about yourself, Mr. Andriani. Your name was given to us by a friend but we know very little about you."

"Well, I'm thirty years old, single, graduated from MIT in computer engineering, originally from California, and now I live in Vegas."

"Did you bring a resume?"

"No, haven't kept one up for years."

Harrington's expression was questioning. "Work experience?"

"After I graduated from college I spent two years with Microsoft. Since then I've done free-lance work for several companies and a few individuals."

"What sort of work?"

"I solve their computer problems."

"What kind of problems?"

"All sorts, but mostly security issues."

"Did you bring any references?"

"No, but I can have a couple sent to you if you'd like. How about I give you a demonstration?" He looked at Dougherty and pointed at the desktop machine. "I take it you have good security in that thing?"

"Of course."

"Your passwords all protected? How about a firewall and antivirus software?"

"Certainly. Why?"

"Good enough that I can't get into your bank statements or other financial documents?"

"I'd be very surprised if you could."

"May I try?'

Dougherty smiled smugly. "Be my guest." He stood up and pointed to the chair behind his desk.

Andriani's long fingers flew over the keyboard like a virtuoso, and in less than three minutes Dougherty's checking account statement was on the screen. A few seconds later it was replaced by his Merrill Lynch stock account.

Dougherty scowled, "How the hell did you do that?"

"I simply granted myself access as an administrator, and incidentally I locked you out. Don't worry, I'll set it back the way you had it and delete the code I just put in. What I did with your computer is kindergarten stuff."

"So, you're a hacker?"

"Sometimes, but I don't run scams or anything like that. I only take on legit things for honest people."

"What about bigger systems like we have at the FBI? Can you get into those?"

"Much more difficult. That often takes many days, even weeks sometimes, but almost always I find a way in."

"What else can you do besides hacking?"

"I play poker. I read people's faces pretty well."

"Do you make a living playing poker?"

"A very good living. When I leave here I'm going to drive up to Atlantic City for a couple of days and check the place out. Actually though, solving people's computer problems is my main source of income."

"How to people find you to fix their computer problems?"

"Previous clients recommend me. I don't advertise."

"How come we could find out so little about you? We have your social security number, driver's license, and passport data and a few other little things, but that's about all."

"I'm a very private person." He looked at Harrington. "I've done two jobs for your outfit over in Europe."

"You know other languages?'

"French, German, Italian, and a little Russian."

They spent another hour and a half talking to Andriani and came away very impressed. After he'd left they decided they really wanted this guy even if he hadn't answered all their questions nor convinced them he was truly honest. They were disappointed when, after running a much more thorough background check following the interview, they still came up empty-handed.

Chapter 4

Tama, Iowa

The radio droned oldies but goodies, and oncoming headlights whizzing by nearly blinding him. Clyde Johnson was having a difficult time staying awake. He opened the window and lit a cigarette. "Lucy, I can't keep my eyes open. How about you do the driving for a while?"

His companion in the right front seat stirred slightly. "Lucy," he said again, "I have to stop for a bit. I'm dozing off here." He pulled the van off on the shoulder and braked to a stop.

Lucy came awake with a start. "Are we there already?" she asked.

Johnson looked over at her. "Nah, it's still another twenty miles or so to Tama. I just need a few minutes." He got out and walked around the car, kicking the tires and humming the last song on the radio. The signal was fading out, and he wished he'd remembered to put a few CDs in the van. This was the end of midterm week though, and he'd gone in at five to put in his eight hours in at the computer engineering building before clocking out. He'd picked up Lucy Waters at her place and they'd set out for a rare weekend of gambling at the Meskwaki Bingo Casino and Hotel just off Route 30 a few miles east of Marshalltown.

Clyde, in his early 60s now, had been a janitor for thirty-odd years. His wife had died of breast cancer some two years earlier and for the first couple of months he tried to sooth the emptiness with booze and gambling. When he met Lucy Waters things got better. Her husband had walked out on her when her children were toddlers. They were all grown now and scattered around the country.

Lucy also worked for the university as a maid in one of the dorms. They gradually became soul mates in a sense, not turning to each other initially in a particularly romantic way, but rather they'd both needed to be with someone in order to remain sane. Lucy and Clyde filled each other's needs pretty well.

Johnson stretched, did a couple of knee-bends, and got back in the car. "Don't worry, I'm awake now. I can drive the rest of the way. I'll want a shower after we check in and then maybe I'll hit the poker tables. You gonna play twenty-one or the slots or the poker machines tonight?"

"Probably the slots. I'm not used to going on a Friday night. With all your seniority you ought to be able to take a day off when you want. Your kids are all grown. Why you keep working them stupid hours?"

I donno. I been doin' it so long it's just like a habit. I like getting to know some of the students pretty well and some of the professors too. They're all kinda like my kids now that my own have up and moved away."

"Why don' you go visit your kids more often, Clyde? I've met 'em, and they all say they wish you'd retire and move closer."

"Hey, they've all got their own lives to live. I like to visit them for sure, but I'm pretty set in how I wanna live and I'm not ready to retire. If I lived closer to them they'd want me to do some things different, and I'd probably wear out my welcome pretty fast."

Johnson put the van in gear and turned back onto the highway. Some thirty minutes later they checked into a room at the hotel, cleaned up, and headed for the tables and the machines.

Clyde watched the action at the seven card stud tables. There were five players at the only one that wasn't full. To the left of the dealer was a frizzy, middle-aged, heavily made up blond who didn't appear to be enjoying herself in the least. To her left was a thin, bald, elderly man with a large stack of chips in front of him. Clyde had seen him here many times and knew him to be an excellent player. Next were two young men, both with beards and large bellies. Clyde took them for truck drivers, many who took a few hours break at the casino en route to wherever they were going. Clyde took the seat next to them, and to his left was a middle-aged man he knew to be a psychology professor at the university. He figured there weren't going to be many easy pickings at this table. Two hours and many of hands later he knew he was right. He was only thirty dollars ahead when he cashed in for a break. He'd learned long ago that his play became too predictable after about that time. He got up and went looking for Lucy.

He found her at the slots slowly feeding quarters into two machines, first pulling the lever hard on the one to her left then softer on one to her right, her usual system. Johnson never quite understood how anyone could stand to play a game the house was invariably programmed to win. Lucy had tried several times to enlighten him, but never with much success.

"How come you keep playing the machines, Lucy? You know the odds."

She always claimed she didn't like to compete against other people, but deep down, even knowing that the house would always win, she played simply because she enjoyed it. As long as she didn't gamble more than she could afford to lose, Lucy regarded this as entertainment and not much different than going out to dinner or to a movie. She was content to usually lose a few bucks but when she hit the occasional hit jackpots she was always able to leave with a few dollars in her purse and no compulsion to give it all back.

Lucy stood up, stretched her back as she looked around, and smiled at the player to her left. "Clyde, this is Mr. Takayama", she said, turning to the quiet middle-age man. "We met him here last month, remember."

Clyde nodded to Takayama and asked Lucy if she was ready for a break.

"Sounds good to me", Lucy said. "These old slots aren't being very good to me tonight. You wanna come along with us Mr. Takayama? The buffet here is pretty good. Clyde and I go to it almost every time we come here."

"It would be my honor," Takayama replied in perfect English with a wide smile. "I don't know many people in your beautiful country, so I take every possible opportunity to meet people and practice my English"

"You sure don't sound like you need any practice, Mr. T, but please join us. Where are you from, Japan?" Johnson was pretty sure that Takayama must be from Japan because of his name. There were many foreign students on the campus and he'd often spoken with some of them and even become fairly friendly with a few.

While sipping their after dinner coffee, Takayama leaned over to Johnson "There's something you might want to think about. The company I work for in Japan and a biotechnology company over here in America are working together trying to develop a heartier strain of rice that will grow better in third world countries where the land has been worked too hard for so many centuries. We sometimes give research contracts to some of the professors who do research at your school. In return we ask they keep us informed about new discoveries that look promising. My company is quite large, and one of our divisions deals with computers. I recall you told me you work in the computer building. Would you be interested in keeping an eye out for us about what projects are going on and let us know what they involve? Now I'm not asking you to steal any secrets or give away any classified information, only asking you to let us know in a general way what sort of research is going on."

This sounded strange to Johnson but he'd heard that such things went on and decided to play along to see where it would lead. "Well, I don't know, Mr. T. I'm just a janitor, so I really don't know that much about what projects are going on. Besides, it sounds like spying to me. I'm not really into that sort of thing."

"It's not actually spying, Clyde. Most of this data gets shipped back and forth on the Internet all the time. Actually anyone could get the majority of what we learn off that information superhighway, but that takes time and you don't always know how accurate the information is. Most large companies nowadays, and even some of the government agencies, retain people at major universities and large companies to keep an eye out for new technologies. If you know what your competitor is up to you can tailor your own sales pitches to counter what they're doing."

"It still sounds like spying to me," Clyde muttered in a low voice, "but I've heard it's a pretty common practice. I know that the faculty always tells the students to be discreet about what they leave lying around the lab or on the computer."

"Takayama smiled. "It's not like stealing national secrets. This is simply how business is conducted these days. It isn't a new practice, either, just more refined and accepted now. Besides, the pay can be quite good. The standard retainer is two hundred fifty dollars a month with a bonus for anything that applies directly to something our company is particularly interested in."

"What's the name of your company, Mr. T?"

"Yokohama Industries."

"Why would your company pay for something it isn't directly interested in?" queried Johnson. "If I were buying information I wouldn't want to be paying for anything I couldn't use."

"Almost all large companies do this now," countered Takayama, essentially rephrasing what he'd said earlier. "Some have formed consortiums to share information. Sometimes one company will hear about something that might interest a partner company and share that information with the expectation the favor will be returned."

What Takayama didn't know was that over the years, in contrast to many others who labored in environmental services, Clyde Johnson had gotten to know some of the professors and students in the departments where he worked fairly well and was interested in the various projects in progress.

"What if someone hears something that might be of interest but thinks it's confidential and wouldn't be right to pass along?" he asked.

"Of course there'd be no obligation to share anything with us that you didn't think was proper. If after a few months we didn't get sufficient information from you we'd let you know that your services were no longer required and we'd look for someone else. Now then, I've heard you've helped some of the foreign students who have trouble keeping up because of the language problems and never take any money for it. I know about that because one of the students you helped a few years ago was my cousin's son. He's now a successful engineer back in Japan. He might not have made it through the first year if it hadn't been for you and a couple of other people who helped him out."

Johnson knew he was being flattered. He'd picked up a fair amount of computer literacy over the years from his contact with students and the ready availability of computers. He was also aware that Takayama's accent had gradually become less pronounced as their conversation had gone on. Something sounded funny about all this and it made him curious. He decided to take his usual course of action when he wasn't sure what to do next.

He stood up and said. "Come on, Lucy. Let's get an hour of play time in before I pass out. Mr. T, I'll give it some thought but I never like to make decisions in a hurry. Maybe we'll see you here again, or let me have your number and if I decide I'm interested I'll call you, okay?"

"That's fine, Clyde. I'm actually planning to be at the university Tuesday and Wednesday. I could check with you then. I'd really like to see that computer lab that my nephew told me so much about."

"Unless I'm working the evening shift I usually get off at four, so if you want to stop by a little after that I'd be happy to give you the dime tour of the campus."

After Takayama left, Lucy turned to Clyde. "Why do you have to think about a chance to pick up an easy two-fifty a month for doing nothing more than everybody else is doin'? I'd grab that offer in a second if it were up to me!"

"Well Lucy, just because everybody else is doing something, or at least our Mr. T says they are, that don't make it the right thing to be doin'. Sides, there's somethin' 'bout that fella I don't trust. Didn't you notice how his English got so much better after we talked a little while? I thought that was mighty strange."

"Your speakin' got lots better when you was talkin' with Mr. Takayama, too, Clyde. I don' see nothing too unusual 'bout that. People talks different depending on who they's talkin' to." countered Lucy.

Johnson left Lucy at the slots where over the next hour she picked up three jackpots and was way ahead for the night. He brooded for the next hour and dropped a hundred bucks. He pushed away from the table, cashed in, and headed for bed, still thinking about Takayama and his offer. He wondered how many of the staff, or even some students, might be on the take.

The following evening, on their way back to Ames, Lucy brought up the subject again. "Clyde, you decides what you gonna do bout Mr. T's offer yet?"

"I'm still thinking it over, Lucy. Gonna keep my ears open and try to learn more about it."

Johnson had a good idea how to go about the learning. After over thirty years of cleaning the lab for Professor (emeritus) William Evans, he was well acquainted with the distinguished gentleman who seemed to consider him a friend, something not granted to but a handful of very longtime University people. Professor Evans visited the lab in the late afternoon three days a week, and often stopped to have coffee and chat with Clyde, partly to keep up with what was really going on among the staff. Evans was the one person he could trust with this conundrum.

Takayama watched them leave and cautioned himself to be patent.

Ames, Iowa

Professor William Evans grunted as he swung open the door of the computer research center. Today it was the dark blue three-piece suit with a twenty year old wide necktie partly covering a white shirt with perpetually rolled up sleeves. He first went to his office where Hazel Stoddard, his secretary for over thirty years, handed him the requisite cup of tea. He was one of the few at the University to rate a private secretary in this era of budget cutbacks. Although he no longer taught any regular courses, he did preside over occasional seminars. It was a holdover from the glory days when he had done some of the pioneering research in computer technology and built the Department of Electrical Engineering, arguably the home of the first true computer.

The Atanasoff-Berry Computer was recognized as the first digital computer and the first to use vacuum tubes. It probably had much to do with the series of patents the university amassed and the steam of income it brought to the school over the years. It was later dismantled, but a replica was built at Iowa State in 2009 that now resided at the Computer History Museum in Mountain View, California.

"You're early today, Bill," Hazel said with her usual smile, "and you're walking much better. Another couple of weeks and you should be able to throw away the cane at least until you need the other side done anyway. How's Martha?"

"She's fine, and the hip is feeling better. I should have had the damn thing replaced a year or two ago. I just was too busy here, and probably a little scared to go under the knife as they say." Evans let out a laugh. "Hell, I'm probably almost as much of a chicken as a surgeon about having an operation."

"I printed out your e-mail and the regular mail is on your desk. There's an invitation to visit London in June to give a lecture on the history of computer development if you feel up to it. I'll bet your wife would love the chance to visit England again. It must be at least three years since you were there. By the way, Clyde Johnson stopped by asking if you'd be in today. He didn't say why."

"I hope he's all right. Do you remember the dates for the London invitation? We have a grandson graduating at the end of May that we have to be here for."

"I pretty sure it's for the second week in June so it should work out."

"I'll jot it down and speak to Martha about it. We don't get as many of these invitations as we did a few years back. Everyone must think we're just a couple of senile old farts by now, or else dead or something. That's what happens when your name isn't first on the papers anymore. Was there any mail that I can't put off until tomorrow? I need to put in a little time at the lab for a change."

"Nothing that can't wait. I typed up replies to a couple of things you might look over so we can get them in the mail. Be sure you speak to Clyde. He seemed anxious to see you about something, and that's not like him at all. I hope there's nothing wrong with any of his kids."

Evans limped into his office and dealt with the letters Mrs. Stoddard had composed, glanced at the London invitation, and then headed for the lab. He was a creature of habit. During his heyday, teaching and administration occupied most of each day. Late afternoons and evenings were his time for research. Although he no longer did any formal teaching or have many administrative responsibilities, he still came to the office at least three days a week. Some habits were difficult to break.

Evans eased his new hip down into his old comfortable chair in the corner. It was here that he had some of his best insights over the years. He began perusing a paper that had been sitting on his desk for a couple of days and when he looked up he saw Johnson standing quietly in the doorway.

"C.J., how are you? Hazel said you wanted to see me. Been standing there long?"

"No, only a couple of minutes. Never understood how you could concentrate so hard on something as you seem to."

Evans eyes narrowed. "Nothing wrong with the kids, is there?"

"The kids are all fine. It's something else, and I need your wisdom on this one," Johnson sighed. "Lucy and I went to that casino in Tama this weekend for a little poker and some foreign guy started hitting on me to become a spy."

Evans looked over the top of his half-frames. "Tell me what this is all about, Clyde. I have a little trouble picturing you as a spy. Exactly what did this person want you to spy on, and on behalf of whom?"

"It went down like this. A guy we've seen there once before comes up to Lucy and makes some small talk. When I go over, Lucy invites him to get a bite to eat with us. He makes like he doesn't speak English very well, but he does. I know he's from Japan because of his name; it's Takayama, Hidehiko Takayama. After a little small talk he tries to get me to become a spy, except he doesn't want to call it that. He offers to give me two hundred and fifty a month to let him know what sort of research projects are going on here at the university. He tells me a lot of people do the same thing for companies sponsoring their research. He gives me this song and dance about how I helped out a nephew of his when the kid was a student here and says he wants to return the favor. I don't know what the deal is with all of this so I say I'll think on it. He told me he'll be on campus tomorrow and the next day but didn't say what for."

"Did he give an indication of who's behind him?"

"He gave me a name, Yokohama Industries, and said it was a conglomerate, that it owned several smaller companies. One was a biotech company developing different types of rice. I called him on that. I said that I worked in the engineering building, not biology or something. He said he knew that but some departments here have research contracts from them."

"What else did he say?"

"Well, I told him that most of the stuff we do is pretty open to anybody who wants to know about it. You can find out about many of the projects right off the web site. He says he knows that but it's too much trouble. He says it's cheaper and more cost effective to pay somebody like me to do the work for them."

"As you well know, some of the things we do at the school are damn sensitive. The information flowing through here could be worth a lot of money to some people. Anything else this Takayama had to say?"

"One more thing, I think I mentioned it before, but he claims there are companies paying people here and at other schools as well to spy for them."

"I suppose it's possible his company is just a shell for a foreign government," muttered Evans. "Did he give you any names of people here who are on the take?"

"No, sir."

"I'm glad you came by and told me about this, CJ, and I think it would be an excellent idea for you to become a spy." Evans smiled.

"Who knows, you might find a second calling. In the meantime I'll talk to a couple of people in a general sort of way to see what I can learn. Let me know what happens after this guy comes to see you again. Don't appear too anxious, but do go along with him. Don't push him for a lot of details at first, but see what you can find out little by little."

"I don't know if I like this, but I'll give it a shot if you think it's the best way to go."

"I don't like it either, CJ, but I'm damn sure we don't want to ignore it."

Evans watched Johnson depart and sadly shook his head. The plans for accomplishing very much this day had just flown out the window. He buzzed for Mrs. Stoddard. "Hazel, please run me a list of all private companies and government agencies that our lab has done contract work for in the past five years along with names of the principal and associate investigators."

"Why the interest?" she asked. "I thought you were going to get some research time in today."

"CJ told me he thinks there might be a fox in the chicken coop. I think it's important to see if we can put his mind at ease." Evans pulled off his glasses and rubbed his eyes "And mine too," he muttered softly.

Dalton picked up the phone, "Dalton here."

"Sam, I'd appreciate it if you'd come over to the office. There's something I want to talk with you about."

"No problem, sir." Dalton was one of the professor's younger protégés, and one of his brightest. When the Professor said 'jump', Sam and his colleagues merely asked 'how high'? Some things never changed. He logged off his terminal and hurried outside.

Hazel Stoddard smiled as Dalton entered looking a little out of breath. "He's in his office and he's up in arms about something. He and Clyde Johnson were in there for a long time. When he came out he forgot all about the things he had planned for today and got me started on a task that's going to take hours. Go ahead in, and if you find out what's going on let me in on it."

Dalton nodded and knocked softly on the Professor's door.

"Thanks for coming by, Sam," Evans said, and pointed to the chair next to his desk. "I know you're busy but this shouldn't take long. I want to know if any of the staff receives extra compensation from their grant sponsors or anyone else for providing them information about activities here at the university. I'm a little out of touch with day-to-day operations but I've heard some people are interested in the research we do here, and apparently they're willing to pay for it."

"Sir, almost all of the companies we contract to do research for or jointly have reps that drop around periodically and they always ask questions about what else is going on. In our department we're currently doing a lot of work for McGregor and he's always interested in things besides his own projects. Some reps do provide a few perks like meetings and travel expenses in lieu of payment. Certainly no one in our department takes money under the table, but I can't speak for the other departments."

"I know that, but I'm specifically interested in any staff on a retainer to provide information to outside parties. I'm speaking of private companies that have dealings with the university. Have you heard of that sort of thing going on?"

"I've heard a few rumors about other departments. Some of the things we do here could be of great significance to competitors. At least in our shop security is tighter than Fort Knox."

"Good. Be sure to keep your ears open about someone getting paid to spy on anyone's research on behalf of their grant sponsors, but keep this between you and me for the time being, understand?"

"Yes, sir," he replied.

Dalton headed back downstairs wondering what was going on. This was a side of the man he'd never encountered.

Ames, Iowa

"Harry, do you know anyone in the Physics Department that could help me out with something?" Kate asked. She went on to tell him about the problem.

Hickman gave her Gary Wong's name.

She reached Wong the next morning and explained that she was working on a project and had heard he was interested in magnetic resonance force microscopy. She asked if she could meet with him to learn more about it, and they set up a time for later that afternoon.

Physics was located in an annex of the physical sciences complex. She hadn't been in there since her sophomore year in undergraduate school. She located his lab after several inquiries and introduced herself. Wong wore thick glasses, blue jeans, and a Hawaiian print shirt. His office was even messier than her cubbyhole with piles of books and journals scattered everywhere. He removed a stack of folders from a chair and bade her sit. "How can I help you?" he asked, with just the trace of an accent.

"As I mentioned on the phone, I'm interested in trying to find a way to read the genetic code faster and more accurately than we can at present. My friend said you were working on something I read about on the Internet. I think I have an idea how to package DNA and maybe RNA to make it easier to study, but I need two things."

"What sort of things?"

"First, I need a device that will actually do the measuring accurately and without damaging the sample. Secondly, I need a way to collect and rapidly collate a massive amount of data." Thinking about Harry and the computer, Summers smiled to herself. "I think I may have a lead on the second part of the problem. So far nearly all the methods to study DNA require lots of intermediate steps that are prone to destroying some of the data, or can read only very short sequences at a time. I want to someday be able to read a whole chromosome at a time."

"I haven't taken a biology course since high school. Even the articles in lay magazines about advances in biology leave me baffled. How small is the stuff you want to look at?"

"Really tiny, not like an individual atom or anything on that order, but long sequences of purine and pyrimidine bases attached to a sugar molecule and a phosphate. In each strand there may be as many as a hundred million bases. Inside the cell they're all jumbled up, but stretched out they'd be more than a yard long. I want to split the two strands and wind them up on tiny grooved cylinders so the phosphate and sugar are on the inside and the DNA is on the outside. These spools will have to rotate at a constant speed so each base can be read individually and in order. One big problem is the DNA strands are extremely fragile. It's even worse if you try this approach with RNA since it's much more fragile. Have you ever used magnetic resonance to look at biological material?"

"I haven't, but I know of a couple of groups are trying to do that. It sounds like pretty exciting research. With so much data you'll need way more computing power than we have here in the lab."

"I know," Kate said, "and I think there may be an answer to that part of the problem. Some friends of mine work with computers and I think they might be able to help."

"Let me call a couple of people I know who work with biological specimens and get back to you. Do you have either a phone number or e-mail address where I can reach you?"

"Hot damn," Kate muttered to herself as she waltzed down the steps of the physics building after again impressing upon Wong that her research must be kept confidential. She thought that at least some of the things she'd need were falling into place. With a little bit of luck her idea just might play.

Ames, Iowa

Spring had finally arrived. The days were warmer, the flowers had begun to bloom, and distractions abounded. They gathered in the converted shed at five-thirty on a Monday afternoon, all similarly dressed in a white *gi,* dutifully going through a warm-up of stretching exercises and practicing their *katas.* Oldenberg moved from one to another with individual tips and corrections. In so far as their schedules permitted they tried to do this each Monday and Thursday, even if it meant for most of them returning to their labs or offices on campus later. Oldenberg watched each work through a series of punches, kicks and throws, and in the last fifteen minutes individual matches. He was impressed with the progress the group had made over the last few months.

While cooling off at the end of the session, Oldenberg turned to Summers. "Kate, I checked with my sister, Liz, and she said you could stay with her when you go to that meeting at NIH next week. It's no problem and it'll be a lot cheaper and easier than getting a hotel in DC.

"That sounds great, Dan. Thanks for thinking of me. Say, what do any of you know about nuclear magnetic resonance or atomic force microscopes? I looked up some papers Wong told me about on the Internet and I wonder if either of those things might be helpful with my project."

Oldenberg deferred to Hickman.

"I don't know much about either," Hickman said, "but try Wong again. Did you find out anything useful in your reading?"

"Not really. I'll give him another call."

"Harry, when are you and Brian going tell us what you're working on?" Shelia asked. "It's not like either of you to be so close mouthed."

"C'mon, we've told you before that we're not allowed to talk about it," Hickman replied, seemingly a little irritated. "That's just the way it is, so you might as well accept the fact."

Ames, Iowa

Sam Dalton sat at his terminal staring into space. He'd just gotten off the phone with McGregor giving him an update on their progress. His shoulders and back ached from the last two hours hunched over his keyboard, and his head ached at the thought he'd have to call Tracy and tell her he'd miss dinner again.

"Honey, we have a problem at work and Professor Evans wants our group to meet in his office at five-thirty to discuss it."

"Sam, you know these long days and late nights are getting to be a real pain in the ass. Every time we make plans to do something you end up canceling out at the last minute. I'll call the Williams and make our excuses, but this has to stop. The university can only get so much blood out of a rock!"

"Sorry, hon. I feel the same way, but this project is big. The chance to work on it is a once in a lifetime thing. At least most of the travel part is over. It'll get better soon, I promise."

"Oh yeah, just remember we've been down this road before a time or two."

When Dalton finally put down the phone he ran his hands though his hair. The brown had a couple strands of gray now. He pulled them out whenever he noticed one but realized that soon it wouldn't be worth the trouble. He glanced at the clock and locked up the diagrams he'd been going over. *Dammit, time to get over there.*

Evans sat at head of the table in the small conference room, tie at half-mast, half- frames perched on his nose, and grimacing at his notes. The entire team was there.

"I'm sorry to keep all of you late again," Evans began, "but Clyde Johnson came by to see me the other day and I want to fill you in about something he told me. I've already spoken to Sam about the problem."

He went on to tell them about Takayama and his offer to pay Johnson for keeping him apprised about research projects going on in the department.

"That didn't seem right to him so he came to me and asked what he should do. I told him to play along so with this guy until we find out what he's up to. I also asked Sam to sniff around to see if he can learn if this same thing is happening in other departments. Tell us what you've found out so far, Sam."

"So far it looks like everything in this department is okay. I haven't discovered any reason to think anyone in computer engineering is loose-lipped about the research going on here or that anyone's had a similar offer. That isn't to say that some of the sponsors or their reps don't press the investigators or their staffs for information."

"I'm glad to hear that. What about outside the department?"

"I spoke with a friend in electrical engineering who said he'd heard about an assistant prof who was asked to leave suddenly and that was the reason. Another friend in the physics department says they caught one of the reps looking through the wastebasket in his office."

Evens nodded. "I want the rest of you to keep your eyes open and let me know if you find out about any more incidents. I'm going to have a talk with the president of the university and possibly the campus police about this. Do any of you have questions or other suggestions?"

Hickman raised a hand. "We have security camera covering the outside doors but none inside. It might be a good idea to install some."

"That's an excellent idea, son. You brought it up, so make it happen." He turned to Dalton. "Sam, next week when you fly out to San Jose to brief McGregor about the project's status be sure to fill him in on what we've just talked about."

Evans glanced up at the ceiling for a moment and sighed before continuing. "In the meantime, if this guy tries contact you be sure to let me know right away. I'll tell him one of us will walk him through the Durham building but not the new lab."

Chapter 5

Washington DC

This time the meeting at the EOB was quite different from their first. Dougherty and Harrington had done their homework and fleshed out a semblance of a plan. They arrived well before the appointed time and set up a brief slide show to accompany the presentation. Casper from CIA, Vance from the FBI, Whitman, and finally Senator Slocum drifted in over the next half-hour. Small talk filled the first few minutes before Slocum announced, "Okay, enough of this chit-chat. Let's get down to business. What do you have for us, Agent Dougherty?"

"Over the last few weeks we've learned a great deal about the scope of the espionage problem. We've developed a staffing plan and what we'll need for a budget," Dougherty began. "Like you said, Senator, nobody in government seems to be doing much about the problem at present. We've spoken with some people at Commerce, the AG's office, both our shops, NSA, and Mr. Whitman here."

Harrington put up the first slide. "We don't want to be just another bunch of watchful waiters that does studies and writes reports. If you want us to do something about this problem and make a real contribution, then we'll need enforcement authorization to issue subpoenas and make arrests. That means we need authority and a clearance for the ops or enforcement side."

"The way we see it," Dougherty added, "is we need to concentrate on particularly egregious examples, and these will come mostly via intrusions into electronic databases. Another area might involve bribes to employees of companies with emerging technologies and scientific discoveries. The limits of encryption are still being debated, and export of technology is theoretically prohibited for some of the more advanced stuff, but via the computer is where we believe most thefts will come from. We want to concentrate in that area and respond in kind as part of our mission."

"We need to be sure we're all in agreement about that approach, gentlemen, or there isn't much point in wasting your time on the nuts and bolts of our proposal," Harrington concluded.

Slocum glanced around the table. Whitman nodded. Vance, the FBI's DDI, and Casper both stared ahead impassively. Slocum finally motioned to Dougherty and said, "Go on, I haven't got all day."

Dougherty drew a deep breath and continued, "We'll need several people with an extensive background in encryption and computer security. We have a few names we've given to Mr. Whitman of people currently working for our government in these areas whom we'd like to recruit. Also there are several candidates from private industry we're running checks on. We do want to get at least one or two people from outside the mainstream, individuals you might call grown-up hackers who aren't beholden to any particular government agency at present. We think they'll be among our most useful assets. We'll also need some full-time legal help. All told this comes to a little over a dozen principals plus three or four junior researchers and gofers, two or three secretaries, and a full time administrator for the computer network. That brings the total up to twenty or so."

"How much?" Slocum asked looking intently at Dougherty.

"We figure for the first year three and a half million, possibly four."

"Where will the money come from?"

Whitman answered quickly, "CIA and FBI should share the cost equally." He nodded at Slocum. "The senator believes this problem belongs to both agencies so that seems reasonable."

Vance leaned back in his chair with a scowl. "So, you steal several people from my agency; that means we have to hire replacements. Who's going to pay for them?"

"I doubt that congress is about to pass another supplemental appropriations bill in the near future, so for this year at least you'll have to finance this task force out of your present budgets," Whitman replied, trying to hide his frustration at having to deal with Vance. "The administration doesn't have any discretionary funds to cover it."

The grousing and finger pointing went on for a couple of minutes before Slocum pounded his hand on the table. "That's enough, gentlemen. Let's move on, shall we? Tell me what you meant exactly when you said you want to do something about these particularly egregious problems you might come across."

"That's about the subpoena and enforcement issues that I mentioned," Dougherty replied. "Of course we'd depend on the Justice Department for prosecution."

"I see," Slocum drawled. "I just wanted to be certain on that point. Now tell us more specifically about whom you intend to hire. I haven't had time to read through the resumes you sent."

Whitman raised a hand, "The only one I have a problem with is this Gustavo Andriani." He looked over at Dougherty. "Jim, you didn't give me much background on this guy. How did you hook up with him?"

"Sorry, but we're not allowed to say," Dougherty replied.

Whitman lifted an eyebrow, obviously annoyed. "Have either of you him or even spoken with him?"

"We both interviewed him at length and we have reason to believe he'd fit in and become a valuable asset."

"Well, I'm not comfortable with him. I think you'd do better to look for someone else."

Technically Whitman wasn't their boss, at least not at this point. "He has talents we haven't been able to find in any of the other candidates," Dougherty persisted

"I still don't like it. I want you to keep looking."

"Pardon me, Brad, but I think you should leave selecting the people up to us. We're the ones who interview them and checked all their backgrounds." Harrington countered.

Whitman seemed irritated. "Well, let me talk with Director Timmons first. I'll see what he says and let you know. The others on the list all check out okay. I don't have a problem with those."

On that note the meeting ended with several items yet to be decided.

Ames, Iowa

It was Monday, exercise night, and Cindy, Yukiko and Harry joined the regular inhabitants for dinner, a rather quick affair of leftovers that Sheila had put together. At the end of the meal Oldenberg announced, "I have a little surprise tonight, people. I think each of you is ready for promotion to brown belt so we'll have a little ceremony after the workout."

"I thought we needed to be in a couple of tournaments first," Sheila said.

"Ordinarily that's true, but at the discretion of your instructor, promotions to brown belt may be awarded without formal competitions. Let's run through your kata, do a little sparring, and then try on your new belts."

The group donned their *gi* and migrated to the workout space Oldenberg and O'Leary had put together the previous year. "All right," exclaimed Hickman. "Watch this." He bowed to the group and then began a series of exercises incorporating feints, blocks, parries, and strikes while moving around the mat in a dance-like fashion. He finished with another bow and yelled, "You're up, Brian!"

The remaining five did their thing to a combination of applause and catcalls and raucous laughter. "Next semester will you teach us to be black belts like you, Dan?" asked Kate.

Oldenberg laughed. "Probably not next semester, it usually takes quite a bit longer than that, but you never can tell."

Arlington, Virginia

Claire Dougherty took the Barton Parkway and crossed over the Potomac on her way to meet her husband at the Harrington's in Arlington. Both couples had gotten together a several times since the inception of the project, and she enjoyed Peg's company. Over pizza and beer at Domenico's they talked about their plans for the new task force and the advice they'd received from William Timmons. The NSA Deputy Director had become more or less their mentor, and their wives were glad that somebody was showing an interest in their husbands' careers. They all understood this task force would be a defining step in all their lives.

"If we don't get a decent budget we won't be able to recruit top-notch people and we'll be out at the plate without so much as taking a swing, Dougherty growled. "Sean and I must have vetted forty or more candidates so far. At this point, we're pretty sure on about half the positions. At least Whitman isn't interfering very much although he's reticent about one person."

"You mean the young man you told me about who worked for both CIA and NSA doing the same thing for both agencies using two different names without either being aware of it?" Peg asked. "I thought NSA was supposed to know everything about everybody. How could he pull that off?"

"No, that was somebody else, the fellow who recommended him to Timmons. We asked him about that," Sean replied, "and we never did get much of an answer. I really believe Director Timmons never found out himself. Well, maybe he did and won't own up to it for some reason."

"The way you've both built up this Director Timmons, it's a treat to learn that the man is human," Peg said with a throaty laugh. "When are we going to get to meet this William Timmons anyway?"

"Probably sometime soon," Dougherty replied. "You'd like his wife, Martha, if you ever get to meet her. She gave us a little lecture when we visited his home on the importance of not neglecting our loved ones while we're pursuing the bad guys. She's one hell of a nice lady."

"About time we heard something positive about this new endeavor," Peg said. "How did you come to meet Mr. Timmons anyway? I don't think I'd ever heard of him before."

Harrington told them how Whitman had suggested they speak to him about the task force. "We'd both heard of him but never had the opportunity to meet him before. Timmons was the first person we ran across who was genuinely willing to sit down and give us some sound advice."

Dougherty added, "Most people we approached simply gave us the brush-off or spoke in vague generalities. Subsequently we came to find out that Timmons has a reputation for openness and being helpful. It's pretty amazing considering he's a spook."

"That seems like some sort of oxymoron, a talkative spook," exclaimed his wife.

"He wasn't always with NSA. He started out as an Air Force pilot and then got into military intelligence. After twenty-some years in uniform he moved over to NSA."

"Now that sounds like some folks we all know pretty well," laughed Claire.

It was after eleven when they called it a night. Tomorrow would be another busy day.

Ames, Iowa

The China Moon was nearly empty this warm spring evening. Monday of finals week had a sobering effect on most of the students. Tommy Lee sat in the corner mulling over the chessboard wondering if Hickman might stop by. He couldn't understand how anyone that bright never seemed to graduate and move on. Harry had told him more than once that it was because he enjoyed the college life and taking interesting courses, but somehow Lee couldn't fathom it. He'd seen his share of students come and go over the years and knew there were other perpetual students that hung around the university for a long time, but Hickman was different. He didn't fit the mold. He didn't have long hair or sport an earring or dress funny or make speeches or get into campus politics. He just seemed to float through life doing his own thing, and he was one hell of a chess player. Tommy didn't have long to wait as he saw the lean man in blue jeans and a tie-dye t-shirt saunter in.

"How's it going, Tommy?"

"Finest kind. I've been working on a new strategy, so sit your butt down and I'll bring us a couple of beers. I'm going to whip your sorry ass this time"

"Be one cold day in hell, Tommy Lee. Go get those beers and let me see what you got on the board here." Hickman stared intently at the pieces for a moment then laughed silently knowing this was going to be fun.

The first several moves were furiously fast. Li took a deep breath and exhaled. "I think I've got you, my friend."

Hickman just smiled at for a moment, and then without so much as a glance at the pieces, made his move. "Checkmate in four," he murmured with a grin.

"No way!"

"Go ahead, make your next move."

Lee looked again and pondered. He picked up his rook and moved two spaces ahead, and after studying it again finally removed his hand.

With no hesitation at all Harry moved his queen's knight.

Suddenly Lee began to whimper, "Oh shit, you're right. Why the hell didn't I see that? Where did you learn to play like this? Why aren't you out playing in the big leagues?"

Hickman leaned back in his chair and chuckled. "The chess is only for fun, Tommy. The pros take this little game way too seriously. Besides, I have better things to do."

"Like taking endless courses without ever finishing your PhD?" shot back the wounded Tommy Lee.

"Not taking courses anymore, Tommy. I'm actually writing my thesis."

"Speaking of working for a living, where's Kate?"

"Still in her lab. The poor girl practically lives there."

"You like her, don't you?"

Hickman stared at Lee and sighed. "Yes, I do, Tommy. I like her a whole lot." He stared up at the ceiling for a few seconds. "Guess I'd better get moving. Thanks for the beer and the game."

Washington DC

Dougherty and Harrington met with Whitman to go over civil service pay grades for the support personnel and the allocation of funds for computer hardware and software. The basic budget was done but the portion for outside consultants was still on the table and this seemed to be a sticky point. It was obvious Whitman preferred hiring full-time employees rather than using consultants. Both Dougherty and Harrington had talked this over and were convinced they'd found the right mix. They'd invested too much time and effort to see it wasted, and so they'd decided not to budge on this issue. After arguing back and forth for half an hour, Whitman brought up another concern.

"This Gus Andriani," Whitman began, "why are you so set on him? I tried to call him and left a message but the bastard never got back to me. How did you hook up with this idiot?"

"Sorry, but like I mentioned last time, we're not allowed to say," Dougherty replied watching Whitman's eyes widen.

"Have either of you interviewed him or even spoken with him in person?" Whitman asked.

"Look, like I told you before, we've both interviewed him," Harrington said. "We have reason to believe he'll be a valuable asset."

"And like I told you before, I'm not at all comfortable with him. I strongly suggest you look for someone else."

Dougherty frowned. They were still on the payroll of their respective agencies and technically Whitman wasn't their boss even though he'd more-or-less tried to assume that role. "He has talents we haven't been able to find in any of the other candidates," he persisted, "I still don't like it."

"Look, Brad, we spent two hours talking to this fellow and he showed us what he can do. We really want him."

Whitman shrugged. "Okay, but it's your asses on the line if he screws up. You're happy with the office space you looked at?"

"Yeah, we'll be the only ones in the building and there's enough space to expand if we need to."

"How long before you're ready actually ready to open up for business?"

"Hell, what do you think we've been doing these past few months? How about coming over to see the place? We plan to sign the papers tomorrow."

"I'll try to make it next week sometime. This isn't my only responsibility you know. Now let's go back to the outside consultant business one more time. They can be awful expensive for what you get. Remember, you have to be damn careful with the taxpayers' money, right?"

"Yeah, Brad, we know we're all responsible to the hand that feeds us." Dougherty said. "That's precisely why we need to allocate at least a quarter of the budget for consultants. For the kind of threat we're talking about the help we want just isn't available in-house. We need to be able to hire consultants on an ad-hoc basis if our estimate of the types of problems we'll see is correct. All the names on the list are people who've been used before by one agency or another and received good recommendations."

Whitman shrugged, "I did run the lists you sent me and found nothing taboo on any of them except maybe the computer guy we already talked about. I just want you to realize you won't be able to hire as many fulltime people if you devote so much of the budget to so-called consultants."

The following day Harrington and Dougherty signed off on the office in Alexandria, glad to have that detail out of the way. They could now start making firm offers and putting together the team they'd likely be working with for the next few years. A celebration was in order. Claire and Peg were both duly notified to put on their finest and be ready for a night on the town. Tomorrow they'd all sleep in for a change, but each was certain the next few weeks would be hectic.

"Hot damn," Harrington chortled, "took four months but we're finally in business almost. Have you cleaned your work over at the Bureau?"

"Most of it." responded Dougherty. "Nothing left over that'll take much time. How about you? Is the Director still giving you a hard time about leaving?"

"No, I've got almost everything squared away or passed off to the next victim. I'll move some of my things over to the new building tomorrow or the next day. Funny how nothing much seemed to happen with this project for weeks, then all of a sudden we've got an office and a staff of three in place. I was really impressed by that Ms. Fisher."

"Yeah, she certainly knows a hell of a lot more about running an office than we do, particularly the budget aspect. You really believe she can have phone lines in there tomorrow. Christ, we don't even have a name for this task force yet."

"I hear you, man. Now what should we call her? She reminds me of my third grade teacher."

"We better ask the ladies tonight but I vote for her first name. I mean, we are supposed to be the bosses at the office. Am I right?"

"Right, Peg and I will see you and Claire at Domenico's around eight. I have a table reserved."

Arlington, Virginia

Domenico's, a family restaurant in Arlington that Peg and Sean Harrington visited once a month or so, was one of the few places they dared take the kids when they were little for fear they'd be asked to leave. Domenico was old now and his children pretty much ran the place, but he was always there greeting the patrons by name and passing out candy to the kids at the end of the meal. Sometimes he gave the little ones a tour of the kitchen. Of course the children didn't understand much of what he told them but it kept the parents bringing them back. Every so often as a special treat he'd try to teach them a kid's song in Italian.

Dougherty announced they should be ready to finally open for business in a week or two.

Harrington recounted the day's events for Peg and Claire while they ate. "Whitman finally gave in to our ideas on staffing. Willa is teaching us the ropes. You wouldn't believe how efficient that lady is," he exclaimed. "When we first interviewed her for the job she grilled us about our plans and about how we anticipated treating the staff. Then she wanted to know all about our backgrounds and questioned us thoroughly about the project itself. It was like Jim and I were applying for jobs at her company."

Dougherty added, "It was as if we were back in grade school. Anyway we certainly felt that way after she finished with us." He took a sip of his coffee. "Apparently Willa Fisher is a career government employee who's come up through the ranks and functions like an old chief master sergeant in the Air Force. We gathered she's a widow and probably in her mid to late fifties. She appears to have the know-how to take a brand new team and get it up and running with no-muss, no-fuss. It was a most educational afternoon, and we're not quite sure who works for whom right now."

"Sounds like some of the nuns back in school," Claire said with a laugh. "You fellows damn well better toe the mark or she'll make you stay after class. What have you decided to call this little task force, or are you going to let Sister Willa decide that for you too?"

"That's a real good question," answered Sean with a grin. "We're open to any suggestion you ladies might have."

"Maybe Spies-R-Us?"

"Try Stolen Secrets Agency."

"Not bad," Sean replied. "We were actually thinking about using the Federal Industrial Security Agency or FISA for short. Whitman thinks that one might work okay although we're still not convinced we can't come up with something better."

"Sounds like a winner to me," Claire said.

"When do we get to meet this Whitman or, more importantly now, Willa?" Peg asked.

"Why don't you just pop on down there tomorrow," Sean told her. "See what you think."

Claire laughed. "Sounds like Mrs. Fishers' been running offices forever and you guys are just the new kids on the block. You'd better learn how to say 'Yes, ma'am' or damn well be prepared to pay the consequences."

Dougherty broke in on a more serious note. "Tomorrow we have to actually make final decisions about who we'll offer the last few spots to. Fred Reynolds from the CIA is our first choice for in-house computer guru if he'll take it. He's been running a small group for a couple of years now so he might not want to make the move but we intend to butter him up and see if he'll give it a whirl. We also want to entice Celeste Butterfield to become one of our investigators." He turned to his wife. "She's very bright. You met her at a party once."

"I remember her, a tall, pretty black woman. Told me she played basketball at Howard before she went to law school."

"That's the one," Dougherty said. "Another computer person we want as a part-time consultant is a little strange. He's one that Whitman wasn't happy with. Director Timmons was the one who put us onto the man and we honestly don't know a great deal about him. He purports to be a computer security expert. We must have looked doubtful so he demonstrated how easy it was to hack into our home computer. Didn't take him but a minute or two, and I mean he got our passwords and into our bank statements and tax stuff, everything. I thought we had our system well protected but he showed us otherwise and taught me how to fix it. Out of the half dozen or so candidates we interviewed for the position, he was the only one who seemed to fit the bill. Well, there was another fellow that Timmons told us about whom we really wanted but he declined."

"That one sounded like a real spook and goes by several names. We're not sure even Timmons knows who he really is," Harrington added.

Claire muttered, "I just can't believe that NSA doesn't know the real name of somebody they've done business with. They turn up more info than both the CIA and FBI put together from what you've told us. Why don't you tap his phone or put a tail on him? How can anyone have a secret identity in this day and age where everyone's life history is on a microchip or in a computer somewhere?"

"We found it pretty hard to swallow, too," agreed Dougherty. "We can chase down just about anyone in the whole United States in a few hours if we really put our resources into it. Almost everyone leaves a paper trial, at least if they're employed."

Washington DC

This year's Advances in Genome Biology and Technology meeting was being held at the Ritz Carlton in Georgetown and she was staying with Oldenberg's sister, Liz, at the family residence also in Georgetown only a mile or so from the hotel. The conference had just concluded and Kate stopped to talk with two of the presenters. When she glanced at her watch and saw it was six-twenty. She pulled out her cell phone. "Hi, Liz, sorry I got hung up but I was talking to someone who gave a talk that interested me. Where should I meet you?"

Liz told her not to worry, she'd pick her up and they'd drive instead of walk.

The gallery at the Corcoran College of Art and Design on Seventeenth Street was only about a half mile north of the hotel and they made it in time to hear the artist address the sparse gathering. Marc Henderson was a pencil-thin bearded young man clad in faded corduroys, an African style shirt, sandals and a baggy sport jacket that looked like it might have come from a thrift shop. Liz remembered him from high school where he'd always seemed spaced out. She thought she detected marijuana when she went over to say hi. She noticed his accent was different now and sounded very affected.

The paintings were all large, mostly six to eight feet tall, and consisted of crude figures in various postures on a yellow or lime green solid color background. One had to study the painting for a minute to decide that it represented a figure at all.

It certainly wasn't Kate's idea of great art, but Liz told her he was selling quite well in the local market. No accounting for other people's taste, Kate thought. It also seemed to her that hardly anyone even looked at the paintings. Maybe they had before she and Liz arrived, but somehow she doubted that. Everyone seemed engrossed in intense conversations about one thing or another as they made their way around the gallery.

They stopped at the bar where Liz introduced Kate to the two attendees she knew and they decided to skip the wine.

"Kind of boring, huh," Liz whispered.

"Yeah, it sure is. You think we've been here long enough to leave?"

"Right on. There's a place not far from campus called Third Edition where a lot of my classmates hang out on Friday nights. Let's go." The streets were crowded and they ended up parking four blocks away.

The bar was located in the middle of the block and bordered on one of the less desirable areas of town. They found a couple of empty seats at a table with some of Liz's acquaintances and both ordered a local draft beer. Some of the others at the table were already really well into the sauce and would probably need a lift home. Liz introduced Kate to some of her friends.

"Are you still working out, Kate?" Liz asked over the din.

"Usually two evenings a week for a couple of hours. Dan fixed up an old shed where we meet. He's been teaching us karate. It really feels good to do something physical after being stuck in the lab all day. I've been jogging a little too, mostly early in the morning before I go in. How about you?"

"About the same. I have to keep up with Dan or else I'll never hear the end of it. I am getting better though, got my black belt a few months ago."

"Congratulations. Dan tested us recently and we're all brown belts now. I don't think I'll ever have enough time to go much further than that."

"You never know. It's just like any other kind of regular exercise. I find it more fun than jogging or using the workout machines, although I still do some of both."

They listened to the music and watched the dancing for a while but it was difficult to carry on much of a conversation. Finally Liz suggested they go back the house.

On the way back to the car Kate told Liz about the meetings and her thesis research. "I can't believe how fast this semester is going by. I think I have an idea about how to do gene sequencing faster than the current methods. If it pans out it could be a ticket to about any research post I might want. I still don't know if it'll play, but I think it's got a chance." Kate went on to describe more about her idea as they walked.

The streets were nearly empty now and there were few streetlights, at least ones with bulbs left. They started to walk a little faster but paused at the sight of a man slumped in a doorway. Kate hesitated. "Should we see if he's okay?"

Liz grabbed her arm. "Not a good idea around here. It's warm out and he isn't going to freeze to death like some drunks do in the winter. Just keep on walking."

They hadn't gone far when Kate heard someone behind them and turned around. It was the drunk. Just then another figure emerged from between two cars a little ahead of them. A third figure sitting on the steps of the building just ahead on their right stood up and moved toward them. This sort of thing was in the paper nearly every day, but it was the first experience either of them had with the threat violent crime in any form.

"Looks like we got ourselves some little college girlies. Maybe they got drugs on 'em," hissed the one from between the cars.

He was small, maybe five-seven or eight with long black hair and thin as a rail. "You hand over them purses and watches and stuff we won't hurt nobody," the one they thought was drunk said in a low voice.

"Nobody around here, man! Let's have us a little fun, man. Stick 'em in the van and drive somewhere real quiet. They'll like it, man," snarled the second assailant.

"Shut the fuck up!" the one by the steps growled "Just grab their damn money and move on, you hear me, brother?" He reached for her purse.

Liz wheeled around. It was too dark to get a good look at his face but she noticed the dirty tee shirt and the tattoos on his hands as he yanked on the purse. She managed to hold onto it, and instead of pulling away kicked him in the groin as hard as she could. He cried out and doubled over and she kicked again, this time in his face sending him backwards into brick facade of the closest building. She turned and glanced at Kate who was screaming for help.

Liz doubted the scream was likely to mobilize anyone to come to their aid, at least not soon enough to might make a difference, and feared one or more of the assailants might have a weapon. She also didn't know if Kate was in control or skilled enough to be of help. In a van there'd be no room to maneuver, so if there was any way to stop what she imagined was coming it had to be before they were sequestered in the vehicle. It was amazing how much one could think of in a few milliseconds, and how clear things could become when they had to.

Kate's training, while not nearly as extensive as that of Liz Oldenberg, was not entirely wasted. She'd seen what Liz had done, and as the apparent drunk grabbed her from behind she brought her heel down hard along his shin. He cursed and spun her around slapping at her face, the blow glancing off the top of her head. She countered by striking upward with the heel of her hand, the blow landing hard on his nose and making a cracking sound. He let go and jumped backwards clutching his face and screaming obscenities. Kate kicked him in the groin as she'd seen Liz do seconds before and then planted a second kick on the lateral side of his knee. He collapsed to the sidewalk and started to moan.

"Bastard!" she yelled, and kicked him again, this time in the chest. She turned just in time to see their third assailant face down on the ground. Liz had one foot planted on his shoulder and was wrenching his arm backwards. The man screamed in pain. Liz dropped the arm, grasped his long hair, pulled back hard, and then slammed his face into the pavement. "Check yours for weapons," she yelled. "I'll do this one."

Someone leaned out of a second floor window in a house across the street and Liz yelled, "Call the cops!"

A police car arrived minutes later, and by that time a small crowd had gathered. Liz explained what had happened to the officers and handed him a switchblade she'd found on the one she'd searched.

One of the officers asked if they wanted to press charges.

"Hell, yes," Liz told them. "If we don't they'll accost someone who can't defend themselves and you'll have bigger problems."

"Then you'll need to come down to the station and it may take a while. Sorry about that, I know you've just been through a very difficult time."

The two most severely injured were shortly transported by ambulance to a hospital and the third was taken into custody and stuffed into the back seat of a police car. Liz and Kate followed them to the Metropolitan Police Station on K Street where they filled out incident forms and their statements were taken. They were then told to wait until those were transcribed and ready to be signed.

They each got a cup of tepid bitter tasting coffee out of a machine in the hall and waited for almost an hour before the officer who'd spoken to them earlier appeared. He smiled and ushered them at a small near-by room. "You aren't going to believe this, but one of these clowns has demanded we press charges against you for busting his nose. It's all a crock but I have to question you a little more just to be sure we have all the details right. It's only a formality, nothing you should need to worry about."

"Are we allowed to make a call, sergeant?" Liz asked.

"Absolutely, ma'am, use the phone on the desk."

Instead she pulled out her cell phone and dialed the number for 'Uncle' Bill Timmons. Her parents had always impressed upon her to contact him if any emergency arose while they were away. If this wasn't an emergency, she didn't know what might pass for one.

"It's Liz Oldenberg. Sorry to wake you, sir, but a good friend and I are at the K Street police station being questioned. We were attacked by three hoods who tried to rob us and were talking about other things they might want to do to us. We managed to get out of it okay, but we hurt two of them pretty bad. Now they're claiming we assaulted them. I think we should have a lawyer. I hate to call you like this but my folks told me to let you know if I was ever in any trouble. The officer who spoke to us told us not to worry about it, but I thought I should let you know."

"Liz, are you and your friend all right?" mumbled Timmons, feeling for his glasses and trying to clear the cobwebs out of his head. "Where are you right now? I didn't get that."

Liz again gave him the name of the station as well as the address and phone number. "I think they'll let us go as soon as we finish giving another statement," Liz offered.

"Don't say another word, Liz. I'll get somebody over there right away. Tell the police that someone will be there to assist you shortly."

Forty minutes later Sean Harrington arrived, introduced himself, and showed his ID. "Lieutenant, we both know with things as busy as they are around here that cases like this get shoved on the back burner. We'd very much like to see these guys do hard time. I can run a little background on them and pass it on to you if you have no objection. Also there are some people I know in the prosecutor's office who might develop an interest if you've got any more than this incident to run with."

"I hear what you're saying, Agent Harrington, but we have enough murders and major violence to deal with every day here in the city that unless one of these very lucky young ladies had been killed or something, nothing much will happen to those bastards. However, if you have the interest and if the assistant DA will go along, I'll put somebody on it and see what we can do."

Liz was amazed at how a thing like this could be so easily brushed off. "You mean if this happened to some other college girls who didn't have a friend like Mr. Timmons to call in the middle of the night these punks would just get their wrists slapped and walk? I find that hard to believe!"

"First of all, young lady, if this happened to almost any two other girls, we wouldn't be here having this conversation," the lieutenant replied. "They'd be lying outside somewhere, maybe alive, maybe not. And second, you better believe it. There is so much violence going on out in the streets that all we can do is try to put out the little fires and pursue only the real headline cases. John Q Taxpayer may not like that very much, but that's all he's paying for. Now I need to run over this with both of you myself. It'll take a few minutes, okay? You think you're up to it?"

Liz and Kate gave their statements and thanked the officers and the lieutenant for the sympathy they'd showed. Harrington followed them back to the Oldenberg residence and told them he'd keep track of the investigation and see to it their attackers got what they deserved.

Once back in the Georgetown house both girls let it all out. The trauma of the evening hit them hard and both shed tears as they commiserated. They ended up sleeping until almost ten the next morning, and over a bowl of cereal and black coffee they talked over the events of previous evening meeting. "I know somebody we should talk to," Liz said. "He's my karate teacher, and he's a good listener. Cruz Lopez is this sort of weird guy with a very interesting background. He moved to Washington a few years ago and opened his own dojo."

Kate let out a laugh, her first in several hours. "Lopez, huh? What a coincidence, I've heard about him from your brother. They studied together in Japan."

The dojo was empty when they arrived around two o'clock that afternoon and Liz poured out their tale of woe, including how Kate had heard about him before.

Lopez chuckled briefly and then turned serious, "You were both very lucky young ladies last night; not lucky about being accosted but lucky in the sense you were able to deal with a very dangerous situation. Was there any chance you could have run away?"

"I don't think so," Kate said. "It all happened so fast all we could do was to react."

Lopez shook his head. "I'm sorry you had to go through all that, both the trauma and having to spend hours at the police station. Why don't you put on your gear and run through some warm-ups and then show me what happened and how you responded? It'll help you work off some of the tension I can see in your faces."

After they'd changed into their gear, Lopez watched Kate go through her warm-up routine. "Very good," he said with a smile. "How long have you been studying?"

"A little over a year."

Lopez had them reenact the events of the previous evening and then discussed and demonstrated possible alternatives that might have worked out better. "It's always desirable to control the situation without causing more harm than necessary," he admonished.

"It's difficult to think about that when it's three to two and your attackers have weapons," Kate said.

"I understand that, but it's important after something that traumatic to analyze what you did and consider how else you might have handled the situation."

They chatted for another hour while Lopez regaled them with stories about his past. He invited Kate to stop by for a workout whenever she was in DC.

Chapter 6

Arlington, Virginia

"Sean, how's the case about those young ladies coming?" Hurwitz asked. "You hear anything yet?"

Mrs. Fisher looked over at Harrington with interest.

"Yeah, the clowns who assaulted them all have thick records but mostly for petty theft, never for assault. The DA has agreed to prosecute and told me he aims to put 'em away for a while," Harrington replied.

Willa slapped her hand on the table. "Good. I want to see the bastards do time, lots of time. As a woman I have a lot of empathy for them, probably more than you men ever could."

"Hey, take it easy, Willa. We've all got wives and kids so we do have plenty of sympathy for them. We want their assailants punished as much as you do."

"Sorry," Willa murmured sheepishly. "Who should we assign to follow up on the phone numbers? The faster we get that taken care of the better. Danny has friends over at Justice so he might be the one to take care of that."

"How about having Celeste do it?" Dougherty asked.

"She's pretty well stacked up right now so I'd better take care of it myself," Hurwitz replied.

Ames, Iowa

Clyde Johnson sat on a bench outside the electrical engineering building eating his sack lunch and sipping a Coca-Cola. He looked up and noticed Takayama walking across the lawn toward him. "Hey, how are you, Mr. Takayama?" he called, and slid to one side to make room.

"I'm well, thank you. I haven't seen you or Lucy at the casino lately," Takayama said with a smile as he sat down.

"Oh, Lucy and I only go there about every other month or so. Sometimes I go visit my kids but usually I just hang around the house. Lucy and I go see a movie occasionally but mostly we watch TV or read. Do you read very much Mr. Takayama?"

Please call me Hidehiko or, better yet, just Hiko. In Japan we use last names almost all the time, but in America it's different. It isn't nearly as formal here, and I must say I like that. And yes, I read all the time myself, books, magazines, scientific papers, almost anything."

"What's the name of the company you work for again?"

"Yokohama Industries, it's a large holding company that owns several other smaller businesses. That's common in Japan. We call that type of company a *keiretsu.*"

Johnson wondered what that meant exactly and recalled how he felt uneasy the previous times he'd spoken with Takayama but couldn't put his finger on the reason. "Why did your company send you to America?"

"As I think I mentioned to you before, it's very important for us to understand businesses over here better so we can compete. We don't have many resources in Japan and we depend on trade."

"What did you do before you came to the United States?"

Takayama hesitated and coughed a couple of times. He didn't reply right away.

Johnson noticed the man's expression change. *Something's not right; he looks so damn sad all of a sudden.*

Takayama pulled out a handkerchief and blew his nose. "I was a mechanical engineer for several years and later was promoted to manager of one of the smaller divisions," he said in a low voice. "Something happened that I don't really like to talk about. The chairman of my company suggested I accept this new position."

The expression on Takayama's face suddenly reminded Johnson of the accident and how he'd wanted to torture the man, a drunk who'd drifted across the centerline and hit them head on. His wife and daughter had died instantly. He hesitated for a few seconds then cleared his throat and reached over to touch Takayama on the arm. "I'm very sorry, Mr. Takayama. I can understand how you must feel."

Takayama didn't reply so Johnson asked if he got back to Japan very often.

"About every three or four months," Takayama replied in a hesitant tone.

Johnson thought Takayama was too upset to press for any more information at the moment.

As soon as Takayama departed, Johnson went to see Professor Evans and recounted their conversation. "When I asked him how he happened to be here he suddenly appeared very sad but didn't seem to want to tell me why. I actually felt sorry for the man," he told Evans. "I thought he was going to ask me questions about what's going on here, but he didn't. "

Evans stared first up at the high ceiling then back at Johnson. "That was an awful thing, Clyde."

Johnson nodded. "Yeah, still hurts a lot." He let out a sigh and shook his head. "Anyhow, what should we do about this guy?"

"The next time Takayama mentions a tour let me know and I'll have Dalton invite him to Durham Center. He may not know about Super G yet since there's little public information available. A couple of government agencies and one other university are scheduled to get them for testing, but not until we're satisfied with how the one here performs. McGregor won't formally introduce them until sometime after the first of the year. I doubt this Takayama character knows about the new building so don't say anything about that even if he leans on you."

"I think I see where you're going with this. You want me to stay in touch with him and lead him on to learn what he's up to."

The professor smiled. "That's absolutely right, C.J."

Later that afternoon Evans brought Sam Dalton up to speed and asked him to brief the others.

Ames, Iowa

"You've hardly said a word all meal," Martha Evans said glancing at her husband's half-full plate. "What's going on, and how come you didn't go to the lab today? You know it's one of your usual days. Hazel even called to make sure you were feeling okay."

"No hiding anything from you, my dear. I stayed home today deliberately although I really wanted to be there. You see, tonight they're going to try out the new computer. I wanted Ewen to have the honor of firing it up the first time and I was afraid I'd steal some of his thunder."

"And that's one of the reasons we've stayed married all these years." She laughed and gave him a peck on the cheek. "Despite that crusty façade, you have a heart of gold. Maybe that's why I have so many Christmas cards to answer every year. Speaking of that, have you decided about the invitation to give those talks in England?" she asked with a coy look. "We could take an extra week of vacation for some visiting and sightseeing. I'd especially like to see our old friends in Edinburgh"

"That sabbatical was at least fifteen years ago. How many of those people are still alive?"

"Almost all of them. You don't read the Christmas letters do you? I've suspected that for a long time."

Evans chuckled, "I plead guilty to that charge, my dear. There are well over a hundred of those every year. No way do I have the time to go through them. That's why we still have Hazel."

"Over three hundred a year, husband dear, and I answer all of them myself, not Hazel. A little more coffee?"

"I'll get it," he volunteered, anxious to change the subject.

Ames, Iowa

Precisely at seven o'clock that evening Howland powered up the QD and five minutes later he threw another switch that connected the Super G to the new machine. The purpose of this trial was not to perform any computations but rather only to demonstrate that the machines could communicate with each other.

Ten minutes later, Howland, beaming now, shut down the computers, passed around cigars, and handed each a bottle of cold Corona. "Another month or two and maybe we'll find out if this baby really does what we hope it will," he crowed.

Hickman nudged O'Leary and whispered, "Most excited I've ever seen him."

Boston, Massachusetts

Takayama turned in his rental and made his way toward the shuttle gate. He stopped at a bank of phones. "Moshi moshi, Takayama desu. My plans have changed. I'm catching the shuttle to Washington. I need to do some work on one of the grants we sponsor. Tomorrow I'll try to get a flight to Chicago, and then on to Iowa the following day."

He listened for a few moments then said, "Hai, Matsumoto-sama. Wakarimasu." His company did indeed sponsor grants for a few scientific investigators and did award research contracts to several universities and companies in the US. To see Takayama in action one might take him for a salesman, but in fact he was really a listener. The various grants were merely a tool to place him in a position where he might overhear an array of knowledgeable people discuss some very cutting-edge technology. He thought that were he an American he'd be doing the same thing, but only for some American company. He was anxious to complete his housekeeping chores in DC and Chicago because he was now very curious about what was going on in Ames.

Back when he'd first tried to recruit Johnson it was obvious the man was suspicious. Well, he relished these little challenges and thought it was just too bad the old janitor didn't seem to trust him.

Ames, Iowa

Oldenberg bicycled the two miles to the storefront dojo located in an older section of town where he used to work out regularly until he moved into the old farmhouse. Harada-sensei, the local master, was about forty-five, lean and wiry. He'd opened the dojo some ten years earlier, and Dan was by far his most advanced and serious student. "Oldenberg-san, I've missed you. Where have you been hiding?"

"Mostly trying to complete my dissertation," Oldenberg replied with a little smile. "It takes up almost all my time but I still work out a couple of times a week with some people I rent that old house with. We converted an unused shed into a dojo. Yukiko and I are going back to Japan next week, but only for a few days. I wish we had enough time to visit Ueda-sensei in Dazaifu but there's no way we can fit it in."

"That's too bad. You should really take a little more time to do the things you enjoy. If you keep putting them off you'll regret it later. Why don't you at least bring the people you've been working out with in here sometime and let me see what you have them doing?"

"When Yukiko and I get back I'll ask them and see if we can find a time when everyone can make it. I'll call you, sensei."

Tokyo, Japan

Oldenberg and Yukiko stepped out of the Japan Folk Crafts Museum in Meguro-ku into a heavy afternoon haze that engulfed the city. Yukiko squinted and tugged on Dan's arm. "We need to find an optical shop. A screw fell out of these sunglasses and I need to replace it. Let's ask at that police box across the street."

While they waited in the air-conditioned shop, Yukiko asked, "It's nice to get out of the heat for a few minutes. What did you think of the folk art? What things did you like best?"

"I think probably the old Imari pottery, the pieces with the subtle blue glazes. The other ones I liked were those from Karatsu. When I was in Kyushu I visited a couple of kilns. My mother loves going to them. She's collected so much pottery that she can't display it all at one time. What did you like best?"

"The textiles, especially the *ikat* from Saga Prefecture. Where should we go next?"

Oldenberg glanced at his watch. "It's late and we promised your parents we'd have dinner with them. We might as well head over there."

Although Asakusa was in an older part of the city, nearly all the buildings were post war. Yukiko's parents lived on the fourth floor in a large apartment building with a nice view overlooking a tiny park. While her father guided Dan into the western-style living room her mother recruited Yukiko to help fix dinner in the kitchen. "Dan seems like a very nice young man," she observed with a sly smile. "You two like each other a lot, don't you?"

"Yes, mother, you know we do."

"Well, you know you aren't getting any younger, and neither are your father and I."

"We know that, mother." She took a deep breath. "Would it bother you and father very much if I were to marry a gaijin?"

"Not at all, at least as long as it's Dan. We like him. He's always polite and he's very well educated."

"Yes he is." She hesitated then smiled back. "We've both thought about getting married and talked about it some but decided we should get the next semester over with and be absolutely sure."

Mrs. Kawakami embraced her daughter. "I'm glad. Your father and I would be very pleased to have Dan for a son-in-law. I think we should invite his parents over for dinner."

"That's a great idea. They've been very nice to me and I think they'd like to see us married too."

Ames, Iowa

O'Leary was again bitching about the need for so much secrecy, something he groused about every few weeks.

"Don't knock it, Brian. We lucked into a great opportunity here. Most people in the department would kill for the chance to help build an entirely new kind of computer."

"How many people do you think know about it, Harry?"

"Word gets around, man. This is a pretty small place after all. You can bet anyone who's interested has already found out it's one of the new McGregor supercomputers."

O'Leary breathed an inward sigh of relief. The Super G was okay for some university people to know about as long as they didn't learn about the main course down in the basement. Somehow he had the feeling that Hickman was going to say something else, something more disconcerting. He didn't know quite why he felt that way but there was something about Harry he couldn't put his finger on. "Yeah, I really am glad we got this gig, even if I bitch about some of the restrictions." He changed the subject. "I've been here almost eight years now, and you've been here longer than that."

"Hell, I enjoy school and taking courses. I understood that if I completed all the prerequisites for my degree they'd force me to graduate and then I'd have to go to work." Hickman chuckled. "I solved that problem by never taking quite the right courses to graduate, ergo I wouldn't need to go out and get a real job." Hickman laughed again. "I'm surprised you never reached this state of enlightenment yourself."

O'Leary didn't finish up at the lab until after eight despite promising Cindy he'd make it by seven-thirty at the latest. She was in the kitchen when he arrived and he bent down to kiss the back of her neck. "Man, it's hot out there," he said, hoping she wasn't too pissed off.

"See this stir-fry I made. Now I'll need to warm it up and it won't taste as good. What kept you this time?"

"Howland is really cracking the whip. We're working as fast as we can without making a lot of mistakes. How the two machines interface is crucial. That takes a lot of checking and double checking every damn little detail as we go along."

Cindy dished up dinner while O'Leary took the iced tea out of the refrigerator and poured two glasses. "It's so damn hot out there, what say we take a dip after we eat?"

"Didn't your mother ever tell you not to go swimming right after eating?"

"Sure, but everybody knows that's an old wives' tale."

"I'm hot too, so you want to race a few laps?"

"There's no way you can beat me, sweetie-pie, and you know it."

"Bet I can if you swim the breast stroke and I do the crawl."

"You're on, babe."

It was already dark when they made it down to the deserted pool. They raced a series of three sprints down and back. O'Leary felt sorry for her and allowed her to nose him out on the third try. When he bent to pick up a towel she swatted him on the rump. "That's for letting me win that last one." She laughed. "Next time

I'll make you wear those water wings the little kids wear. We'll just see what happens then."

O'Leary chuckled, "I didn't think you'd notice."

"Oh, I notice everything. They must have added chlorine lately. We'll need showers."

"Who's first?" he asked when they got upstairs.

She smiled at him. "It's big enough. C'mon, you can wash my back."

The shower was almost large enough for two average size people and the water came out cold. Cindy flinched and O'Leary grabbed her to keep her from falling then pulled her tight against his chest and kissed her. "You always wear a bathing suit when you take a shower, my lady?" he murmured in her ear.

"Not usually," she whispered back, suddenly aware of his hardness. She pulled off her top. "Your turn," and then she turned and yanked his trunks down.

Much later, as they lay on her twin bed holding each other tightly, Cindy murmured, "You know, that hurt a little. It was my first time."

"Believe it or not, mine too. I've told you I love you lots of times, well, I love you even more now."

They awoke a little before six as if the alarm had rung. Over toast and coffee, O'Leary said, "My housemates are going to wonder."

"You toad, I'm sure we're the last ones of our little cadre to get it on. Besides, you fall asleep here half the time you come over."

"Yeah, but you always wake me up and send me packing before it gets real late."

Bethesda, Maryland

Summers' thesis advisor had sponsored her for a meeting at NIH about advances in genome technology shortly before the semester was to begin. Although she wasn't ready to present any of her own work, she was grateful for this opportunity to talk with some of the world's foremost experts in the field. She called Liz Oldenberg and they arranged to get together the afternoon the talks were due to end.

The Hyatt Regency, located in the heart of downtown Bethesda, had all the amenities one could ask for, and Summers was glad the department had sprung for hotel and meeting fee. By the time the formal presentations were over she felt she'd learn a great deal, but the best part had been to listen in on some of the side conversations and occasionally ask a question pertaining to her own research. It also allowed her to say hello to a few people at her own level that she'd met in the past and compare notes.

Liz picked Kate up after the last meeting and took her to the hotel to check out. The plan was to meet Cruz Lopez at his dojo and then go out for dinner. She'd spend the next night at the Oldenberg's house and Liz would drive her to the airport for her flight back to Ames.

Lopez was teaching a class when they arrived. After changing, both girls got on the treadmills to warm up and chatted about how things were going.

When Lopez was free they had the chance to chat for a few minutes.

"Cruz, you never mentioned you'd been married," Kate said. "Dan told me when I said I'd probably stop by while I was at the meeting."

Lopez looked up at the ceiling for a moment before responding, "That was a long time ago. Her name was Penny but she called herself 'Flower'. I'm ashamed to say it lasted less than a year. By the time it was over I was happy to see her gone."

"Do you still have any contact with her?" Liz asked.

"No, she ended up dying of a drug overdose a couple of years after the divorce."

"I'm sorry," Liz said, putting her hand on his arm.

"Sometimes things are just destined to happen," he sighed. "You can't roll back the clock."

The evening ended on a lighter note when they all returned to the Georgetown house and ordered a pizza.

Ames, Iowa

O'Leary and Cindy had wrangled a few days off near the end of the summer to visit her family in California and O'Leary had been lucky to hitch a ride out with Ray Brown who was to ferrying a pair of McGregor Industries executives to San Diego for a meeting along with several boxes he'd picked up in Ames. Again, Brown invited him to the cockpit. O'Leary climbed into the right seat, slipped the headphones on, and studied the controls and gauges to refresh his memory. The voice in the headset instructed him to taxi out behind an American 737 and hold short of 28R for inbound traffic. Brown checked the wind looked out over the runway and then said to O'Leary, "You up for trying a takeoff, kiddo?"

O'Leary hadn't expected this but quickly answered that he was.

"Okay then, give it a little juice and ease off the brakes. Don't rush anything." O'Leary followed a good distance behind the larger aircraft and waited. The 737 lifted off two minutes later and then it was his turn.

"Gulfstream 876, you're cleared for takeoff. Contact Departure Control on 101.71. Have a good day," came the voice from the tower.

"876 rolling," responded Brown. "Okay, Brian, time to go. With the light weight we have on board you can rotate at a hundred and thirty knots. I'll talk you through it, a piece of cake."

Given this was his first takeoff in the G4, O'Leary was perspiring more than a little. He wasn't afraid since he knew Brown could take over at the first sign of a problem but he wasn't about to let that happen. He turned onto 28R, pushed the throttle forward, and released the brakes. It felt like a long time before he saw the gauge hit 130, though it was really only a few seconds. He heard Brown's voice in his headset.

"Begin to rotate. That's it, nice and smooth." Moments later Brown told him to retract the gear. "Okay, start easing back a little on your throttle but not too much," he said a couple of minutes later as they passed through four thousand feet. "Okay, now go ahead and contact Departure."

O'Leary keyed his mike, "Departure, Gulfstream 876 for San Diego. Request altitude and heading."

"Gulfstream 876, climb to twelve-zero, air speed 250 knots, and heading two-seven zero. Contact Omaha Center on 101.20. Good day."

"Contacting Center on 101.20."

The flight was smooth the whole way out to Southern California. O'Leary flew most of the way including the first part of the final approach but Brown took over for the actual landing. They taxied to the private gates on the southern side of the airport where Brown tapped him on the shoulder. "You did very well, Brian. I'll give you another lesson sometime. You must be starting to rate in the scheme of things for the boss to have me divert."

"I wish, Cap, but it wasn't me. It's what's in the boxes I brought on board. Those guys in back need it for a meeting. I'm just the courier. Thanks again for the chance to fly this bird. Someday I want to take regular lessons and upgrade my ticket. It's a hell of a lot of fun driving this puppy around."

"Always has been for me. I couldn't imagine a nicer way to spend my time. I get to play all the great courses on a super per diem. See you two. Take care."

With that O'Leary and Cindy were back on the ground waiting for her mother to come pick them up.

Ames, Iowa

Hidehiko Takayama landed in Des Moines after several grueling days of travel and realized this visit would have to be brief. He knew it was one of new supercomputers from McGregor Industries and understood they were already starting to take orders for the machines although delivery wasn't expected to begin for several more months, so why all the secrecy? He'd seen some of the speculation and claims in the trade journals causing him to wonder why they'd sent a prototype to this particular university. He suspected that there was something more to all this but so far was batting zero on validating his hunch. Determined to find the reason, he decided to lean on Johnson a bit harder.

He found an unoccupied spot in the waiting area and pulled out his cell phone and the small laptop computer he carried everywhere. It contained the names, phone numbers, addresses, and brief summaries of communications with his array of clients and informers, all in a code he kept locked away in his head. Some thirty minutes and four phone calls later he shut down the computer, put away the battered phone card, and made his way to the Hertz counter.

Takayama climbed the stairs to the front porch of the white frame house a few blocks north of town admiring how well Johnson kept the place up.

Johnson didn't appear surprised to see him, and this didn't escape his attention. A fleeting thought crossed his mind. Just who was playing whom in this game?

"Hello there, Mr. Takayama, I have the day off because I worked on the weekend for one of the young fellows. Come on in for a minute. How have you been?"

"Very well, thank you. I'm sorry I didn't call ahead but my company wanted some last minute changes in a contract we're negotiating for some research your school of agriculture is supposed to do. Anyway I thought maybe you had some new insights about the computer that's being installed in that new building. I heard it's one of the Super Gs from McGregor Industries. Have you had the chance to look at it or heard much about its capabilities?"

"I've heard it's powerful and very fast, better than anything else on the market. I understand they put the prototype here to get any bugs out before it actually goes on the market."

"Is there any way that you could arrange a tour for me?" inquired Takayama.

Johnson frowned. "I don't know. They still have all this security business in place so only the regular people who work there have the necessary badges and codes to get in. I heard the official unveiling should be after Christmas sometime. I don't understand how they already have so many orders for machines that expensive sight unseen."

"It's probably because of McGregor Industries' reputation. They have most of the worldwide market for supercomputers so I suppose people purchase them on that basis alone. Just like everyone else, my company and its' partners are most interested to know more about this new computer and I was hoping you could get me in to talk to the people working with it."

"Well, I wish I could help you out on this, Mr. T, but I'm not really in the loop. Listen, if I hear any more I'll let you know."

"I understand. If you do learn any more about its specifications please let me know, okay?"

"Sure, I can do that."

"Say, how about I take you and Lucy out for dinner to express my gratitude for your help."

"You treated last time, so this one it should be on me."

"I much appreciate that you wish to reciprocate, Clyde, but I'm on an expense account and it would be very difficult for me to explain that to my superiors. What time would be convenient for you, and where should we go?"

"There's a restaurant called the China Moon near the campus that's very good, and it's not crowded this time of the year with most of the students gone."

"I've eaten there once and thought the food was good. Do you like it?"

"Lucy and I both like some of the Asian dishes on the menu, particularly the Chinese ones. She gets off at five so would six-thirty be okay? I'll let her know and she can meet us there."

Takayama bade Johnson good-bye and got back to business. A couple of phone calls netted appointments with two people in the facilities offices for the following morning. He went into town and had some business cards made up identifying him as a part time writer for an obscure architectural magazine. This was the part of his work that he truly enjoyed. It reminded him of the ancient Chinese strategy game of *Go*. He thought that if he could get a look at the construction schematics for the new computer building he might get an idea what this secrecy business was all about.

Takayama arrived at the China Moon a few minutes early, ordered a bottle of Pete's Wicked Red, and sat down at a table close to the front to wait for Johnson and Lucy. They arrived a few minutes later and each ordered the Chinese special of the day.

Takayama made a mental note to treat Johnson and Lucy to a weekend at the Reservation if this panned out. *Just maybe Johnson is going to earn his retainer.* It was much too premature to offer an increase in the retainer to better set the hook, but it would show appreciation on a personal level for services rendered.

The next morning Johnson stuck his head in the door to Professor Evans' suite the next morning and asked Mrs. Stoddard if he might have a word with him.

"Yes, he's here. Let me buzz him." She pushed a button on the intercom. "Clyde Johnson is here, says he needs to see you." She turned to Johnson and nodded. "Okay, go on in."

Evans, with sleeves rolled up and coffee mug in hand, peered over his half-frames as Johnson entered. "Is this about our friend, Clyde?"

"Yes, sir, I just had another visit from Takayama. He seems very interested in the new computer building and asked if I couldn't get him in for a tour. I reminded him that I'm just the janitor and told him security is tight. I'm pretty sure he smells something big is going on."

"What do you think he knows so far?"

"Pretty much what everybody else does, that it's a prototype of the next generation McGregor supercomputers, but I think he suspects there's more to it. There's already much speculation about its performance specifications."

"So, what do you think we should do about him?"

Johnson pondered for a moment and then smiled. "I have an idea. He treated Lucy and me to dinner last night. I'll keep playing dumb but tell him you've given a couple of outsiders a limited preview. I suggest to him that, since his company is a big donor to the university, you might be willing to reciprocate by showing him the Super G. Hopefully that might satisfy him and get him off our backs." He waited as the professor mulled this over before adding, "Maybe you could suggest you'd have Professor Howland and the others do some research project for his company in exchange for a big donation. That would give you the chance to size up this character. What do you think?"

Evans frowned and seemed to contemplate briefly. "I would like to find out how much he suspects and what he's up to. I'll talk it over with the rest of the team first. If we decide to go ahead, we'll have to be sure nothing important is going on at the time."

That afternoon Evans spoke with his principal investigators and they agreed Johnson's idea might be worth a try.

That afternoon, at the physical plant offices, Takayama presented himself as a member of an architectural group putting together a magazine spread about recent construction at the university. This had been coordinated with both the magazine mentioned and the architectural firm thanks to one of his affiliates. It was helpful to have a multitude of contacts that asked few questions, knowing that one day Takayama would likely return the favor. A secretary helpfully pulled the construction plans for the buildings he'd inquired about and provided him with a list of the construction firms engaged in the projects. He jotted down the names of three out of state companies that in turn had done work on the new computer facility over a matter of several weeks. Unusual, he thought as he spread out the first set of prints. Takayama made sure he was alone before he pulled a small camera from his briefcase and photographed the plans.

He next walked twice around the building housing the Super G before strolling over to the Union for lunch. As he munched on chicken wings and sipped a coke, he suddenly had an idea. If Johnson couldn't get him inside the new computer building it suddenly occurred to him that maybe a more direct approach might work. He smiled and mentally gave himself a pat on the back.

Back at his hotel, Takayama entered the photos he'd taken into his laptop. As he studied the blown up images of the blueprints for the new computer center he realized there was something funny that he didn't quite understand. The sizes didn't match up. There was space unaccounted for in the plans. He pulled off his glasses and rubbed his eyes. When he looked them over again he picked up the other discrepancy. A full subbasement had been excavated but no notation about what it was for and nothing in the plans about wiring nor why the underground walls, ceiling, and floor were double thickness nor why there was five foot crawl space between the basement and the first floor. *What the hell's going on in there?*

Late that evening he called Matsumoto-san in Tokyo and shared his suspicion there was more to this new computer than they were letting on. He suggested that his boss arrange for a fax to be sent to Professor Evans requesting a meeting with Evans.

The following morning Takayama placed a call to Professor Evans' office. Hazel Stoddard acknowledged that she had indeed received a fax from the offices of Yokohama Industries that morning regarding a request for a meeting between Takayama and the Professor. Yes, the professor would be happy to discuss the project in question. Would it be convenient for Mr. Takayama to come by around four o'clock this afternoon? Did he need assistance with transportation or accommodations?

Promptly at three forty-five Takayama, dressed in a dark suit and conservative tie, presented his card and a small bouquet of flowers to Mrs. Stoddard for her help in arranging the meeting on such short notice. After buzzing the inner sanctum she escorted him to Evans' office.

Evans stood and came around his desk with a slight but noticeable limp. "Aha, yes. Hazel told me you were coming. I don't get very many visitors these days. I think they keep me around for show mostly. Please tell me how we might be able to help you and your company."

Takayama outlined a rather simple computational problem that the branch office could easily have handled on its own. He was a little surprised that the Professor asked him to repeat several obvious points two or three times and began to relax just a little. Finally Evans told him that someone in the department could probably help with the project. He would ask some of his colleagues to recommend a graduate student who needed a project to work on. His secretary could handle the details if Mr. Takayama would just leave the proposal with her. "Is there anything else we can do for you?" he asked.

"Well, sir, now that you mention it, I understand you're testing one of the new McGregor computers. My company is considering purchasing one, but it's so much money and there's so little hard data out on it that we're in a quandary whether or not to commit that much capital. I know it's a presumption on your time, but I would like to see it and talk with someone in your group working with it if that would be possible."

"Access to that machine is restricted, but the team has let me show off some parts of it now that most of the installation work is over. I'll give them a call and see if it would be all right for you to peek in for a few minutes." He glanced at Mrs. Stoddard, "Hazel, will you please get Sam Dalton on the line?"

Evans picked up the phone when the light came on. "Sam, would it be okay to bring one of our department's new clients by for a few minutes? His company is thinking about buying one of those machines when you fellows get all the bugs worked out, and he has a few questions for you. Yes, thank you so much. We'll be right over."

"You're in luck, Mr. Takayama. They're not very busy right now. This old hip is acting up again so I think we better drive."

At the entrance to the new computer facility Takayama watched Professor Evans fumble through his pockets and then turn and smile sheepishly at his guest.

"I must have forgotten that damn card again." Evans pushed the intercom button by the door. "Sam, could you come open the door for us....Yes, I forgot the little card again.....No, I don't remember where I put it....I know, Sam. I'm sorry."

Dalton opened the door, smiled at Evans, shook hands with their guest, and then escorted them past the series of offices that faced the street and across the hall where he punched a code in a box by another door and motioned them into the lab. "Ewen, Sal, this is Mr. Takayama. Professor Evans wants to show him around." He pointed toward O'Leary. "That young fellow over there is one of our grad students. We understand your company is thinking about purchasing one of these monsters. Sal tells me they have quite a few firm options already so it might be quite a while before anyone ordering one now could actually expect to take delivery."

"Precisely why I so much wanted to talk with you and be able to see this. There hasn't been much put out by McGregor Industries about the actual specifications on this machine or what it will cost.

My company would certainly appreciate anything you could tell me about its capabilities."

Ewen Howland smiled and spoke up, "This represents a rather remarkable leap forward in computer capability. As you may know, computer capacity or capability doubles about every six months. This simple formula holds true for the average PC, but not for these so-called supercomputers. With those, things remain pretty static for a long time then capacity jumps by a factor of ten or so. I think you could safely say this machine right here is about ten times as powerful as any in general use today."

Takayama took in an audible breath, deliberately exhibiting awe. "Well, can you tell me in layman's terms what that means?"

"I think so," replied Howland. "Every task is faster and easier to program than ever, and the bottom line is it will cost roughly only two or three times what the current machines do for a ten-fold gain in performance."

Hernandez interrupted, "More than that. Many tasks that can't be done on the current machines this one can at least take a crack at. Modeling chaos theory might be one example."

"What sort of marvelous breakthrough made it possible to accomplish this huge leap?" Takayama asked.

"Not any one single thing," Howland responded, "More a whole series of little things, just as it's been for over thirty years now. Things have gotten smaller and smaller so they run faster, use less energy, and they're more reliable thanks to better manufacturing tolerances."

While listening, Takayama noted that the lab didn't fill the entire space outlined in the footprint of the plans. Also the lab was directly over the apparently empty basement level. He could spot no obvious entry to that area however he'd seen both a stairway and an elevator in the hall on the copies of the blueprints. He decided to gamble. "This building appears much larger from the outside. What's downstairs?" He caught a quick exchange of glances between Dalton and Evans. O'Leary noticed this as well.

Dalton answered, "More offices. The basement space is used for storage mostly."

Takayama tried a different tack. He turned to O'Leary. "It must be quite a thrill for you to take part in this project. What do you think of all this, young man?"

"Oh, it's a thrill, all right," O'Leary replied with a grin. "Mostly I'm here to learn and be the gofer for my elders here."

A few minutes and several questions later Hernandez checked his watch and turned to the Professor. "We need to get back to work."

"What was that all about?" O'Leary asked once the visitors had departed. "You all seemed tense as hell. Who was that guy?"

"You've probably heard us talking about him," replied Howland. "He's the one Professor Evans thinks might be a corporate spy and I think he may be right. What's your take, Sal?"

"I agree. Something about that guy makes my sphincters tighten up. I think we'd better let McGregor in on this."

Arlington, Virginia

At last the office was up and running, but they still seemed stuck in first gear since hardly anyone knew the agency existed. Almost all of the few inquiries thus far had been misdirected and had to be turned over to the appropriate agency. Dougherty, Harrington, and the rest of the staff were using the time to research the activities of related departments and network with others in government. They also were devoting three afternoons a week to computer security tutorials given by invited speakers.

Willa picked up the phone on this beastly hot afternoon. "Federal Industrial Security Agency, Mrs. Fisher speaking. How may I direct your call?"

"Good morning. This is Angela Torres with McGregor Industries. Doctor McGregor is in Washington and would like to have a word with someone in your office."

This call was certainly a surprise. A major corporation calling a start-up task force wasn't anything she'd expected. "Certainly, can you tell me the subject of interest so I may direct your call?"

"Doctor McGregor didn't tell me what this is about, only that he wants to meet with a senior member of your agency."

"James Dougherty and Sean Harrington are our co-directors. I'm sure that either or both of them would be happy to speak with him. Would he like for one of them to call him or would he prefer that they meet him somewhere?"

"Doctor McGregor is free this afternoon. He'd prefer to come by your office, say around three o'clock."

"Of course, that will be fine. I'll tell them to expect him."

Willa hurried into the conference room, essentially a classroom these past few weeks, and motioned to them. "You'll never guess who just called."

"My wife, she always calls about this time and wants me to pick up something for her on the way home," Dougherty laughed.

"Nope, Ted McGregor of McGregor Industries, that McGregor, well, his secretary anyway. He'll be here at three o'clock."

"Wow!" whistled Harrington. "We go a month with hardly anything, and now all of a sudden we get a surprise visit from the CEO of a Fortune 500 company. Did you get any idea what this is all about, Willa?"

"None whatsoever."

"He's coming himself?" asked Dougherty.

"That's what I just told you. Do you want me to pull up whatever I can get on him and his company?"

"That's a good idea," replied Harrington. "Do it."

Willa showed McGregor into Dougherty's office promptly at three. Dougherty and Harrington both rose, and after introductions Ms. Fisher exited leaving the three men to themselves.

"It seems a little odd to see the head of a large company here," began Dougherty. "Usually we deal with security types. How may we be of service?"

"I'd like some information on a particular person." He pulled a photo from his briefcase and handed it to Dougherty. "I want your promise that what we speak about in here is strictly between us. If you agree, I'll fill you in on some background about this person that should enable you to understand my rather unusual approach."

Both men quickly agreed.

McGregor explained that a man named Hidehiko Takayama representing Yokohama Industries, a subsidiary of a Hong Kong outfit calling itself Pan Asia Limited, had shown a great deal of interest in the new computer his company was developing. "I decided to come to you rather than the FBI or CIA because believe I'll receive more personal attention here as opposed to the larger agencies."

He went on to tell them about the new Super G computer and why he didn't want his own security people dealing with this particular problem. He also told them about the meeting his engineers had with Takayama at the lab and handed them another photo of the man along with a set of fingerprints taken from a coffee cup Takayama had used along with a list of those working on the new computer.

Dougherty and Harrington, impressed, glanced at each other before Dougherty responded, "We'll see what we can find out. How should we contact you, directly or through someone at your firm?"

"You can reach me directly at this number. Leave a message and I'll call you back. If you don't hear back from me promptly, call this number and ask to speak to Ewen Howland or Sal Hernandez. They'll know how to get in touch with me directly."

"All right, sir. We'll get right to work on it," Sean Harrington replied. They shook hands and McGregor departed.

"What do you think, Sean?"

"I don't think he's telling us everything. There's already a lot of info out about this new computer. Hell, they've already started taking orders for it, so why does he want our investigation to be kept quiet? He's obviously worried about something."

"I agree. Let's see what we can find on this Takayama character."

Chapter 7

Las Vegas, Nevada

The temperature was well over a hundred when Hickman checked in under a different name at the Luxor, his appearance very different than when he'd left Des Moines early that morning. He now wore faded Bermuda shorts, a pale blue loose-fitting t-shirt bearing a game company logo, scuffed up sandals, thick tinted eyeglasses, and a black wig. The tan was fresh from a bottle. Before going downstairs he looked in the mirror and smiled. *What a hell of a sorry spectacle, ought to fit right in.*

Hickman wended his way between rows of old ladies pulling slot machine handles in the smoke filled lounge on his way to the main convention hall where the unimportant part of the meeting was taking place. He stopped for a moment and glanced around looking for people he knew. Once he stepped through the door, he'd become an entirely different person. The few in the next room who knew him by sight would address him as Zeus. The younger ones wouldn't know him except by reputation. Zeus's rep as a hacker got started while Hickman was still in high school. He'd managed to penetrate almost any system at will back then, but ever since that time his known escapades had been few and far between.

He pulled a cigar from his pocket and stuffed it in the side of his mouth, unlit as always. He wasn't more than a dozen steps into the hall before a loud voice called out, "Zeus, how the hell you been, man? Damn good to see you again."

"Stinky! Good to see you too, man. I saw that stuff on the net about those oil guys last spring and knew it was yours. Finest kind, man! You really stuck it to those sleaze-balls." Then, with no more than a brief nod, Hickman moved deeper into the room.

Every year at this convention he ran into some of the same people plus a few new ones. The main difference now was the addition of all the suits. Computer security was a big business, and a good many of the people in that field had been those same hackers with the magic touch on the keyboard. They could find a way to go almost anywhere in a virtual sense. These were often the best people to either develop a new security system, or at least vet an existing system. For the golden few, they were sought after to help track down other hackers. Zeus was one of those chosen few. The suits were here to size up prospective employees, those special hackers whom they might need to turn to during the coming year. Harry was making his annual, and possibly last, appearance at this event to touch bases with those representatives from the FBI, CIA, and NSA as well as many private companies.

Ames, Iowa

Kate Summers slouched back in her chair and closed her eyes as she attempted to visualize how the latest scheme might play out. She imagined a four centimeter long six millimeter thick ceramic rod etched with microscopic grooves. She'd fasten the 5' end of a single strand of DNA to the inner end of the rod. If the rod could be made to turn at a constant speed all she'd need now was a way to read the sequence of the individual nucleic acids as they came into view. Of course either the rod itself or the viewing apparatus would also need to move linearly at a constant speed as well.

Kate spent the next hour running computer simulations on rods of varying diameters. She hoped to present Gene Donaldson at the microfabrication lab with as many design options as possible. She saved her work to a disc and deleted the simulations on the hard drive. It was unlikely anybody would look at it anyway but she was taking no chances. Kate hoped to be the first to try this method, and if it worked the way she hoped, to publish it as her thesis. Next she did a quick search for articles on miniature ceramic etching techniques to be sure she hadn't overlooked anything. Google came up with several matches for her inquiry which she printed out for later study.

On the way back to the house she called Donaldson. "Hi, Gene, it's Kate again. I think I've figured out a way to do this. I was kinda down in the dumps and this guy I worked out with gave me a pep talk. He told me to go back over some of the first things I'd tried and see if anything clicked. Well it did. I went back to the spooling idea that we talked about. I've read some articles on microfabrication and molecular beam epitaxy. I think we should try etching a ceramic rod that will turn at a constant speed to line up the DNA in a spiral. Then we read the sequences with that pulsed cantilever apparatus Gary Wong told me about."

Donaldson took a long minute before he replied. "Kate, look, it sounds like it just might work. Unfortunately I'll be away for a few days. I'll get back to you as soon as I return."

"Where are you going?"

"My wife and I are going to visit family and we'll be gone about ten days. I wish we could stay longer but we have to be back by then for a meeting."

"That sounds great. Have a good time," she said, hoping the disappointment in her voice wasn't obvious.

"Hi, Mom, it's me. Sorry I didn't get a chance to call last weekend."

"That's okay, honey. We know you've been busy. Your father and I are fine. When will get out here?"

"The next semester starts soon so it'll have to be next weekend or the one after."

"Did I tell you that your father and I ran into Todd and his new wife? She seems very nice, and they're expecting a baby. He said to say hi to you and asked what you were doing."

"That's nice." Kate replied in an even tone. "How are the crops doing?"

"So far, so good. We've had some rain. Hope the prices hold up. Your dad's been working real hard. I wish he'd take on a hired man if he can find someone who's reliable. He shouldn't have to work such long hours."

"Long hours are part of farming, Mom. You know that better than anybody."

"Guess I should by now. We go back some four generations on this farm."

"Well, I'd better get back to the books for a while. Say hi to Dad for me."

San Jose, California

Takayama checked into the Marriott on South Market near the convention center, his favorite place to stay when he was in the area. His first appointment was with John Tompkins, a mid-level manager at McGregor Industries, whom he believed had personal problems and might become a source of information. He'd called Tompkins a few days earlier to request a meeting and hinted that it might be mutually profitable.

He saw a man stop at the desk and then turn to look in his direction. As the heavy-set man approached Takayama stood and offer his hand. "Mr. Tompkins, it's very kind of you to meet with me on such short notice. What would you say to a drink before dinner?" Tompkins florid face suggested the man imbibed more than his share, and Takayama hoped it would loosen his tongue.

"Sure, a whiskey and soda sounds good."

"A whiskey and soda it is then, and please, call me Hiko. How are things going?"

"Oh, business is a little slow, but not too bad. Is there something I can help you with?"

"There is, I ran into a couple of engineers at a university in the Midwest who are doing some work for McGregor Industries. Since my company already sponsors research in the agricultural college there, it would help greatly to learn more about these people who work on a different project that we're interested in. If I give you the names, could you check into their backgrounds and what it is they're working on now? I'd be most appreciative."

Tompkins showed no hesitation. "Just tell me their names and I'll see what I can come up with."

"Sal Hernandez, Ewen Howland, and Samuel Dalton."

"I can't say I've ever heard of them. What is it you want to know?"

"Oh, anything new you've heard about. How's your family, by the way? Did you decide to take that trip you mentioned on the phone?"

"No, the money's a little tight right now and our kid has some problems."

"Sorry to hear that. Has he been giving you a lot of trouble?"

Tompkins stared down at his plate and muttered, "Has he ever."

Just then a waitress came out and told Takayama their table was ready.

Takayama ordered the catch of the day. Tompkins ordered steak and another whiskey sour. "How long have you been with McGregor Industries, John?"

"Almost fifteen years now."

"Doing the same thing?"

"Pretty much, but it's awful tough to climb the ladder there unless you know the right people."

Takayama had hoped for more expansive comments to get a feel for how useful Tompkins might be but his guest seemed to become more morose as the minutes passed. When the waiter came to clear the table Tompkins ordered a beer.

After desert and coffee and an after dinner drink a somewhat wobbly Tompkins took his leave.

Takayama went up to his room and got on the phone, his notepad in front of him. He'd told Tompkins there was no rush and where he could be reached if and when Tompkins learned anything. He watched the news before turning in early. He'd decided to hold off on offering Tompkins a retainer, at least for the time being. All this travel was beginning to get to him.

Around noon the next day while he was waiting to board a flight to Boston Tompkins called. "I looked up those names you gave me last night, Hiko. The only thing I could find on them is that both Howland and Hernandez have done some consulting work for our supercomputer division a couple of years back. They never actually worked up here in the Bay Area although they did spend a few months with an affiliate called Avant Associates. Apparently it's based in Ontario, California."

"Thanks, John, that's helpful. Do you know anything more about this Avant Associates?"

"I've never heard of them before and I couldn't find anything else in our files."

Takayama thanked Tompkins again for the scant information and asked him to call if anything else turned up. *Shit, another dead end.* He tried searching on his computer for Avant Associates without success. He finally called information in Ontario to ask for a phone number for the company and was told there was no listing for anything by that name.

A few minutes later his cell phone beeped. It was his Matsumoto's assistant telling him he was needed in Tokyo the following week for a meeting with someone from Pan Asia Limited, the Hong Kong outfit that now essentially owned Yokohama Industries following the decline of the yen.

Ames, Iowa

It was lunchtime and she should be attending the noon lecture but Summers was too excited. Kate stuffed the notes and references in her backpack, gulped down a sandwich, and hurried over to the physics building to see Gary Wong.

Wong was in the office he shared with another grad student. He looked up and smiled. "What's on your mind, Kate?"

"It's about the DNA sequencing. I need to pick your brain. It's about an idea I showed to Donaldson." She pulled out her notes and explained what she wanted to do. She watched as he read through the loose papers, often asking her to decipher the writing.

"Sorry, penmanship isn't one of my strong points and I was in a hurry when I jotted down some of it. Do you think if Gene can put together what's on those sketches we could give it a try?"

"Hmm…it might be doable but it'll take some time. I think we have all the basic components but getting time to use them will be a challenge. Donaldson's lab has a waiting list."

"I was afraid of that."

"Let me copy your notes and I'll see what I can do. Give me a call in a couple of days."

"That's okay, but only if you promise not to share any of this with other people," Kate replied hesitantly and with a worried look.

"No problem, I can keep my mouth shut."

Kate walked back to her cubbyhole in the biophysics building and smiled at Dewey.

"I made some progress today, my friend. Gary Wong says he'll give me a hand with the project."

"Glad to hear it. Show me."

"I'm in a pinch for time right now, Dewey," Kate said without looking him in the eye. "Sorry, gotta run."

Tokyo, Japan

Takayama ordinarily traveled to Japan every three months or so for consultations at Yokohama Industries but this summons came less than two months since his last visit and he wondered why. At least this trip offered respite from the daily grind and would give him a chance to visit his aging parents. He caught a late night JAL flight out of San Francisco in business class, nodded to the elderly man in the seat next to him, slipped off his loafers, took the eye shades out of the amenities bag, and leaned the seat back hoping for sleep to come quickly.

Eleven hours later, while the giant 747 completed circling and began descending toward the runway at Narita, Takayama patted his face with the *oshibori* the stewardess handed him and cinched up his blue striped necktie. He was glad he'd have time to rest and organize his thoughts before the meeting with Matsumoto and the Chinese.

The offices of Yokohama Industries, Ltd. were on the ninth floor of a large but unpretentious office building in Shinjuku. The outer office staff greeted him with bows as he made his way to the conference room. A secretary escorted him to the meeting room and brought him *oocha*. Soon Matsumoto entered accompanied by Chen, an elderly heavyset Chinese male, and two younger men he took to be assistants. More tea was brought and ritual greetings exchanged, and polite inquiries were made about the health of family members. In this elegant room business was never rushed.

Matsumoto took his place at the head of the table. In Hong Kong the older Chinese man to his right would be occupying that spot and Matsumoto would be to his right. Matsumoto cleared his throat. "Takayama-san, we're happy to have you with us today and we're most eager to know what you've learned about that new computer and the other projects. I noted you modified your itinerary on two occasions to more closely observe whatever is transpiring at that university. I trust you have information to share."

"Thanks to my contact there I was recently given a tour of the building where the computer they call a Super G is located. Unfortunately all I have to present today are the reasons that led me to conclude that something else of great importance is taking place at that facility. Historically universities tend to tout their research but they have not done so with this project. There must be a reason but details have been minimal. This led me to obtain copies of the blueprints for the building. There's a great deal of space unaccounted for, including a large below ground area with unusually thick walls that shows up on only some of the plans and seems devoid of any obvious function. The work on this structure was completed in record time by three out of state construction firms that do not regularly perform work for the university, again most unusual."

Takayama took a sip of water and continued. "The secrecy surrounding this facility is beyond any I'd expect to be accorded to a next generation computer. Only a select few faculty members have been allowed in the building. I was fortunate to see the computer in action, and although I'm no expert in computers it didn't appear to be that unusual. Even from the inside I couldn't account for the extra space and my inquiries were brushed off. I believe the group building this supercomputer is also doing something else they haven't revealed, I suspect that is because the management at McGregor Industries doesn't trust the people in their primary research lab in San Jose for some reason which remains obscure."

Chen rhythmically tapped his Mont Blanc pen on the polished table and shook his head. "Takayama-san, this is all very interesting, and I take it you believe we should give this project a higher priority and devote additional resources to it. I'd feel better if you had some idea about what you're looking for."

Takayama nodded politely. He spent the next hour giving them a rundown on his other activities. When this was over Chen asked several pointed questions about his expense account.

After Chen and his assistants left, Takayama joined Matsumoto in his office to talk about the meeting.

"Did you find him as detestable as I did?" Matsumoto asked. "I wish we'd never sold out to those Hong Kong bastards. Imagine that pig questioning your expenses!"

"I most humbly agree with you Matsumoto-sama. Neither of the two men with him said anything. I wonder if they were merely bodyguards."

The following morning Takayama took a train to Mashiko for a brief visit with his parents. He was pleased to find them in reasonably good health and took them out to dinner that evening. He returned to Tokyo the next day for another meeting with Matsumoto.

"I'm worried about you, Takayama-san," Matsumoto began, sipping his tea and taking a moment to examine the cup "I can understand why you don't like Chen, and I assure you I find him despicable myself. Unfortunately they do own the majority share of Yokohama Industries so we must treat them with respect."

"You're correct, as usual, Matsumoto-sama. I must accept that."

Matsumoto's tone softened. "Mr. Chen has seen the wisdom of your suggestions and will send a small team to assist you in learning more about the computer. They are to be under your direct control. I insisted on that."

"I don't believe sending a team is a wise decision on Chen's part. There's something important going on in that building, I can feel it." Takayama scowled. "This may be the most important project we have going right now and we have to be careful. I don't believe the people working there are suspicious by nature, but they're all intelligent and I'm sure it wouldn't take much to tip them off. Chen's people will only complicate matters."

"As I said, they are to answer to you. Be sure to let me know if they give you any trouble."

Ames, Iowa

It was a rare night when all the housemates were home for dinner at the same time. Kate button-holed O'Leary, "Brian, I've talked to Gary Wong and he pointed out that if my spooling idea works I'll need a computer powerful enough to read the data. We don't have anything in the biophysics department that's fast enough. Is there any way I could get time on the new computer you're working on?"

O'Leary knew she meant the Super G since no one outside the project knew about the QD. "I don't know. We're really busy in there but I can ask the guys and see what they say."

"Please do. Tell them this could be a real breakthrough."

O'Leary sighed. "Okay, I'll present it to 'em."

Harry Hickman came over later for a group workout and O'Leary asked him what he thought about Kate's request.

"She's been working very hard and has high hopes, but I'm not sure they'll go for it with all the security concerns."

"I know that, but we should test the waters. Back me up as much as you can."

"Hey, I want her project to succeed as much as she does. Let's float the idea together."

"You got it," O'Leary replied and gave him a fist bump.

Arlington, Virginia

Things were picking up at the FISA offices with several open cases plus a few new inquiries each week, most fairly routine and referred by other government agencies that didn't want to be bothered. Timmons, with his multiple contacts, had spread word of their existence and people were starting to call. That was fine with Dougherty and Harrington after months of dealing with organizational setup issues. Danny Hurwitz was giving the staff weekly briefings on the law as it related to computer technology and everyone was getting up to speed.

Harrington buzzed Mrs. Fisher. "Willa, we hear anything from McGregor yet? We sent him a preliminary report last week."

"Not yet, you ought to give him a call. I'm sure he hasn't lost interest."

Harrington pulled the file and asked Danny Hurwitz to join him, shaking his head at the way their motherly office manager took charge of everything. While they went over the data Harrington jotted notes about what they'd learned so far.

Later that afternoon, McGregor called back and Harrington told him that Takayama had been in the States for almost a year on behalf of Yokohama Industries which was part of a larger company called Pan Asia and was based in Hong Kong. "He's thirty-seven years old, was a mid-level manager handling contracts and has been with them since he graduated from college. Takayama was married but his wife and child both died shortly before he came to the States. His immediate superior is a man named Yosuke Matsumoto, a vice-president for technology and engineering."

"What happened to the wife and child?" McGregor asked.

"We don't know how they died. Possibly it's what prompted his assignment here. He rents an apartment in New York City but spends most of his time on the road visiting various corporations and colleges. We pulled his travel records. Since he's been in the States he's visited Iowa State University several times. His company has made several donations and sponsors a small research contract with their College of Agriculture in an attempt to develop a hardier strain of rice."

"Where else has he gone?"

"He's made several visits to California. I'll have his travel data faxed to you."

"Who does he see in California?"

"John Tompkins is a name that popped up. Tompkins actually works for you but we're not sure exactly what he does."

"I'll find out what and let you know. It's not uncommon for overseas companies to try to buy inside information about research and developments going on in other companies or big universities. Keep me informed about whatever else you learn. I appreciate all your help."

At lunchtime Mrs. Fisher, Harrington, Dougherty and several others gathered in the conference room. At Willa's behest everyone was walking the stairs now. She'd become the de facto number three person in the fledgling agency, or maybe the number one depending on one's point of view despite what the locator board in the hallway said.

Dougherty commented, "Whitman's telling me his boss wants a progress report but so far we don't have much to show him."

"Tell him we're just getting started and that we have several open cases," Mrs. Fisher said. "You can even say that they were mostly intergovernmental referrals, but that a few have come directly from private industry. That should keep the wolf away from the door for a while."

"Probably the best answer," agreed Harrington.

"Okay. I'll e-mail him back with that. Danny what do you have for us?"

"Well this one started as a non-government referral, at least indirectly. It seems that someone's been trying to break into an experimental computer system at MIT," Hurwitz replied. "They've been real careful about not leaving any clues and it has the group up there extremely worried. Their system took some hits in just the last few days. Seems like a pro job since nobody was supposed to know about this particular project. That's what's got them stymied."

"That reminds me of the McGregor thing. Do you see any similarities there?"

"Some, but not enough to go on yet. Fred Reynolds is going to catch the shuttle up to Boston tomorrow to talk to them in person. He'll fill us in when he gets back."

"You know, Sean, the way it's been going most of the inquiries we've seen have been computer related. I think Timmons' was correct, we do need to beef-up our in-house computer capability."

"We need to show that we can close a case with what we've got on board and then we can scream that we need more resources," Harrington replied. "Willa, what do you think?"

"I agree. You need a little carrot to dangle in front of the keepers of the purse strings. You were smart though to hold out for that budget authorization item to cover consultants."

As they all started back to their offices Dougherty stopped Willa. "Peg and Claire apparently have plans for us Friday night at Domenico's. You care to join us?"

"Sure, the food was good the last time, and besides, I have to make sure you boys are being attentive to your better halves."

Later that afternoon Harrington walked three doors down the hall to the office of Danny Hurwitz. "Danny, you have anything more on that MIT thing we spoke about?"

"Not much. Those guys have to be really worried about something to be calling us. They've got tons of in house talent they could tap. It's reminding me of the thing with McGregor."

"Right, and like McGregor he hasn't confided just what it is he's trying to protect. I wonder if the same thing will happen to Reynolds."

It'll be a wild goose chase if that's the way it goes down. You'd think that if they really expect us to help they'd be a little freer with the details. I used to think the agency was secretive but they've got nothing on these guys."

"When we talk with McGregor about Takayama again, what do we tell him? Danny doesn't think we have legal grounds to sue him or the outfit he's working for. Maybe we could try to get him deported but even that might prove difficult."

"If we can establish that he's paying people to spy for him it might constitute grounds for either approach. It may be difficult to get a conviction but deportation shouldn't be a problem. I doubt his company wants that kind of publicity. They'd probably just replace him with someone else. That would probably only set them back only a couple of months and we might not tumble to who his successor is right away. We really need to catch this guy trying to acquire something that's on the restricted export list or maybe highly government classified documents to make a real stink over it."

"You get the FBI office in San Francisco and ones in the other areas he's been visiting trying to keep tabs on him at all?"

"No, I don't want to risk spooking him without more to go on."

Ames, Iowa

O'Leary decided his best bet might be Hernandez. He and Harry were now on a first name basis with their professors, except for Professor Evans of course. "Sal, you know Kate Summers, one of my housemates. I think I've mentioned before that she's researching a new method for gene sequencing. It'll require a more powerful computer than what's in the Biophysics building. She wanted Harry and me to ask if she could get time on our computer." O'Leary watched his mentor's eyes narrow and a frown spread over his face.

"I'd have to talk that over with the others and you'll need to give us complete details about her project before we could decide. Things are busy here and there are security concerns. She can't be allowed to find out about the QD under any circumstances."

"We understand that, and I'm sure she can be trusted."

Hernandez sighed. "We'll see, Brian. Now drag your sorry ass downstairs and get back to work on the damn wiring. I want to see some progress today."

Arlington, Virginia

Dougherty stopped by Harrington's office. "Take a look at some of these numbers. After we talked about the new inquiry this morning I pulled the Takayama folder on a hunch. He's made a lot of trips to Boston, and some of these numbers are on the MIT campus. One of them belongs to a tech in the computer engineering department. There were several calls to that number."

"Interesting coincidence isn't it? Better find out what he does up there."

"I'll give Reynolds a call, have him get a list of employees and see if this guy's name pops up."

Dougherty hit the intercom button for their office manager. "Willa, see if you can get Fred Reynolds on the phone for me. We have something he might want to check on while he's up there."

"Good thought, James, but sometimes the things you ask for are only a couple of clicks away," Willa said with a grimace. "That might save the staff a lot of phone calls."

Dougherty shook his head and hit the off switch.

That evening Willa Fisher met her bosses and their wives at Domenico's to enjoy some pasta and a couple of the old man's bottles of Italian wine. During the conversation Willa mentioned Reynolds' trip up to Boston.

"Damn, guys," Peg said, "why don't you go and take us with you for a change instead of sending Fred. It's been months since we've been back to New England and we could use a little vacation. Willa, the next time a junket like that comes up, don't let 'em pass it by. At least let Claire and I know about it"

"I've told them the same thing. The office will still be here if they take a day off now and again."

Dougherty laughed. "We're just waiting for a case to pop up in Vegas or some exotic place."

"Won't hold my breath on that one," muttered Claire. "Peg, let's plan a real vacation ourselves and tell these sticks-in-the-mud when it's a done deal."

"Right on. Maybe rent a yacht in the Caribbean this fall."

"Yeah, or go up to New York to see a show or two."

"Hell, why not go to London for a week and see a whole bunch of shows?"

"Sounds like trouble, Sean," Dougherty growled. "They're like bulldogs when they come up with an idea."

"Yeah, the next thing they'll want is a new wardrobe for the trip."

Peg laughed. "Now that you mention it, honey-pie, there are supposed to be some good sales this weekend. How'd you like to come shopping with me instead of watching some dumb football game on the tube?"

Ames, Iowa

Wong Soon-Long and Chow Quang-Li arrived in San Francisco at the end of the long flight from Hong Kong, glad to be back in the States where they'd both obtained masters degrees several years earlier, Wong in business at UCLA and Chow in electrical engineering at San Francisco State. They were then hired by Pan Asia partly for their English-speaking ability. More importantly they'd each impressed Chen by their willingness to take orders yet still show initiative.

The flight from Hong Kong had been uneventful. They'd traveled under the names Samuel Long and Norman Chow and cleared customs without difficulty. Their first stop was in Chinatown where they contacted a man who provided several items they'd dared not carry through customs. The following day they purchased a late model secondhand car. The drive across country, interrupted by a couple of brief sightseeing detours, took four days which gave them time to work on accents and formulate a plan.

Back in their Hong Kong office, nestled among other nondescript high-rises on the Kowloon side, were scores of men and women who spent their days poring over newspapers, wire service reports, and business magazines which they summarized for the analysts. In another land this sort of office could just as easily have been the CIA or the FBI. Finally there were the Longs and the Chows, people with special backgrounds willing to go the extra mile for the company and do whatever it took to accomplish the objective of the moment.

Upon arriving in Ames, they checked in at the Hampton Inn on South Dayton before driving to the campus where they spent a couple of hours walking around and listening. They managed to pilfer a university phone directory and decided to have dinner at the Commons in the Student Union. "Should we call Takayama?" Chow asked.

"No, let's learn our way around first. I think Chen was far too optimistic about how long this assignment might last. Tomorrow we ought to look for an apartment."

The next day they found a furnished two bedroom unit on Campus Avenue two blocks from the university. They spent the rest of the day stocking it with all the little things they'd need including rice, vegetables, pork, and a few staples although neither was inclined to cook. They also arranged for a telephone and internet service.

The carrot for this present assignment was all that mattered at the moment. Should they be successful they'd be given several weeks off at company expense, maybe even bring their families over, maybe even visit Las Vegas or New York. Based on the information in Takayama's reports, a major computer engineering project going on in Ames and they were determined to learn about it before it made the front page of the Wall Street Journal.

Ames, Iowa

Takayama, recently back from Japan, visited his contacts in several other cities before arriving in Ames. Now it was time to meet the team from Hong Kong that Matsumoto told him would be coming to assist. He'd been assured he'd be in charge but wondered how far that charade would go should there be a major disagreement. He put in a call to his office in Tokyo to ask for their names and phone numbers. He was surprised to be given a local number along with numbers for their cell phones.

When he dialed, a voice answered that sounded almost Midwestern. They agreed to meet at the Student Union that afternoon.

Takayama found a table in a relatively quiet corner and waited. Fifteen minutes passed before two Chinese males approached. Both were of average height, lean of build, casually dressed, and wore glasses. Takayama could detect nothing at all particularly distinctive about either one.

"Mr. Takayama?"

Takayama stood and held his hand out. "Yes, I'm Takayama."

Chow smiled and shook his hand. "I'm Norman Chow. It's nice to meet you." He pointed. "This is Sam Long. We were sent to help test your theory that there's something of great interest to our company in this pretty little city. We're at your disposal."

Takayama wasn't sure he believed that but felt required to go along with the charade. "It's nice to meet you too. You're English is excellent by the way, did you study in the States?"

Long told him where they'd gone to school, that they had families back in Hong Kong, and were delighted to be in the US again.

"Where are you staying?" Takayama asked.

"We rented an apartment just off campus in case this takes a while. The official reason for our visit here is to study American teaching methods that may be of interest to scientific educators back in China. We have letters of introduction to help get us in to see people on campus. So far we've just been learning our way around."

"Again, thank you for coming to help," Takayama said, careful not to betray how he really felt. "I hope that together we can obtain additional useful information. I realize this trip is probably inconvenient for you and I'm sure you've been briefed on the problem. My superior requested help with this matter since he believes what's going on here is far too important to leave to an isolated agent such as myself."

Takayama understood that Long and Chow knew that he was lying, but at least at this stage elected to be polite and not point it out. "I've prepared a list of people working at the computer lab you should become familiar with. I believe these people are testing the new McGregor Industries supercomputer and I've included my impressions about the principals."

Both nodded without comment.

Takayama went on, "It's most important not to let any of these people realize they're being watched. Among the names on the list is a contact who is employed in the computer lab, a Mr. Clyde Johnson. Although he's merely a janitor, Johnson knows a great deal about what goes on in that building, much more than he lets on. Professor Evans is the director of the facility. You may have heard of him. He's semi-retired now but he's in his office three days a week."

He concluded by giving them a list of others working there including Howland, Hernandez and Dalton. "Those last two names, Hickman and O'Leary, are graduate students. Their full names are Brian O'Leary and Harry Hickman. They're probably less sophisticated and therefore might be easier to compromise but I wouldn't underestimate any of these people. I also have a list of some of the secretarial and other junior staff which I'll print out for you."

"We appreciate your preparing this information, Mr. Takayama," Long said. "By the way, we expected you yesterday. Were you detained?"

"No, I had to make a quick stop in California to visit a location where two of these men apparently worked in the past but it turned out to be deserted. That only intensified my suspicions about the value of what's happening here."

Long told Takayama they may want his help in placing some equipment in certain places. "Will that janitor you mentioned be helpful?"

Takayama shook his head. "I doubt we can count on Johnson. I did get him to accept a small retainer, albeit with some reluctance on his part. What sort of equipment are you talking about?"

"The first thing we need are bugs, you know, passive listening devices, inside the building and possibly taps on their home phones. They sweep the lab periodically so it's better to avoid tapping those phones. We'd like to try a voice activated listening device and don't want to use a radio transmitter since they're easy to detect. Are you familiar with ac line carrier signal monitors?"

Idiot, of course I know about those things. Takayama forced a smile. "I've heard of them."

"They splice a high frequency low amplitude rider onto ordinary power lines which can be read from the line outside the building providing we can tap in fairly close to the circuit box. Can you get us wiring diagrams for the building?"

"I filmed as many of the plans as I could while I was in the construction office. That's how I learned about the large empty space in the basement. Nothing in the plans I saw indicated what it would be used for. They may not be up to date so I don't know how much we can rely on them."

Long asked, "Did you see any electric clocks or proprietary electrical devices in the lab that could be switched out for new 'upgraded' ones?"

"There are clocks on the wall and I did see a radio."

"That's a start, how about desk lamps?"

"I'm not sure," replied Takayama. "I think there might have been."

"Lots of equipment must go in and out all the time. If they're building some new kind of computer the parts have to come from somewhere," Long mused. "How do they handle the trash? If we look through that we might learn something. Maybe your janitor friend will tell you."

"I'll see what I can do," murmured Takayama.

The quizzing went back and forth for another half-hour. It was apparent these weren't ordinary businessmen. Despite what he'd been told it was becoming very clear this was their operation and they'd follow his orders only when it suited them.

Once Long and Chow departed Takayama sat for a while sipping coffee, staring into space, and scowling. He'd begun to lose his appetite for some aspects of his work and hadn't felt this melancholy since his wife died. *"Bastards,"* he muttered under his breath.

Chapter 8

San Jose, California

Despite his reluctance to leave the two newcomers from Hong Kong to their own devices, Takayama needed to make his rounds. This time it was a quick trip to California. As soon as the US Air 737 taxied to a stop Takayama grabbed his bag out of the overhead bin and made his way to the lounge. Tompkins had intimated on the phone he had something of interest, so Takayama lost no time in getting in touch with the rotund man to set up a dinner meeting. Tompkins liked to eat and drink, especially drink. After completing his calls he proceeded to the Avis counter and picked up the keys to his rental.

Tompkins was waiting in the bar at the Marriott on South Market when Takayama arrived a little after six, and it seemed the man hadn't wasted any time getting there after work. Tompkins' face appeared flushed even in the dim light and there was an empty basket of chips and a half empty beer glass in front of him. Takayama wondered how many of those Tompkins had already put away.

"John, it's a pleasure to see you, as always," he said with a big smile. "How's the family?"

"Fine," Tompkins muttered with a sigh and a pained look. "Well, things aren't really so fine. My oldest got busted for selling marijuana to an undercover cop. We didn't have any idea he was doing anything like that. Jesus, they want to put the poor kid in jail and I don't know what we're going to do. He's always been kind of a wild kid, but this is the first time he's ever been in trouble with the cops. My wife is beside herself."

Poor bastard. Takayama grimaced and shook his head "I'm sorry, John, I hope things work out. Did you get him a lawyer?"

"Yeah, we got him a lawyer. The guy charges a goddam arm and a leg but won't promise anything. Says if he's lucky maybe he can get him off with probation. I can't understand how they can throw someone in jail for what he did, not that I excuse it or anything. I know it's wrong and all that, but jail? Christ, he doesn't need that!"

"I wish there was something I could do or advice I could give you but I'm afraid we don't have much experience with his sort of problem in Japan. It goes on there but to a much lesser extent than it does here. The penalties are extremely harsh in my country when it comes to drugs."

"Well, it just doesn't seem fair to my wife and I, that's all. I don't know what we're going to do. You want something, a beer maybe?"

"No, perhaps I'll indulge a glass of wine with dinner. What time is our reservation?"

"Seven. Do you mind if I order something?" asked Tompkins, motioning to the waitress.

She brought another beer and set in front of the man in the rumpled suit who eagerly grabbed it and gulped down a mouthful, some dripping down his chin. As much as Takayama wanted to shift the conversation around to the purpose of his trip, he was an astute reader of people. He needed to listen to Tompkins and his problems for now. Later there'd be time to find out whatever it was that Tompkins wanted to tell him. He leaned forward resting his elbows on the small round table in the darkened lounge and waited expectantly. "Please refresh my memory, John. Where is son working, or has he been going to school?"

"Oh, he's been going to school but only on and off. He started out in engineering three years ago at Cal State, had a scholarship even. It just seemed too hard so after a year he switched to business. That only lasted a semester before he dropped out again. Since then he's worked at a bunch of odd jobs. He worked at a video store for a while but that closed up. He did deliveries for a pizza place until he got held up one night. Since then he's been a clerk at a little convenience store part time, nothing regular. He did go back to a junior college and took a couple of courses but that was only for one semester."

"How old is he now?"

"He's twenty-one, but you know sometimes he acts more like thirteen. When his mother and I try to talk to him it goes in one ear and out the other."

A waitress approached and indicated their table was ready. Takayama felt relieved when the Tompkins didn't order another drink, partly allaying the fear his rotund informant would soon become incoherent. Takayama asked for the fish of the day, halibut with rice and herbs along with a salad, while Tompkins ordered steak with potatoes and gravy. He was usually a talker but tonight had other things on his mind.

Over coffee Takayama gently reminded him of the purpose for their meeting. "John, I believe you had something you wanted to tell me."

"Oh, right, I almost forgot. It was about the Super G. Donato and Reeves, two of the main guys who worked on the project initially, were bitching the other day about how they didn't get to actually build the damn thing."

"Please go on."

"Well, it seems they thought since they'd helped to develop a good part of the plans for the machine they should be overseeing the actual building and couldn't understand why that part of the project was sent down south somewhere."

"What do you make of all that? Why would it be moved?" Takayama asked.

"Hell, I don't know."

"John, folks are always talking about their work with their family and friends. All of us in the info business make our living trying to stay one step ahead of the competition. You know that. What's different about this computer?"

"Only two things it could be, more memory or more speed. I don't have a damn clue which, hell, maybe both things."

"Did they mention anything else?"

"No. Wait a minute. I did hear that they were concerned about the shielding on the prototype, something about stray interference crashing 'em. That's never been a problem before, so I don't see what the fuss is now."

"What things might make more shielding desirable?"

"I don't know. Hell, I'm no engineer. Maybe he's afraid that some of them will be sent somewhere that has lots of interference or something."

"Anything else you can think of?"

"Maybe they're doing something new that might require it but I have no idea what that might be."

Takayama now had more questions but no answers. He picked up the check as usual then bade good night to Tompkins and wished him well with his son's problems, He'd hoped for a little more concrete information out of this trip but often he came up empty. It reminded him of the fishing trips he'd shared with his father those occasional Sunday mornings many years ago.

Ames, Iowa

Long and Chow, glad Takayama was off on another of his jaunts, studied the blueprints for the new computer facility hoping to discover a way to plant a bug or video camera inside the building. After much discussion they concluded security was too good and a break-in wasn't feasible. Long tried to tap the phone lines on the outside but found they were buried and couldn't find an access point.

They'd had high hopes for a device that could record voices from vibrations off the windows. That didn't work because of the double-paned glass. Another avenue not meeting with success was old-fashioned trash sifting because all they found in the recycling were bags of shredded paper which were carted off to the incinerator every day.

"How about trying their homes?" Chow asked. "Do you have that address list?"

"Right here," Long replied. "Who do we start with?"

"Howland, and if he's home we try Hernandez or Dalton."

"What about the two graduate students?"

"Let's save those for last."

"I think they might be the best choices."

"Why do you say that?"

"They're more likely to talk with their friends about what they're doing at work."

Just before noon Long and Chow drove by the house where the students lived. It was so much more palatial than their apartments back in Hong Kong and a far cry from the dormitories of their own student days, and wondered how they could afford it. The mid-morning sky was overcast. "No cars or lights on and plenty of trees block the neighbors' view. You ready?" Long asked.

They entered through the rear and saw a pile of dirty dishes by the sink. Chow frowned, "I can't believe they don't lock the doors."

"Well, we're not in Hong Kong. Where should we put the bugs?"

"I'd say one here and one in the living room. You don't want it near the refrigerator or the microwave so I'd say up in that high cupboard."

They placed the second Enigma Elite VR behind a drawer in a small table next to the sofa. "Shall we give it a try?" Chow asked.

"Sure, I'll step outside and dial. The battery should be good for at least three months since it will be on standby most of the time. I programmed it to turn completely off between midnight and four pm since they'd likely be asleep or at school during those hours."

Long stepped outside and dialed the number on the device that looked like a tiny cellphone and was set to send its signal to a recorder in their apartment.

"It's working okay," Chow called.

On the way back to their apartment Chow drove by the houses belonging to the principal investigators. He saw cars in the driveways and decided to hold off on those for now.

Later that evening Long listened eagerly to the digital recording trying to make sense of the different voices. He heard Summers say. "Brian, I spoke to the people at the microfabrication lab today, and they said they'll mock up some spools for me. They should be ready next week. I've got my calculations partly worked out. Wong says he'll be ready on his end in a week or so. I'm almost ready to give it a try."

"That's great, Kate. Hernandez told me he'll clear time on the computer for you. Things are going smoothly now, nothing pressing that should interfere. You really think you're going to be able to read someone's genetic code just like that?"

"What the hell are they talking about?" Long asked.

"I don't have a clue," his partner muttered. "Shut up and listen."

Kate's voice continued. "I still have to extract the DNA and do some preparation to stabilize it. I'll need to fasten it to the spools in the proper orientation. That's the idea of the micro-grooved spools. If I got the calculations right the MR microscope should be able to feed the data directly into the computer and leapfrog all current methods. God, I hope it works!"

"How will you know if you've got it right?"

"There are lots of known sequences. We get the computer to match them up. If there's a good correlation we'll know we're in business. I'll bring you a list of public domain web sites that put out sequences we can download onto your machine to run correlations once we get some data."

"Isn't there a lot of variation in DNA from different individuals? I mean everybody's different, right?"

"Yes, but not nearly as much as you might think. Most everybody's genes are nearly the same, over ninety-nine percent. Even between humans and a lab rat the vast majority of genes are the same."

"Hard to believe, but if it works you might even make the front page of Fortune magazine someday," O'Leary exclaimed. "Maybe we can tell people we knew you way back when."

"It won't be long, maybe only three or four weeks if everything goes smoothly."

"What's on for dinner tonight? It's supposed to be your day to cook."

The conversation ended at that point.

Long hit the stop button and they exchanged glances. "It's your turn to cook. What's for dinner?"

"Maybe some leftovers. I'll look and see."

"Again? We should have gone out."

While checking out the student's house Chow had seen several photos of people he didn't recognize. He assumed these were of the occupants and had snapped pictures of them with the camera on his cell phone. He showed them to Long and pointed, "I think this one with the brown hair is Kate Summers, the girl that was doing most of the talking about DNA."

Long hesitated and frowned. "You know, what she was talking about might be more important than that damn computer. It sounds like this girl is working on a new way to read the genetic code, and apparently she thinks it's going to work."

Chow glanced at his notebook. "She's in the biophysics department. Her office is in a building that they call the Dawson Annex. Let's see what we can find out there."

Early the next morning Chow wandered through the Dawson building and found Summers' name on a door on the third floor. He made his way to the break room just off the lobby where he noticed a bulletin board with class schedules and messages and several photos including one of Summers and next to that another of Dewey Jenkins. *That's the girl, the brown-haired one."*

He got a cup of coffee from the machine and pretended to read a magazine while he waited for her to arrive. A little after eight he spotted her speaking with someone out in the lobby. He followed her upstairs at a discrete distance.

Long was similarly engaged at the computer building watching the parking lot and waiting for the staff to drive in. He zoomed out the lens on his small camera and snapped several images of each one. He also jotted down the make and model of their cars and license numbers. For what was supposed to be a quick and simple job this was taking a long time, and so far they had little to show for the time invested. He knew their boss back in Hong Kong wouldn't be pleased. At least finding out about the possibility of using the new computer to decipher the human genome would be enough to keep Chen off their backs a while longer. Their reputations, not to mention all their perks, were at stake if they didn't produce results.

They met at the Student Union for lunch to go over what they'd learned. Long then walked across campus to the microfabrication laboratory located in the mechanical engineering department where he again adopted his casual observer pose hoping to pick up additional information about the girl's project. He found a bulletin board that listed the various courses being taught this semester and the instructor's names and office hours but nothing relating to the microfabrication lab.

In the lower level he came across an area with vending machines and tables. Long figured he might as well sit down and watch for a while. He dropped three quarters in the machine and parked himself at an empty table. He quickly decided he didn't have a clue what the people nearby were talking about. Frustrated, he swallowed the last of his coffee and departed.

In the meantime Chow drove slowly by the homes belonging to Howland, Hernandez, and Dalton. Again it seemed that someone was always home. He also drove again by the house where O'Leary and the Summers girl lived and didn't see any cars in the drive. He wanted to establish their schedules as best he could.

Later they met back at the apartment to commiserate. "You have any ideas about how we can speed things up?" Long asked.

"For starters, we get on the Internet and look at all the sites that the biophysics department has running to see if anything comes up about the girl's project. I doubt she's doing it all on her own. There didn't seem to be anyone home when I drove by her place around noon so no point in listening to the recorder until this evening. In the meantime let's see what we can find on the internet about gene sequencing."

"One of us ought to go to the library and see if we can find a simple text on the subject, or maybe try the bookstore in the Union. Any idea why they call that area across the street Dogtown?"

"Damned if I know. Let's go over there and get something to eat."

On the way they browsed through one of the bookstores and bought a used Introduction to Genetics text. They didn't find much pertaining to sequencing techniques.

"Could you bring us menus and tell us what kinds of beer you have?" Long asked the waitress at the China Moon.

"Bud and Michelob on tap but one of our local favorites is Pete's Wicked Red by the bottle."

"Okay, two bottles of that please."

Chow glanced around while they waited and his gaze settled on a couple sitting at a table across the room. He nudged Long with his foot and pointed at them, "That's Summers and Hickman from the computer lab," he whispered.

Long nodded.

Instead of the young waitress, it was Tommy Lee, the proprietor, who brought the beer to their table. "Hi, I'm Tommy Lee. I noticed you both in here last week. Are you here for a conference or something?"

"Pleased to meet you, Mr. Lee. My name is Long, Sam Long, and this is Norman Chow. We're here to observe American instructional techniques on behalf of our university back home."

"I'm glad to meet you. I sometimes practice my poor Chinese with the students. My family's been here for three generations so I have to struggle to remember much of the language. We do have a couple of authentic Chinese dishes on the menu."

"We've eaten here before and thought the food was very good," Long replied. "Our boss suggested we adopt American versions of our real names to make it easier on the people we meet. Chinese names seem to confuse Americans."

"I can understand that. My parents gave me a Chinese middle name. I used it when I visited China a couple of years ago. We still have relations we keep in touch with over there."

"Where is your family from, Mr. Lee?" Long asked.

"Near Beijing."

"Our families have been in Hong Kong for at least two generations," Chow said "Mine came originally from Shanghai."

"Gentlemen, let me get our kitchen to whip up something that might pass for Shanghai cuisine. It's the least we can do and it won't take long. I'll also have the waitress bring some Chinese beer. I keep some in the back but it isn't popular in Iowa."

"Thanks very much. It's nice to have some authentic Chinese dishes for a change. Say, who is that young man looking at us from that table over there?"

"Oh. That's Harry Hickman, one of my regulars. We sometimes play chess if we're not too busy. The girl with him is Kate Summers. They've been going together for a few months."

Chow and Long thought this light meal at the Moon was the best food they'd had since their arrival in the States, exactly what they needed to lift their spirits, especially after having the opportunity to see Summers and Hickman together in person.

Ames, Iowa

The new semester was half over and O'Leary worried about the thesis and how long it might be before he and Harry would be allowed to publish the work. They were testing applications for the Super G which was running quite well at the moment. The quantum dot machine also seemed to be coming along reasonably well since Hickman came up with a redundancy program to solve the error rate problem. There were still some bugs to be worked out, but nothing insurmountable. Professor Evans stopped by a couple of times a week despite his earlier efforts to stay away for fear of infringing on the staff's turf. He greeted the three principals and ambled over to O'Leary's corner.

Evans stared at the picture of the winsome brunette perched prominently on the desk. "Cindy is a beautiful young lady, son. When are you two going to tie the knot?"

"We've been talking about that, Professor, but things are so busy here it's hard to plan."

"We all grow older by the day so don't put it off too long. Some things more important than these damn computers."

O'Leary smiled, "I hear you, sir."

"Is Harry teaching you all about computer security?

"Quite a lot, sir."

"How's the thesis coming?"

"We're so busy in the lab that neither Harry nor I have much time to work on them."

The professor gave O'Leary a pat on the shoulder, then called out, "Evan and Sal, what are you working on today?"

"We're playing around with an algorithm to crack large primes as part of an anti-cryptography program," Hernandez replied. "If the

QD works like we hope, the government will want to get their paws on it. Sal thinks we can break almost any key in a matter of days now just using the Super G. The program can not only break the multipliers, it stores the results in memory to simplify future searches."

Evans nodded approvingly and smiled. "The QD might enable us to access any secure site in the world in a matter of minutes. I thought that was still a ways off, but wouldn't it give the establishment fits"

"Only until we get the parallel processing on the QD going. That sucker should run like greased lightning on problems like this."

"Do we have any projects going at the university that could make use of this new technology?" Professor Evans inquired.

It was O'Leary who somewhat unexpectedly blurted out, "Yes we do, sir. I have an idea."

That got everyone's attention. "And just what might that be, Brian?" Evans asked.

"I spoke with Professor Hernandez about it and he said he'd talk with you about it. Kate Summers, one of my housemates in the Biophysics Department, thinks she's developed a better way to read genetic code. She's been working on it for a couple of years and thinks she's found a way to read it directly from a long strand of DNA without breaking it into little pieces. And the computer can not only store the code as it's being read off, it can compare the results to a library of known sequences to verify accuracy."

"You didn't promise her time on the QD did you?" Howland asked sharply.

"Of course not. She doesn't know anything about that, only the Super G."

"And just how much does this housemate of yours know about what the Super G can do?" Dalton asked.

Oh boy, I stepped in it now. "Nothing, Harry and I haven't told her anything more than that we're working on a new computer that's faster than anything else here at the university, and that we're anxious to try it out on some practical projects. Doctor McGregor told Harry and me to keep our mouths shut about what we're really working on and I have, and I'm sure Harry has too. I didn't even tell my folks about it, not that they'd have any idea what I was talking about anyway."

Howland asked him to explain Summers' project in more detail.

Here goes. "It's about trying to read an entire strand of DNA. You guys have all heard about the human genome project. Well, this is a way to do the whole thing right now. If it works out Kate could eventually be on the cover of Time magazine picking up a Nobel Prize."

"Not if it means compromising this damn project, she won't, at least not until we're ready to go public with the quantum dot. The biology types might not appreciate the computing power needed to do that sort of thing in real time but some computer jocks will and our cover could be completely blown. We need to really think this through before we proceed."

"Damn, I hadn't thought about that angle," O'Leary croaked, slapping his forehead with both hands. "You really think somebody could get an idea about what we're doing by guessing at the computer power required for Kate's project?"

Hernandez frowned. "You can bet your ass somebody will. What do you think, Professor Evans?"

Evans cleaned his glasses while he considered the alternatives. "I agree there's risk. Still, her project could turn out to be extremely important. I think we might have an out here."

"What's that?"

"First we talk with her as a group. If she seems reliable, and if it's okay with McGregor, then we clue her in about the stakes involved and work out an agreement to delay any publishing she might have in mind. If she isn't willing to cooperate and agree on that point we can the whole idea. Brian and Harry, it's the same type of thing you had to sign when you started. You think she'd find that acceptable?"

"I'm pretty sure she'd go along with it but I think she should hear it all from you to be sure it sinks in."

"And she has to understand that no one regularly working on the project gets inside this building, and that includes Kate herself, right?"

"Yessir, guess I didn't consider the ramifications. I just thought this would be the ideal real-world test for the machine."

"It probably is, Brian, but we need to tie up all the loose ends before we give the go-ahead," Howland cautioned. "If it works, and if we time it right, it could be a real breakthrough for demonstrating the value of the new technology. It could be the best advertisement we might ever hope for, so let's not screw it up. Now tell us about anybody else who's in on this."

"Okay, Kate is working with Gary Wong. He's just finishing his PhD on magnetic resonance force microscopy in the physics department and knows about her project. I don't think he has any knowledge about what we have over here except the general scuttlebutt that it's a new McGregor Industries computer. I haven't talked to him myself. Kate doesn't understand anything about how the machine works or what it can do. The other person who's helping her is Gene Donaldson in the microfabrication lab."

"All right, that's good. And nothing from outside can get through the firewall, correct."

Howland nodded in acknowledgement.

"Anybody else have a question?"

The group batted possible objections around for a few more minutes before Evans sighed and glanced at the others. "Sounds all right to me, the rest of you okay with it so far?"

Each nodded their assent, and so it was settled, at least for the time being.

O'Leary breathed a long sigh of relief. *Another lesson learned.*

After a short break they migrated to the basement level to watch the QD attempt to crack a security code. There were many varieties and levels of computer security in individual computers and networks all over the world, and usually these involved the multiplication of large prime numbers. Even if one knew the product, it was an extremely time-consuming task for even the largest computer to factor these in order to decipher the actual code, in some cases theoretically longer even than the life of the known universe. Each hoped this limitation was about to change. Hernandez punched up the factoring program, typed in two very large numbers, multiplied them, entered the product in the QD program, and punched 'Run'. They watched as numbers whizzed across the screen, aware it might take days or weeks or months to get a result if it worked at all, yet they sat there still as mice fascinated by the sheer audacity of the experiment.

Ames, Iowa

While the group toweled off after finishing their karate practice Kate looked at Shelia whose turn it was to cook and asked, "What's for supper?"

"Lasagna and a salad, won't take long."

Sheila asked Hickman to reach up in the high cupboard over the sink for a large salad bowl. As he groped around the inside he touched something he didn't recognize and asked her to bring a step-stool and flashlight.

He pulled out the bowl and handed it down, then shined the light on it. He suddenly put a finger to his lips and herded everyone outside.

"What's the matter?" Cindy asked once they were all gathered on the front porch.

"There's a bug up in that cupboard."

"So, kill it," Sheila laughed. "You're not afraid of it, are you, Harry?"

"It's not that kind of bug," Hickman said, "and yes, I am afraid of it. It's a listening device. When's the last time anybody actually looked inside there?" He glanced around at the others.

"Probably not since we cleaned when we first moved in," Dan said. "I was the one doing all the high stuff and I didn't see it.. Anybody else remember seeing it up there?"

"Not I," Kate volunteered. None if the others had noticed it either.

"So, do we just take it out and chuck it?" Sheila asked.

"Not yet, because where there's one there may be more. We each need to take a room and go through it very thoroughly. Nobody talks until we've checked the whole house. Don't call out if you find something, just show it to me."

The search took over an hour but it did turn up another device behind a drawer in the living room. "What now?" Kate asked.

"They're the same. I'll look 'em up on the internet before we do anything. Kate, you sometimes talk about your research in here; that needs to stop. You all need to check your offices for similar devices as well. We don't want to tip off whoever put 'em here otherwise we'll never catch the bastard. Even though you're all pretty good with security, I don't want anyone using their computers in here until Brian and I check them out."

"That's going to be a real pain in the ass," Kate mumbled.

"That's the way it has to be," Hickman insisted. "I'm going to snap pictures of these things, then I say we go out to eat and hash this over. First Brian and I have to check for phone taps. There's the one line in the kitchen and the three others used for the computers, right?"

Kate nodded.

"Good. I'll check the phone itself and the box outside. Brian, you check the lines in the cellar. We'll do a more complete examination later."

They discovered no problem with the phones and a few minutes later they all headed to the China Moon.

Tommy Lee greeted them. "You here for a game, Harry?"

"Not tonight, Tommy." He glanced at the chalk board near the entrance. "Bring us a pitcher of today's special if you'd be so kind."

Lee shook his head thinking Hickman looked much more serious than usual. In fact they all seemed subdued.

Hickman said, "We should check out Yukiko's and Cindy's apartments too. Brian can help you with that. I'll do the same at my house then I'll get in touch with people from the lab to clue them in."

"The first thing we have to do is put a good security system in each place and be careful to keep them locked at all times, "O'Leary added.

After they finished eating Hickman drove to Howland's home and called him from his cell phone. "Meet me outside for a minute."

"It's cold out there. It's okay to come in."

"No, better we talk out here."

Howland stepped out wearing a heavy parka. "You sound worried, Harry. What's going on?"

Hickman explained what they'd discovered back at the house.

"Dammit, we checked everything the whole time the lab was under construction and we've swept it many times since then so I doubt we have a problem there. Is there any chance those things could have been placed before any of you moved in?"

"No, this particular device has been on the market for less than two years so we can forget that idea. I suspect this has to be related to what we're doing at the lab or more remotely possibly related to Kate's project. I instructed her not to talk about it anywhere in the house and I'll help check out her office tomorrow."

Howland said he'd let the others know about this new problem right away and promised to do it where there was no possibility they could be overheard.

San Jose, California

McGregor was due at a R&D budget meeting when his cell phone buzzed. It was bad news. He listened intently while Ewen Howland explained the problem Hickman had discovered the day before.

"You have any idea who planted the devices?"

"No sir, not so far anyway. This morning we searched our homes and Hickman came by to double check. He knows more about security than the rest of us."

"Hickman impresses me, Ewen, but you say he left the ones in the house where they were? You think that's a good idea?"

"He didn't want whoever placed them to know we found 'em."

"Probably a smart move. You think it might be that Takayama person you told me about?"

"Possible, but I doubt it. He may prod Johnson for information but doesn't strike me as someone who'd do this. We think it's somebody else, possibly someone working with Takayama."

"How about that student's project, are you going to hold off on it?"

"I spoke with Professor Evans about it. He sees no reason to unless we find bugs in the lab itself, and O'Leary and Hickman sweep that regularly."

"All right, have them keep that up and be sure to keep me posted." He thought maybe he'd hire Hickman when this project was over.

Ames, Iowa

Hickman, Oldenberg, and O'Leary spent the better part of the next weekend installing a security system at the farmhouse that included a way to automatically send a signal to each of their cell phones if someone tried to enter without punching in the correct code. They deliberately didn't change the locks for fear whoever planted the devices might notice and be warned off.

"How about the outbuildings, the garage and sheds?" Oldenberg asked.

Hickman said he'd put in motion sensors that would turn on a recorder if someone was speaking and maybe include video recording capability.

"What about the professor's homes?" O'Leary asked.

"We'd better upgrade those as well. They'll be some real late nights for a while."

Arlington, Virginia

Mrs. Fisher picked up the phone and pushed the flashing priority button. "Certainly, ma'am, please hold and I'll get Mr. Dougherty line on the line." She buzzed his office. "James, you have a call from McGregor."

Dougherty felt a little intimidated. He still wasn't sure why McGregor had picked the fledgling agency to look into his security concerns about the new computer project.

"I spoke with Professor Howland yesterday and I wanted to touch bases with you. Is there anything new on your end?"

"I already know what this is about. A couple of things, first the lab and the homes of all lab personnel are being checked on a daily basis until this can be sorted out. Additional security cameras have been installed. Also, from Takayama's visa application and registrations at hotels he's frequented, we've learned that he represents a company called Yokohama Industries Limited. We're trying to find out more about that outfit. By the way, did you get the printouts of phone records I sent?"

"That's partly why I called. "Unfortunately the two you underlined work for me. One's an engineer who worked with the Super G development team. We'll keep a close eye on him. The other is a manager named Tompkins who I've learned has family problems. I doubted he knew anything about the project in Iowa, but when we went over his phone logs and expense chits we learned he's spoken with this Takayama on at least two occasions."

Dougherty thought things were beginning to come together. "There's another coincidence you might find interesting. We had an inquiry a few days ago from another university about an attack on a new computer system that's under development. We don't know all the particulars yet, but phone records show Takayama has spoken with one of the technicians there on several occasions."

"Damn," McGregor muttered. "What do we do about Takayama? Are there sufficient grounds to have him arrested?"

Dougherty didn't think that was a good idea. "Well, probably grounds for deportation, but charging him in court would be based on circumstantial evidence and shaky. The downside is Takayama could be easily replaced and it might take a long time to identify the replacement. The best bet is to keep a close eye on him and try to ascertain the full extent of his activities. We know he visits many places on a regular schedule, and keeps in touch with a lot of people by phone even more often. He might lead us to bigger fish."

"Sounds reasonable," McGregor replied after a brief hesitation.

Dougherty felt McGregor didn't sound entirely convinced. "Maybe surveillance on him can be stepped up. I can see if the Bureau will give us a hand."

McGregor hesitated again. "Let's hold off on that for the time being. I'm worried about any more people learning about our research projects. How about having someone from your office shadow the guy?"

Dougherty, worried as always about committing much of their meager resources to a single case, even one as important as this, replied, "Let me speak with Sean and I'll get back to you on that."

As soon as he got off the phone, Dougherty refilled his coffee cup and went over to Harrington's office to tell him about the conversation with McGregor. "What do you make of it, Sean?" he asked.

"I think you're right. I say we up the surveillance on this clown. If we respect McGregor's desire to minimize the number of people who know about his project we should send someone from our office out there."

"I suppose so. Who do we send?"

"Celeste Butterfield. With her experience at the Bureau she's good with investigations and Reynolds or Hurwitz can back her up. Both of us should keep a close eye on this too."

Harrington buzzed Celeste and asked her to meet them in the conference room and bring the folder on the McGregor case and also the one from MIT that Hurwitz was working on.

Once everyone was seated Dougherty gave a quick synopsis of the two cases and opened the floor for discussion.

"This Takayama, whom we believe to be a spy, is involved with the two most interesting inquiries we have at present," observed Hurwitz. "That's too much to pass off as a coincidence. It deserves a closer look."

"Our thoughts exactly," agreed Harrington. "Where do we take it from here?"

Butterfield perked up. "One of us ought to fly out to Ames, meet the people involved, and shadow Takayama whenever he's there. Danny is already looking into the one in Boston so I guess I'd be the logical person to send. Do we know where he is right now?"

Dougherty glanced around the table but nobody had the answer. He turned to Willa and asked if she'd have one of the staff check with the airlines for flights he might be booked on.

Harrington added he'd cable the CIA officer in Tokyo and ask for any info he might have on Yokohama Industries.

Ames, Iowa

Hickman had spent the better part of the afternoon helping his bosses re-examine their homes inside and out for evidence of bugs and phone taps. As expected the lab had come up clean but he knew he'd be stuck with this task on a frequent basis until they found out who'd planted the devices. All lab personnel were now using cell phones exclusively but one landline was left on and dedicated strictly to taking incoming calls and messages.

O'Leary, tasked to perform a more thorough search of the house, traced the phone line that ran down into the basement from the connection box outside to a splitter in the cellar and then followed the wires to where they terminated but found nothing out of the ordinary.

He next turned his attention to the computers beginning with his old rarely used desktop. O'Leary ran a security program and found no viruses or malware then did the same thing with the rest of the group's computers and they also appeared clean. He called Hickman. "I didn't find anything wrong at the house but I did think of something. I think it might be worthwhile to try and lift prints off those things. That might help identify the bastards."

"Not a bad idea," Harry replied. "I know a guy who might help. His name's Don Bricker, a police detective here in town. I met him a couple of years ago when he was investigating some thefts at the physics building. I've run into him a few times since then."

That evening a beige Ford pulled into the farmhouse drive and a stout, balding man got out and waved. "Hey, Harry, long-time no see. Who's your friend?"

"This is Brian O'Leary. We work together."

"So, did you get your PhD yet or are you still screwing around?"

"No, we both finish sometime next year. It depends on how the project we're working on goes."

"Oh, top secret stuff, huh?"

Hickman laughed. "Sort of."

"Show me those things you found. You said there's two of 'em?"

"Yeah, we rechecked everything again today. Remember, no talking once we're inside."

Bricker opened the trunk and took out a large briefcase. "Let's start with the first one."

O'Leary brought a stepladder and a flashlight. Bricker was thorough. It took almost an hour for him to take pictures and dust for prints. After that he insisted they recheck every room along with the basement but found nothing else suspicious or missing.

"Whoever did this were pros, probably didn't leave any prints. The other thing is that these aren't local bugs. I've heard about this type before. They're made in China. You guys see anyone who fits that description around here lately?"

"There are lots of Chinese at the university. Most of them are in graduate school, some are faculty."

Bricker lit a cigarette. "The smart ones, right?"

"Most of 'em are damn smart," allowed O'Leary. "When will we know if you find a match?"

"I doubt we'll find anything usable. If we do get lucky I'll run 'em through Interpol and see if a match turns up."

"Are foreign nationals fingerprinted when they enter the United States?"

"Some countries, but you'd have to goggle it."

"Are you willing to speak with our bosses and give us some advice on how to proceed here?" Hickman asked.

"No problem."

Ames, Iowa

The following afternoon they met in the Professor's office. Hazel brought in coffee and soft drinks and whispered to the Professor, "Do you want me to call Clyde Johnson? You said you wanted to keep him abreast of things."

"No, I'll talk to him later." Evans turned to Hickman. "Harry, please run over what we know so far for Detective Bricker and bring us all up to date?"

Hickman recapitulated how they'd discovered the bugs at the farmhouse and how the rest of their homes tested clean so far.

Bricker asked if they had any suspects.

"There's this Japanese man, Hidehiko Takayama, who's been buttering up one of our employees and asking about what's going on in the lab," Dalton replied. "I can't think of anyone else and neither can the others."

Bricker cracked his knuckles. "I don't presume to know what it is you're working on, but based on what I've heard so far I'll hazard a guess it's some advanced computer technology. It's possible they've already gotten whatever it is they want, but I doubt it. If they had, they most likely would have removed the bugs by now. If you tamper at all with them they'll know it immediately so until you decide on the next move you should leave everything just the way it is. If you change your pattern of communication they'll probably pick up on that too. You need to make a couple of decisions. Now you say the only suspect you can think of is this Takayama?"

"He's the only one so far," Hickman replied.

Howland asked, "You told us the equipment you found was of Chinese origin. Does that mean whoever is doing this is probably from China, or could they be from someplace else?"

"Like where?"

"Say maybe Japan?"

"Possible, but as far as I know this particular device hasn't hit the market here in the States so it's likely it hasn't in Japan either. I recently read an article about newer types of bugs but this is the first time I've actually seen one like those."

"How specialized would someone have to be to install the device?"

"Anybody can easily learn how and it wouldn't take long. But for someone to do it without being detected makes me think it's a pro we're dealing with here."

"If someone went to all the trouble and risk of placing the bugs, wouldn't they have to spend a lot of time listening to be able to find out anything?" Hernandez asked.

"Yes and no. They're voice activated and probably set to record only when someone's actually speaking. It would still take quite a bit of time to sort through all the extraneous conversation to find anything useful. I'd guess maybe a couple of hours a day. Why do you ask?"

O'Leary brought up the point that Takayama spent very little time at the university which suggested that he may have help.

"Excellent observation," Bricker said. "You know if he has any friends at the university besides this Clyde Johnson?"

"No, but CJ told me he periodically visits somebody else here at the university," Dalton said. "I think it's someone in the agriculture department but I don't have a name."

Professor Evans interjected, "Hazel, I think we should let Detective Bricker take a look at your place to see if there are any bugs there just as a precaution."

"How about bugs in our cars." Dalton asked.

"Unlikely, but I'm willing to help you check them out," Bricker said. "You should consider putting hidden cameras on the bug locations in the house O'Leary and the other students rent because sooner or later whoever planted 'em will want to remove the evidence."

"Makes sense. What else should we do?"

"You've already got cameras covering the lab entrance, and I noticed another one in the lobby that might pick up someone hanging around who doesn't belong. Does anyone ever look at the tapes? First, are they just live monitors or do you save everything on tape?"

Hickman said they kept the tapes and either he or O'Leary had been tasked to look at them every morning.

"That's good. Next put a tail on Takayama whenever he's on campus. Find out who he talks to at the Ag school. If you don't have anyone I can give you a couple of names of retired officers who'd be willing to help."

"What else?"

"You need to make a decision about just how much of this you tell anyone outside your immediate families. The more people who know about this increases the chance of a leak; conversely, the more eyes and ears the more likely you are to find who he's working with. This decision could cut both ways so that's up to you."

"How about feeding them misinformation," asked O'Leary, "or maybe trying to set a trap? Saying something that could make them tip their hand maybe?"

"Anything more specific than that?"

"No, but Harry and I will give it some thought."

"Then bring it up again when you flesh something out. For now the best thing is to keep your eyes and ears open." Bricker glanced at his watch. "I'd better get going. Harry, call me tomorrow or the next day and let me know how you're coming along."

Arlington, Virginia

The FISA group had gathered in the first floor conference room to run over current cases. Harrington told them he'd been in contact with the embassy in Tokyo and asked the CIA officer there about Yokohama Industries. "He called back yesterday and said it's a holding company that owns several businesses including a collection of rice farms, an import-export business, a medium-size information services company, and an architectural firm among other things. It's a little hard to understand how all those things fit together. Yokohama Industries was bought out a couple of years ago by a Hong Kong company called Pan Asia, Limited. It may be a front."

"A front, a front for whom?" Butterfield asked, suddenly more interested.

"He suggested the Hong Kong outfit might itself be part of a mainland company. That's still a soft assessment, but probably accurate based on public records."

"We'll need to research those companies and learn more about how they operate," Butterfield said. "I understand public records in China can be deceptive."

"If you follow Chinese stocks you'll probably know that from the way they bounce around so much," Reynolds added with a pained look. "I lost big on one my broker suggested a few months back."

Butterfield suppressed the urge to rub it in and instead patted him on the shoulder. "Maybe I should make a trip to Tokyo and Hong Kong," she said, trying to maintain a straight face. "I could check out Takayama's company up close and maybe learn more about this parent outfit at the same time."

Harrington laughed, "Nice try, Celeste, but for the time being I want you to learn all you can about Takayama, where he goes and who he sees. The guy really does seem to get around."

"Certainly looks that way. Some long range audio and video equipment and an extra ID might come in handy in case I spot the guy, although that's probably unlikely."

"Okay, talk with Willa and see what she can round up for you."

Ames, Iowa

O'Leary had swept Cindy's apartment and deemed it free of any bugs so the group had agreed to meet there to talk more about the problem.

"How was your patent course final?" O'Leary asked as he slipped off his parka and gave her a kiss. They'd invited everyone over to her place so they could speak freely.

"I thought it was fairly easy," Cindy replied. "I doubt I'll use it very much but it'll be good background for what I'm doing here. Any progress on who placed the bugs?"

"Harry and I are still trying to figure that out. We're still being careful not to talk about what we're doing whenever we're inside. I hope you are too even though your place checked out clean."

Cindy wanted to know if they had any other ideas.

O'Leary mentioned that he doubted Takayama was the one who planted the bugs. When she pressed him about why he felt that way he didn't have a good reason, only a gut feeling.

The rest of the group drifted in over the next half-hour. Kate and Harry brought the pizza and beer and Sheila had made a salad. Dan and Yukiko put an extra leaf in the kitchen table and brought it into the living room. Despite concern about the bugs they all had everyday things to talk about before they got down to business. Finally Kate said, "Harry filled me in earlier. Let's have him bring us all up to date and tell us where we go from here."

Hickman tapped a spoon on his beer mug. "Here's the deal, so far only the house seems to be compromised. We've searched the labs both where Kate's working and the new computer building and those are clean, likewise Mrs. Stoddard's and all the professor's houses. For now Brian and I will continue to sweep those on a daily basis. Detective Bricker, a friend of mine on the local police force, is giving us a hand. He tried to lift fingerprints from the two devices we know about but I haven't heard if they found any."

"How long you think?" Kate asked, drumming her fingers nervously on the table and worried about how any delay might affect her project.

"Like I told you on the way over, Brian and I are going to place some more surveillance cameras around the house. We think whoever planted the bugs will eventually want to get rid of the evidence. Of course that won't help us right now, so we all have to be extra alert for anyone who looks out of place, someone who doesn't fit in, and we have to let each other know right away if we spot something or have any ideas. Kate, you've been dealing with Gary Wong on your thesis project so I think you need to caution him again not to talk to anyone about your project. Be sure you don't mention anything about the computer lab. We haven't told the rest of you what we're working on because we promised not to. Wong knows a lot of physics though, so the less specific you can be about what we do here the better. The same goes for Donaldson at the microfabrication lab as well."

"I'll go over to his office in the morning and take care of that. I don't trust the phones right now," muttered Kate. "If somebody tries to steal my work, they're going to pay for it, dammit!"

"It's often someone in a lab who leaks or sells information about what goes on there. In this case the person being recruited told Professor Evans about it and now acts as sort of a double agent," Hickman replied. "It isn't someone any of you know, none of the regular staff. The person we're concerned about is Hidehiko Takayama, at least that's the name he goes by here. He travels around the country talking to people who work in various research positions trying to gain information about what they're doing and reports back to his company in Japan. I don't know all the details, but that's what it sounds like so far."

Yukiko, silent up to now, spoke. "You mean you think it's someone from Japan who's behind this?"

"I'm afraid so, Yukiko, but I don't think it matters very much where he's from. This sort of thing goes on a lot more than any of us have ever thought about. I think people from our country probably do the same thing other places. I know they have in the past. I'm aware your country has received more than its share of bashing on this issue from our government because of the trade imbalance."

"That may be so, but it's still is an embarrassment when it's someone from my country."

"We don't think he's totally on his own in this. He travels a lot so it's likely he wouldn't have the time to be the one doing the bugging. Like I mentioned before, that's partly why we haven't removed the bugs yet. We want to catch whoever else might be involved."

"Any thoughts on who that might be?" Oldenberg asked.

"Not so far," admitted O'Leary.

"So we all keep our eyes and ears open from now on, that it, Brian?" Sheila opined. "I mean there are thousands of people on campus. A lot of them are from overseas. It could be anyone."

"Yeah, but what we want to watch out for is someone who seems particularly interested in us, or hangs around for no reason," Hickman said. He turned to Yukiko. "I hope you're not mad at me for singling out Takayama."

"Not at all, I was just surprised since crimes like this are so uncommon in Japan."

"You seem to be enjoying the Monday night workouts, Yukiko," Kate observed, changing the subject.

"Yes, especially after what happened to you and Dan's sister in Washington. I hope I never have to go through anything like that."

"I hope you don't either. Thank the good lord for Dan teaching us karate. I didn't believe it at first, but I think this regular workout regimen helps get us through the bad times like when these bugs suddenly popped up."

Ames, Iowa

"Not too bad a flight this time," Takayama mumbled as the little Mesaba commuter plane touched down only thirty minutes late. He buttoned up his coat, glanced at his watch, and approached the Hertz counter where he handed the clerk his Five Star Gold Plus card. "Nasty weather out there this afternoon."

"Certainly is, sir. TV says it'll snow tomorrow. Your car is ready. I'll have it brought right over."

Forty-some minutes later he pulled into his space behind the small one-bedroom apartment he'd recently rented in Ames, happy to find the driveway and walks had been shoveled out. Takayama heated water for tea and glanced at the messages on his phone. He should contact the two men from Hong Kong but wanted a few minutes to himself first. He poured the hot water into an old Imari teapot he'd picked up in a second-hand shop, put a few crackers on a plate, and turned on the TV to catch the nightly news. Finally he could put it off no longer.

He called but got only a generic message. "Hello, this is Takayama. Please call me." He left his cell number just in case.

Long returned the call a half-hour later and invited Takayama to stop by. This was the first time he'd been in their apartment. "Looks nice," he said as he looked around at the throw rugs and a few posters tacked on the wall. It seemed like they were planning on staying awhile.

"Thanks," Chow said. "We believe this job may take longer than we anticipated because something else has come up. What do you know about genes or gene sequencing or the human genome project?"

"Not much, biology isn't my strong point. Why?"

"We bugged two rooms in that old house west of town where one of the students who works in the computer lab lives. We overheard her talking with one of the other students there about using the computer for a project that involves gene identification, or at least that's what we surmised."

"That doesn't surprise me. I'd guess the new computer would be very useful to other departments for research."

"Just suppose that the research this girl is doing resulted in a new faster way to learn to the genetic code, to read the DNA itself, what might something like that be worth?"

"That's one of the hottest topics in science today, would surely be worth a lot. What else did you learn about this project?"

"Very little, and that's the problem. It's the same with the computer. Most places you can just walk right in and find someone who'll brag about what they're doing, but not here with these projects."

"If it were easy the company wouldn't have sent you here," Takayama observed. "What have you tried so far?"

"I've been hanging around the building where the girl works and listening," Chow replied. "We did use our cover to speak with a couple of administrative types but didn't learn much there either."

"Well, we did find out one thing," Long added. "The girl spent a summer at NIH and we're trying to find out what she did there. Do you have any contacts there?"

Takayama ran a hand through his hair. "No, but I'll make a couple of calls to people who might. You have any other ideas?"

"We've got some long-range audio-visual equipment that we tried out on the computer building but it didn't work because all the glass is double-paned. We'll give it another try on the girl's office," Chow said, "but I think they probably have the same kind."

"Any luck putting a bug in either lab?"

"No, not so far. Security is too tight at the new computer center. We're about out of ideas. You want to go get something to eat?"

"No thanks, Takayama said. "I'll get something later."

Chapter 9

Ames, Iowa

Christmas lights were flicking on all over town. Finals were due to start in just over a week. Chow and Long had both experienced the Christmas holidays as graduate students and they were in reasonably good moods. They'd developed a file on the four students renting a house together along with Hickman, Yukiko Kawakami, Cindy Murray, and several of the staff in the new computer building. They'd heard Summers mention her project on only one occasion shortly after they placed the bugs. Today Chow planned to bump into Dewey Jenkins and strike up a conversation, something at which he was quite proficient.

Long turned left and headed toward the microfabrication laboratory and Chow continued to the biophysics annex where he found a table in the lounge and sat down. He knew the location of the office Jenkins and Summers shared and that Jenkins frequently took breaks in the lounge. He went there and waited for almost an hour until his target came in, dropped coins in the machine, and sat down at a nearby table. Chow got up and walked over. "Excuse me, but would you mind if I ask you a question?"

Jenkins, happy to have but one final left, looked up at the lean Chinese man. "No problem." He held out his hand. "Dewey Jenkins. What can I do for you?"

"A colleague and I from China are visiting the university to learn more about post-graduate education in America, specifically differences in teaching techniques between here and my country. I obtained my masters here in the States in a similar area a few years ago. May I ask what you're studying?"

Jenkins, known for his garrulousness, was happy to oblige. "I'm researching ways to speed up nerve regeneration. I hope to finish my thesis in another year or so."

"Do you have an office here in the building?"

"I share one with another person."

"Is he working on the same thing you are?"

Jenkins laughed. "He's a she. And no, she's doing gene research, real cutting edge stuff."

"She must be very bright."

"She is. You know, that girl changed majors three times as an undergraduate. Can students do that in China? Are they allowed to change majors?"

"It's frowned upon," Chow replied with a chuckle. "What is she doing exactly?"

Jenkins knew he wasn't supposed to talk about their projects but this was someone from overseas whom none of them would ever see again. "She thinks she has a way to sequence genes faster than they're doing it now."

"That sounds like it could be a major advance."

Jenkins nodded and said he needed to get back to work.

Chow had hoped to find out more about what Summers was up to but it confirmed what they'd learned from the bug and was enough to convince him they were onto something big.

Chow walked over to the Student Union thinking about how he might learn more details about her research. He made his way to the cafeteria and saw that Long had already been through the line.

"How did your morning go?" Long asked.

Chow told him that Jenkins confirmed the Summers girl was working on a new a way to decipher the genetic code. "If it works it could be worth a fortune. Who did you talk to?"

"I spoke briefly with a Gary Wong. He's a grad student from Taiwan. I learned that his area of interest is in magnetic resonance force microscopy, and Summers has been talking with him. I didn't dare press him until I learn more about what those things are for and how they work. What's that?" He pointed at Long's tray.

"Tuna fish sandwich. Tastes good; give it a try."

Chow made his way through the line settling for a bowl of soup, a slice of pumpkin pie, and tea. When he returned they mused again about how they might bug both the computer lab and Summer's office. Takayama had cautioned them about the tight security in the computer building but Chow figured that if he got there early before any of the staff arrived he'd go through her desk and photograph anything of interest might and possibly plant a listening device.

Long said he'd stop by the library and see what he could learn about magnetic resonance force microscopy.

Ames, Iowa

Snowflakes were falling by the time O'Leary returned to the lab after checking the professors' homes for more bugs. He was back at his desk munching on a sandwich when Dalton and the others returned from lunch.

"Everything clean?" Dalton asked

"Yeah, but how am I supposed to get any work done on my thesis with these additional chores?"

"We've all got to suck it up until we figure out who's behind it. I'm sure you and Harry will figure out something."

O'Leary almost choked on his Pepsi. He was being had and he knew it. McGregor wanted to know how they planned to deal with this problem, but none of the senior staff wanted to be bothered with it themselves. As the saying went, shit flowed downhill. Well, he'd make 'em sweat when he figured out something that would take a little effort on their part. He put on a big smile. "I guess I'm the closest to this kind of thing so I'll work on it this afternoon but somebody else will have to enter the data and do the run you had scheduled for me. That's okay, right?"

"Touché', kiddo!" Dalton answered. He, too, knew when he'd been had.

O'Leary slouched in his corner cubicle chewing on the end of a pencil after the morning meeting and pondering what else they could do to find out who planted the bugs. Maybe Harry's friend, Bricker, would have some ideas. He decided they should install a program that would detect and trace attempts an outsider made to get into their computers at home. Another thought occurred. He'd taken two computer security classes in his first year of grad school but now realized he knew little about the practical aspects. He logged on to the Internet, punched up Google, and typed in 'recent advances in computer security'. After several minutes his efforts were rewarded when he came across a site dealing with recent advances in computer security with many links. He began downloading files and printing them out for further study, suddenly realizing he didn't know nearly as much about hacking as Harry or probably even some high school kids.

O'Leary noticed Howland get up and walk over.

"You look deep in thought, Brian."

"I was considering other things we ought to be doing and realized how little I know about any of the practical side of computer security. I mean I've taken courses that I thought covered the subject well but I still don't know very much about it. Compared to Harry I'm a novice when it comes to hacking."

Howland sighed. "That's life in the real world. The material you studied in class is all just background. I felt the same way when I first started. You acquire the practical stuff as you go. Look at this as a chance to learn, not just some extra scut work we piled on you. You got it not just because we're a bunch of lazy sons-of-bitches, which we might be, but mostly because you really are a lot closer to this now than the rest of us. We're honest enough to admit that a lot of this crap has already passed us by."

"C'mon, Ewen, you could pick this stuff up easy and you know it. I understand you can't possibly keep up on everything, and what you're doing carries a higher priority than this security business."

"You're correct there. Most networks hire a systems administrator to handle all that. I've talked to a couple of those guys, and they say that nobody listens to 'em when they preach simple things like using strong passwords or even turning off the computer when they disappear for the night. Hell, I never paid much attention myself until we started working on the new Super G before Sal and I broke off to try and develop the quantum computer. McGregor made sure we changed our ways when we started in on that, I'll tell you."

O'Leary showed him a webpage about bugs available on the internet.

Howland smiled. "We ought to buy one and try it out on our Mr. Takayama, see what he has to say for himself."

Ames, Iowa

"Dewey, about that Chinese guy you told me about, he hasn't been around again, has he?"

"Haven't seen him for a couple of days. You ready to try this thing out?"

"Absolutely." Kate had a DNA sample from her own hair that she'd separated into single strands. The objective now was to attach a sample to the grooved glass spools Gene Donaldson had made in his lab and rotate it at a constant speed with the tiny motor he'd built. If the strand didn't break or get tangled up she'd use the nuclear magnetic force microscope in an effort to visualize the individual nucleotides.

"Okay, Dewey, turn on the motor."

She peered at the screen. "Damn, it came off," Kate muttered a few seconds later.

It took several tries to obtain a solid bond between the DNA and the spool. The denatured strand seemed to adhere and follow the grooves when the tiny motor ran very slowly but when they increased the speed it wouldn't track properly and the specimen broke. They tried three more times, all with the same result.

Kate moaned, "At that rate it'd take a week or more to wind an intact sample."

"What are you going to do?" Jenkins asked.

Discouraged but not ready to give up, Summers said, "I'll ask Gene Donaldson to fabricate some different size rods and see if there's a smoother motor I can try. If we increased the rotation speed more slowly that might help also."

"Yeah, I thought it looked good for a minute there. Maybe those changes will do the trick," Jenkins said encouragingly.

Ames, Iowa

Chow learned that Summers taught a Tuesday morning lab section simply by looking on the bulletin board in the snack bar. He spent a good part of the morning hanging around the biophysics building waiting for Jenkins to leave so he could get a look inside her office. When he saw Jenkins go into the snack bar he pulled his hat low over his face and hurried up to the third floor.

The small office was cluttered with books and folders scattered around and a full ashtray sat on Jenkins desk. He ended up not finding anything helpful and thought it strange there was nothing remotely connected to gene sequencing. He decided not to leave a bug there. *Wonder if that son-of-a-bitch was bullshitting me?* Frustrated, he quickly departed taking care to avoid the cameras. It didn't occur to him until later that Summers might be aware she was being watched.

Long had considered speaking to Wong directly but when he learned Wong was from Taiwan and might harbor a certain animosity toward people from the mainland he gave up on that idea. He thought it a shame that those damned islanders wouldn't admit they were really a part of China. It was however becoming clear that Summers might be making use of Wong's project in her own work.

His next stop was the administrative offices in the physics building. He spoke with one of the secretaries and asked for a course list. When she asked if he was a student he told her that he was visiting the university to learn how teaching techniques in America differed from those in China. When she swiveled around to her computer to bring up the information he watched her keystrokes in an attempt to pick up her ID and password. He wasn't quite sure but thought he'd caught it.

They met at the China Moon for lunch. It was fairly quiet this time of day with most of the students in class or the library or their dorms or apartments. Long and Chow had been in Ames over three weeks, and though they were increasingly more comfortable speaking English again, they were frustrated with their lack of progress on learning what was going with the new computer.

Tommy Lee handed him two bottles of Tsingtao beer. Long took a swallow, and burped. "Really good," he called over his shoulder as he walked back to their table.

"Any luck searching the girl's office?" he asked.

"I waited almost an hour for the Jenkins kid to leave but I finally got into their office. I didn't find a damn thing about her project."

"I'd have thought you should have at least spotted some books on it or something."

"There was nothing there. How did you do with Wong?"

Long told him he'd decided to hold off for the time being. "I think I found a way to get into student records. Remember we tried accessing those last week and didn't have the right clearance? Well, I think I captured a password from one of the secretaries in the Physics Department by looking over her shoulder. We could do it from the apartment but I think it's better if I use one of the computers in the building just be sure she isn't logged on at the same time."

"I'm planning to go back there tomorrow and maybe hook up with Wong then. We'd better decide who else we should look up and in what order of importance in case I don't have time to get through everything.

Chow suggested he start with Summers.

"Yeah, that makes sense. Did you make any progress with that microfabrication lab?"

"I know the building it's located in now but I haven't approached anybody there yet. I'll go back tomorrow and nose around some, see if I can find somebody to talk to."

"We might as well listen to the damn tapes and get it over with."

That evening they watched the women's basketball team lose a close one to Baylor and then spent an hour listening to the tapes, fast-forwarding through most of it. They were disappointed not to learn anything they didn't already know. "Damn, these people must lead some pretty dull lives," Long said.

Ames, Iowa

Kate, ready to get back to work, hummed the Alicia Keyes tune 'You Don't Know My Name' as she hurried up the three flights of stairs. She'd just spoken to Donaldson who'd told her he'd have some time over the holidays to see what he could do about a different motor. She hung her parka on the back of the door and saw Jenkins leaning on his desk with his chin in his hands. "What are you thinking about, Dewey?"

"I think there must be a bug in my software. My data isn't making any sense."

"Where's the hang up?"

"That's the problem, I just don't know."

"Don't get so down on yourself. You'll figure it out."

"Sure, Kate, easy for you to say. Oh, remember when you told me to keep quiet about the thing you're working on? Your own project I mean. I'm afraid I let something slip out yesterday."

That caught her attention. "Say what?"

"There was this guy I met in the lounge during a break. He said he was from China and asked me about what I was doing. Then he asked me if we ever worked with people in other departments and I told him sometimes we did joint projects. He inquired about Gary Wong and what he was working on."

Jenkins hesitated, wondering if he should continue, then he shrugged. "I'm sorry, Katie, but somehow I mentioned your name and that you were doing a project about gene sequencing. I was so damned wrapped up with my own problems that I completely forgot about what you told me."

Summers, surpassing a sudden urge to strangle him, took a deep breath. Instead she forced herself to say, "That's okay, Dewey. Tell me about this person, everything you can remember."

"He was Chinese, didn't tell me his name but he did say he was here to learn about American teaching techniques for his university back home. Seemed like a nice guy."

"Can you describe him for me or tell me anything else about him? And if you happen to see him again would you point him out to me?"

"Sure. He looks just like any of a thousand other guys around here. He's medium height with black hair and he smiled a lot. Spoke perfect English, much less accent than most of the Chinese students around campus."

Summers saw his expression change to that of a dog being berated by his master.

"I hope I didn't mess anything up for you, Katie. I know you cautioned me not to say anything."

"It'll be all right, Dewey," she said, again trying to smile. "I just wanted to keep everything about my research quiet in case anybody else is working along the same lines. You know, all the glory goes to those who publish first. I wouldn't mind meeting this man sometime. Did he say anything else?"

"No, we only spoke for a minute."

"Have you ever seen him around here before today?"

"Umm…I think I saw him down in the atrium a few days ago."

"Dewey, this is important. If you see him again please don't tell him anything more about what I'm doing. If he shows up when I'm not here I want you to call me right away. Don't tell him you told me about any of this."

"You think he's some kind of spy or something?"

"That's exactly what I think, so if he approaches you again don't let on that I think that, you hear?"

"Gotcha. I can do that."

"Counting on you, my friend."

Summers stepped out of the office and hastily pulled out her cell to call Hickman. "I might have something on the person we're looking for." She proceeded to fill him in on her conversation with Jenkins and asked if he thought it might be the same person who'd placed bugs in the house.

"It's possible, but he could be just what he told Jenkins. Was Dewey able to give you a description?"

"Not a good one. He said he didn't get the guy's name but he'd point him out if he sees him again. He told Dewey that he and another man are here learning American teaching techniques to take back to their university in China. Is there some way we can check up on them?"

"I'm sure there is. I'll pass this on to the others right away and find out if the university has any record of them."

"Harry, call me back as soon as you know any more, will you?"

"Sure thing. See you later."

"Hey, people!" Hickman slapped his hand on the desk and called out to the others in the computer lab. "We may have a break here." He told them about what had just happened with Kate and her project.

"Do we know who he is?" asked Dalton.

"No, said he's here to learn about American teaching methods in universities. I'd like to see if there's anything on him in the university database but she doesn't have a name."

"Without a name or something else to go on that'll be difficult."

After considering the possible implications, Dalton said he and Harry would go over to the Professor's office and ask Mrs. Stoddard if she'd try to find out the man's name.

Professor Evans wasn't in the office but Mrs. Stoddard was there as usual. "Sam, you seem all worked up about something. Did you catch that spy so we can all get back to normal, or at least what passes for normal around here?"

"Haven't exactly caught anyone yet," Dalton admitted, "but we do have a lead. Harry, go ahead and fill Mrs. Stoddard in on the phone call."

Hickman quickly recapitulated Kate's call for her.

"Ahhh, I see. And now you came over here to see if I can find out anything about this person for you. I'll be happy to try but it might take a while. You may as well go back to the lab. I'll call you."

Later that afternoon she phoned Dalton. "Sam, I learned there are two men from China who registered with the university claiming to represent a company named Pan Asia Limited in Hong Kong who allegedly sent them here to study American teaching techniques. I looked up Pan Asia and learned they own Yokohama Industries in Japan, the outfit Takayama works for. Looks like you'd better be careful. I got their address here in Ames and phone numbers from the university's record system if that will help."

Dalton immediately assembled the group in the computer lab to digest this new information. O'Leary proceeded to pass out copies of the pictures that Mrs. Stoddard had faxed over.

"So how does this help us and what should we do about it?" Howland asked. "Do we complain to the university administration or to the police?"

"That's one approach," Hickman replied grimly. "These must be the ones who planted the bugs, but two can play this damn game. We now know where they live and I found out the apartment next to theirs is going to be vacant after the holidays. I think we should rent it and find a way to listen to their conversations. If they speak in Chinese I'm sure we can find someone to translate for us."

"What will that cost?" Howland asked.

Hernandez scowled and tugged on his ear. After a moment's reflection, he said, "The cost of renting the damn apartment is miniscule. I think Harry has the right idea."

Howland decided they should run it by Professor Evans first. In the meantime he said he'd ask Mrs. Stoddard to see what else she could find on Long and Chow.

As they broke up, Howland took Hickman and O'Leary aside to discuss some of the problems they were facing with the QD. The physical transfer of data between the Super G and the QD took place along many thick fiberoptic cables leading to the basement level, but the interface between the two machines was still a problem. The fundamental programming languages for the two computers were very different and they were still experimenting with the translator programs that were designed to allow them to work in harmony. This appeared simple on paper but was proving to be anything but. Howland had thought they were fairly close to having that particular item worked out and now knew that wasn't the case.

When they were finished, O'Leary returned to his desk and nursed a glass of iced tea while considering what else they might do about Long, Chow, and Takayama. He was beginning to think they should ask the FBI or some other agency to help. Maybe they could be declared persona non grata or something and kicked out of the country, but first they needed to be sure they had the right culprits. *Wonder if we asked for help how much we'd have to reveal and what McGregor would say. Cindy's a lawyer; she should know.*

Arlington, Virginia

Shortly before quitting time Willa Fisher punched the intercom line, "Jim, Danny on line two from Boston."

Dougherty picked up. "Danny, you find out anything new on that case at MIT?"

"Yes, but I had to agree what I tell you has to remain strictly within our shop. They have some kind of fancy new computer up here they're working on but wouldn't give me any details. That makes me wonder if it's anything like McGregor's machine. They're still in the design phase, haven't actually begun building it yet."

"Does it sound important enough that it might entice someone to try and steal the plans?"

"The people here think so. I spent the last couple of hours with Doctor Clifford Benjamin, the project director. I told him we had reason to suspect that Homer Spires, one of his techs, might be on the take. I emphasized that what we have on him so far is only circumstantial and based partly on that other case we're investigating. I also advised them to tighten security by changing the locks, restricting access to the lab, and installing more video cameras, but actually their security looks pretty damn good."

Dougherty thought Hurwitz was making at least some progress. "Butterfield tapped into Takayama's plane reservations and learned he's going to be in Boston tomorrow. She could come up and give you a hand."

"I was planning to fly back tonight but now I guess I'd better stay over and see what happens. I think your idea about having Celeste fly up is a good one."

"Okay. I'll tell her to ask Willa to make the arrangements."

Boston, Massachusetts

Hurwitz got the word the next morning that both Takayama and Celeste wouldn't arrive until late afternoon so he had a good part of the day to kill. He thought about driving the rental car, but after negotiating his way from the airport to the Le Meridien hotel in Cambridge he became convinced that all Boston drivers were maniacs. Instead, he took the T across the Charles River to the downtown crossing and then the green line out to the Boston Museum of Art on Huntington Avenue. He'd visited it with his parents many years before and was anxious to see it again.

The museum was all he remembered it to be and he particularly enjoyed the large Asian Gallery. Later he had a light lunch in the museum's New American Cafe. Rather than take the subway directly back to Cambridge Hurwitz chose to walk along the Fens then toward the Charles and down Newbury Street to the Boston Commons and on to the financial district finally ending up the infamous Durgin Park.

The waitresses really did seem to treat their customers like dirt, and the red and white-checkered tablecloths looked like they'd seen better days. "What do ya want?" she asked in a barely understandable South End twang without the hint of a smile.

Hurwitz stammered, "Strawberry shortcake and a Sam Adams, please."

"Bottle or draft?"

"Draft."

"Can't hear you, mister. Speak up."

"Draft," he mumbled louder. He turned his back and waited for Butterfield to call.

As he scraped the last morsel of dessert off the plate his cell phone chirped. Butterfield told him Takayama had reserved a room at the Four Seasons on Boylston Street across from the Public Garden and said to meet her there.

Hurwitz found her in the lobby across from a bank of elevators, one eye intermittently glancing at a newspaper and the other watching for Takayama. "Let me fill you in on what's going on," he said. "Our suspect at the MIT computer lab is Homer Spires, mid-thirties, single, high school educated, and self-taught in computers. He apparently thinks himself quite the computer whiz. His user name in some of the chat groups is 'keystroke'. No police record, but his name turned up on a list of hackers the Bureau started back in the nineties. We have a recent photo of him courtesy of the DMV. A credit check hasn't turned up any large debts or unusual spending habits."

"Did you give them Spires' name, Danny?"

"Yeah, Doctor Benjamin said they'd assign him somewhere else, keep him away from the touchy things. I told 'em we didn't have enough on the guy to do anything yet, and that he might lead us to bigger fish. They were okay with that."

"Good. I've brought along some equipment for long range listening and recording." Butterfield patted her briefcase. "It looks like a laptop but it's more than that, has a directional microphone and it's extremely sensitive."

"Nice. What else you got in there?"

"Besides my brass knuckles? I have a pen with pepper spray, a can of Mace, and my service revolver." She watched Hurwitz's expression change. "I'm just kidding, no brass knuckles. I did bring a couple of bugs we can plant that'll send signals to my laptop. I can also plug this into any phone, scrambled of course, and send the info back to the office."

Almost an hour had passed before an elevator door opened and Takayama stepped out. They watched him head to the opposite side of the lobby where he set down next a man with long hair pulled back in a pony-tail. Butterfield observed them with a small compact style mirror she was ostensibly using to powder her nose. A few moments later Takayama and the man entered the fairly crowded lounge off the lobby and found a table.

"That's Spires all right," Hurwitz whispered. "Let's go in and find a table but not too close to 'em."

Butterfield found a decent spot several tables away and ordered a Shirley Temple. Hurwitz asked for a cup of coffee. She slipped the laptop out of her briefcase and placed the mike on the table pointing it at Takayama. She punched a couple of keys and slipped a tiny piece of plastic in her ear, then handed a similar one to Hurwitz. Next she pulled a tiny camera from her purse and snapped off several images. In her earphone she heard Takayama ask, "So, how's the job going?"

"They just started me working on a new virtual reality system. You can be in this room they program with projections on all the walls that makes you think you're really in the middle of it. Hell, I've seen a lot of folks come out of there looking about ready to upchuck."

"Tell me about that computer project you mentioned in the email. Have you figured out what it's about?"

"Not exactly. During the short time I was in that lab I never learned what they were actually doing. It's been off limits to everybody except a few senior people but I did hear someone say it'll be months before whatever it is will be finished. I also got the idea they're worried because suddenly security got tighter with more guards and weekly badge changes. Whatever it is, nobody's talking."

"This is interesting," Hurwitz whispered. "He doesn't have a clue to what's going on there. I guess we can put Dr. Benjamin's mind at ease a little."

Butterfield frowned. "Don't tell him just yet, Danny," she whispered. "Better wait until we've finished the investigation."

"You're right. I guess there's no reason we have to say anything yet."

They watched as Takayama picked up the check and slipped an envelope to Spires.

"Celeste, did you get that?"

"I think so," she said, patting the small camera. "Guess we can call it a day. I've got the feeling Spires really didn't know much about the project and he's just shining Takayama on to keep his retainer coming."

Hurwitz laughed. "Serves the bastard right."

Arlington, Virginia

Dougherty, after speaking by phone with Butterfield and Hurwitz, called McGregor to discuss the similarities between the case in Boston and his project in Iowa. "I plan to send one of our agents to Ames after the holidays and offer our assistance like you suggested. She's a lawyer and her name is Celeste Butterfield."

"Can the local police handle this?" McGregor asked.

"We don't think so. This is an espionage case involving foreign nationals. Even if the cops arrest them their embassy would probably have them on the next plane back to China."

"Do you think that might happen even if you or I talk to the State Department and Homeland Security ahead of time?"

"Maybe, but we don't want to take that chance. Having somebody from our office on the scene gives us flexibility if anything goes wrong. What we hope for is to catch them doing something grossly illegal and nail 'em."

McGregor felt uncomfortable but allowed that the advice made sense and left it at that, at least for the time being.

Ames, Iowa

With the holidays coming up the students were excited about having time off to visit family. They still avoided talking about many things in the house because of the bugs. Instead they met once in Cindy's apartment and another evening at Yukiko's. The big news was that three couples had announced their engagements, all within the past week. Shelia thought it must be catching, and wondered if the same thing would happen to her when she visited her boyfriend on the east coast for Christmas.

Long and Chow, knowing they wouldn't make much progress with nearly everyone gone for more than a week, booked plane tickets to Las Vegas for a few days.

"I'll bet a hundred bucks I come out more ahead than you do."

"You don't stand a chance. Hell, you'll probably lose. Make it five hundred and you're on."

Chapter 10

Tokyo, Japan

Her father greeted them as they slipped off their shoes and shed their coats in the vestibule before stepping up into the apartment itself. Dan bowed and Doctor Kawakami grasped his hand. "We're delighted you could come, Dan. Our other children should be here shortly and my wife is preparing a special meal to welcome you and our daughter."

Yukiko soon stepped into the kitchen to help her mother who looked at her for a moment before asking with a shy smile, "Do you have anything special you'd like to tell me?"

Yukiko, quite sure what this was all about, smiled back. "We were planning to tell you at dinner but I guess I can't wait. Dan asked me to marry him, and I said yes. Please don't say anything until everyone's here though."

Her mother let out a little gasp and pulled a handkerchief from the sleeve of her yukata and dabbed her eyes then gave her daughter a hug. "Your father is so very impressed with Dan-san. I'm so happy I could cry." She buried her head against Yukiko's shoulder. "I love you, daughter," she whispered. "I'm certain you'll both be very happy together."

Her brother, Junichiro, and sister, Tamiko, arrived shortly thereafter and asked Yukiko how school was going and how she liked living in the States.

"It's a lot of hard work and late nights, but I'm enjoying it very much. How about you two?"

Juichiro groused about the workload but said he'd done very well on his exams."

At the end of the meal Yukiko said she had news she wanted to share. She stood up and tip-toed over behind Dan and put her hands on his shoulders. "Dan has asked me to marry him and I accepted. We'd like to be married here in Tokyo."

Her mother was very glad to hear that and wondered if it would be at the local temple or at the embassy. She decided she'd be happy either way.

The next few days passed quickly. It was agreed upon that the couple would tie the knot the following summer and that there would be two ceremonies, one at a Buddhist temple and the other at a Catholic church. They also made plans for a short honeymoon but it was too early to decide on where yet.

The evening before they were due to fly back to the States Yukiko's whole family had dinner at the embassy with the ambassador and his wife and their daughter Liz. Everyone was delighted at the news and seemed to get on well together. No one seemed at all surprised.

After coffee and dessert, the women retreated to the kitchen. Dan followed his father into the study. "Yukiko is a lovely young woman, and we like her very much. I can't imagine a better match. We're sure you'll both be very happy together. Be sure to remember her birthday and your anniversaries. Little things like that are important." He grinned and added, "Your mother and I can hardly wait for some little Oldenbergs to come along."

La Jolla, California

Cindy's mother picked them up at the San Diego airport and fought the rush hour traffic on the I-5 north to La Jolla. On the way she asked how O'Leary's thesis project was coming along and if Cindy still liked her job with McGregor Industries. Then she asked if they had any news.

"We weren't going to tell you this until Dad was here, but I guess we can tell you now. We're engaged."

The next few days played out very similar to Dan's and Yukiko's visit to Japan. There was a party at the country club and lots of planning for the wedding. Her mother accompanied them to the Mary-Star-of-the-Sea church to meet Father Sanchez and pick out a date.

Mapleton, Iowa

Hickman chauffeured Kate to Mapleton in the red 550 Maranello 5.5 liter Ferrari that he drove only on special occasions. Her father was duly impressed and wanted to know how he could afford it. Kate had told him she wasn't sure but knew that he had patents on some computer software and had done some consulting.

After lunch Kate's father hinted, none too subtlety, that he'd really like a ride in the Ferrari.

"No problem," Harry said. "We can take a spin around town. You drive. You'll want to be careful when you step on the gas because it'll accelerate faster than anything you've even driven."

Upon reaching town they stopped to pick up a part for one of the tractors and were immediately surrounded by several people who asked about the car. A couple of them sat in it and wanted to know how fast it could go.

Harry smiled. "I've never actually put the pedal to the metal so I can't give you an honest answer. I understand it can probably hit one-fifty or so." He went on to answer a few more technical questions before they headed back to the farm.

On their way back Kate's father, probing a little, said, "I'm impressed with your knowledge about so many things, Harry. You're a little older than Kate, aren't you?"

"Only by two or three years. I enjoy going to school and learning things but in a year or so that'll come to an end and I'll actually have to go to work."

"Will you teach?"

"Maybe, but it's more likely I'll be primarily involved with research."

"Kate mentioned that your parents are deceased."

"They were killed in a traffic accident when I was twelve. An aunt took me in and finished raising me."

"I'm sorry. That must have been tough."

"It was." Harry shook his head but didn't elaborate further.

Hickman stayed on at the farm for two more days after Christmas but had to get back to work in the lab. Kate remained at home a couple of more days before going back to the grind.

Ames, Iowa

Takayama awoke when the flight attendant announced over the intercom for everyone to bring their seats to the upright position and prepare for landing. Once he'd retrieved his luggage and rented a car, one of his first calls was to Clyde Johnson. They agreed to meet for dinner that evening. Takayama had developed a guarded respect for this taciturn janitor who seemed more down to earth than most of the others he dealt with.

When Takayama got back to Ames he called Long but got no answer. He fixed a pot of tea and turned on the TV. *I wonder if they've made any progress on that computer or the girl's project.*

Clyde and Lucy were waiting for him at the China Moon. Clyde asked, "What have you been up to, Mr. T?"

"I just got in from Boston. We have a project going on with MIT and I have to keep up on how it's progressing. Sometimes I wish that the places I cover weren't so spread out. I must spend half my life on airplanes."

"I've only been in an airplane twice in my whole life," Lucy said. "You remember where we met first at the casino in Tama? You mentioned something about going out to Vegas. Well, I've been trying to talk Clyde here into going there for a real vacation instead of that Reservation place we always go," Clyde just tells me maybe someday, but I can't never pin him down." From the look on his face she could tell this irritated him.

"Never said I didn't want to go, Lucy. It's just hard to find time, that's all," grunted Johnson.

Takayama picked up a menu "If Clyde can find the time we could all fly out there."

Johnson only grunted and didn't comment.

The Moon's daily special had combos for two, three, or four people and wasn't particularly busy this evening. They ordered the combo for three with a side order of egg rolls and a pot of tea.

"Doesn't all the travel get to you, Mr. T?" Lucy asked.

"Ah, yes it does. Sometimes when I wake up I don't even remember where I am."

"How did you get started in this line of work?" Lucy persisted.

Takayama sighed and stared up at that ceiling for a moment. "That's a long story."

"You don't need to tell us if you don't want to," Johnson said.

"That's all right." He placed his hands on the table and stared at them for a few seconds before continuing. "In fact it might do me good. It was before I came to the States. We'd been married for almost three years and were very happy. My wife was pregnant with our first child."

He coughed and hesitated again before he could finally continue. "Unfortunately our son was born with a heart defect and he died shortly after birth."

Lucy reached over and put a hand on his arm. She thought he looked as if he might cry. "I'm sorry, Mr. T. It must have been real hard on you."

"But that wasn't the end of it." Takayama said when he finally looked up. He took a sip of water and blew his nose. "It was one of those freak things that you read about but nobody thinks will ever happen to them."

Johnson thought the words had seemed to catch in his throat and noticed his eyes were closed.

"A few days later, while she was still in the hospital, my wife's leg swelled up. It got huge almost overnight and had this ugly purplish-blue color. The doctor said it was a blood clot in her veins and started her on a medicine to thin her blood." He reached for his handkerchief and dabbed his eyes then took another sip of water. "Three days later she suddenly had terrible pain in her chest and said she couldn't breathe. The doctor told me that the clot in the swollen leg had broken loose and traveled to her lungs. They put her on a breathing machine right away but she died a few hours later. I became so depressed and I couldn't bring myself to return to work. My superior was helpful but finally suggested a job change might be beneficial. He sent me over here and I'm extremely grateful to him for that."

Johnson noticed how much Takayama's hands shook when he reached for the water again. "It's hard to lose someone you love,

Hiko," responded Johnson. "I know something about that myself. The first couple of years after my wife died were really hard."

"Next time instead of going out, Mr. T," Lucy said with a tear creeping down her cheek, "I'm going to have you over to my place and feed you some down-home Southern cooking." She knew Clyde believed Takayama to be a spy but to her he was just a man, and at least when he was with them, a very nice man.

They all picked at their food without saying much. At one point Lucy reached over and touched Takayama's hand.

Later, as they sipped tea, Johnson asked somewhat pointedly, "Does it ever get to you, the kind of work you do? There's so much information in print and on the Internet nowadays do you really need all this travel and being away from home?"

"It bothers me sometimes. Dealing with you is easy because we both know and respect there are lines we won't cross. Most people I meet aren't like that at all. Some have gambling debts or a grudge against their company or something that makes them a good target for someone like me seeking information."

Lucy noticed the faint smile, the first since he'd told them about his wife's death.

"Yes, there's free information available, and for every person like me companies have a dozen analysts back home keeping up on press releases and trade journals. They often come up with more useful information than those of us in the field, but you have to understand what's out there for free is what the companies want you to have. Besides, much of it is false."

Takayama took a deep breath. "You also need to understand that Japan's culture is different. I believe what I do is for the good of my country. We're a small nation in terms of land and natural resources so the only way we can keep up with the rest of the world is to stay a step ahead with technology. That's why I do what I do."

"I've read about the cultural differences. Is it true that the Japanese government sponsors some of that?" Johnson asked.

"To some extent. More often companies like mine cooperate with similar firms in other countries. Sometimes that bothers me a little. I feel comfortable in what I do for Japan but I don't feel good about it benefitting other countries, say like China."

Everyone was silent for a minute before Lucy finally said, "You must love your country to stay here in the United States for so long. Do you have any brothers or sisters?"

"No, only my parents."

"How long do you think you'll stay in America?' Johnson asked.

"I'm not sure."

They ordered more tea. Takayama seemed to have recovered, and the conversation took a lighter turn.

Ames, Iowa

Later that evening Takayama called Long and Chow and agreed to meet them at the IHOP for breakfast the next morning. As he scraped the snow off the windshield his thoughts turned to the previous evening's meal.

While he waited for Long and Chow to arrive, Takayama sat leaning forward with his elbows digging into his knees and chin in his hands. He'd revealed more about himself and his work to Johnson and Lucy than to all of his other contacts combined and wondered if he really should have done that.

The two Chinese came in a few minutes later and each ordered pancakes with bacon and eggs. Takayama settled for orange juice, a bran muffin, and tea.

"Any progress the past week?" Takayama inquired.

"A little, but so far no breakthroughs. You have any luck in Boston?"

"Not much. So tell me what you have learned since the last time I was here."

"Well, we confirmed the Summers girl was working on a gene research project. We know she has help from a couple of other departments and we have names of some the people she's working with."

"What about the computer project?"

"Nothing significant," Long said. "We listen to the tapes every night but they don't seem to talk much about their work. They do occasionally mention little things in passing, but never anything new or helpful. I think that's strange and it makes me wonder if they found the bugs."

"If they did, why would they leave them there?"

"No idea. Did your man in the Bay Area have anything of interest?"

"He says the principals on the project there are pissed they weren't invited out here to help set up the computer. I've been following a project at MIT and wonder if it might be similar to what's going on here. They're both about computers and well-guarded."

"So, any chance of your friend Johnson helping?"

"I doubt it. He's not the kind to lean hard on anyone."

"Any ideas from your analysts back home?"

"Nothing useful at all. How about from your people in China?"

"They're always pumping us for results but the minute we ask for help the bastards come up empty. We've talked about some other approaches we might try," Chow said.

Takayama raised an eyebrow. "Oh?"

"We could search the student's house again. We've also thought about trying to break into the main computer lab but that would be much more risky and we'd need clearance from home for that."

Takayama shook his head. "That would have to be a last resort. Did you order any more long-range listening equipment?"

"Yeah, should arrive any day now," Long said. "I wonder if they know about us and they don't want us to know they know. We better not sell these people short. I mean this is the toughest assignment we've had in a while."

Chow announced that he had an idea. "They've got key pads by the doors of the new building. If we placed a video camera somewhere we might be able to see what numbers somebody punches in. There's a janitor and a guard there in the evening but I don't know if they stay there all night or not."

"Good thinking, Norm." Takayama was getting used to calling his confederates by their American pseudonyms. "Have either of you tried to establish a presence in the main computer engineering building itself, like sitting in on a class or getting acquainted with a few students to see if you can pick up anything?"

"I've been there twice this week and I was impressed watching them tape some extension classes," Long replied. "I do think that approach might be useful back home."

"Get to know a couple of the instructors and maybe you can pick up something about the new building," Takayama added.

Ames, Iowa

On the drive back to Ames, Hickman thought about ways they might induce Takayama and the two Chinese into doing something clearly illegal and catch them in the act. He spoke with O'Leary about it the following morning and asked him to talk to Cindy about having everyone over to her apartment to talk over some ideas.

Several days later they met at Cindy's place for supper and to make plans.

Hickman explained that he'd learned where Long and Chow lived, and that the apartment next to theirs was vacant. "I spoke with the people in the lab about a way we can learn more about these guys. Howland gave us the go-ahead to rent the place and said the expenses can come out of the lab's budget. Brian and I want to plant a bug their apartment to find out what they're really up to. All we need now is somebody they don't know to actually rent the place."

Yukiko glanced over at Oldenberg and then turned to Hickman. "Since they're unlikely to recognize me, I should probably be the one."

"Wait a minute, Yukiko," Oldenberg objected. "If somehow they found out what we're doing things might get dicey. I don't want you getting hurt."

"I don't think there'd be much risk and I'd hardly ever be there anyway. You've all been so nice that I feel I really should help out."

The group talked over the risks and ultimately decided to go ahead with the plan and that Yukiko would indeed be the logical choice.

"Brian and I will get the necessary equipment, install it for you, and teach you how use it," Hickman said. "We must assume they know Dan, so any time he goes over there you'll need to be sure our friends aren't home. And Brian, don't you dare park that old wreck of yours anywhere the apartment."

The following day Yukiko signed a rental agreement on the sparsely furnished apartment until the end of the June. The following day O'Leary, Oldenberg, and Hickman helped her move in and began setting up the listening gear after Yukiko had called to let them know her new neighbors had just driven off.

Sheila had talked her advisor into letting her borrow an old Olympus endoscopy unit from the veterinary clinic which she brought over. She showed them how to set it up and hook it a video recorder. "Where will you put it?" she asked.

Yukiko told her the apartments were mirror images of each other and looked over at Hickman. "What do you think, Harry?"

He walked around studying the furniture arrangement and then measured the length and width of the living room before making some calculations in his head. "What's your guess, will it be set up like this one?"

"I don't think any other configuration would work," Kate said after looking around for a minute.

Harry slid the couch a couple of feet closer to the window and crouched down to tap on the baseboard in a few places. Satisfied, he fixed a three-quarter inch hole-cutter to his drill and made a circular opening slightly above the floor and then extended it through into the adjacent unit. "We'll save these pieces so we can patch the holes later."

Sheila connected the camera and video recorder then threaded the scope into the next apartment using the two rotary controls to look into the next door apartment from different angles. "Nothing's in the way," she exclaimed. "TVs on the opposite side, edge of the sofa blocks out about half the room. No pictures on the wall, only a couple of Playboy centerfolds. C'mon over here, Yukiko, and let me show you how to use this thing."

After everyone had taken a quick peek Hickman examined the floor just below the hole. Fortunately there was only a trace of sawdust from the drilling. He jury-rigged a short piece of flexible tubing to the vacuum cleaner and used this to clean it up. He next drilled smaller holes to position a small microphone flush with the baseboard just behind the sofa and showed her how to turn on the devices "One of us will have to review the tapes on a daily basis."

Finally he handed Yukiko a panic button device that would call his and Oldenberg's cell phones if there was any problem.

Ames, Iowa

Takayama slipped off his shoes and made a slight bow as he entered their apartment.

Long smiled at the Japanese custom. "We were busy today and haven't had time to fix anything for dinner," he told Takayama. "We called out for a pizza if that's all right with you."

"I already have plans," Takayama mumbled, although he really didn't have anything special on for the evening.

"We did bring up the possibility of trying a break-in and finally heard back from our office. Our boss didn't say yes or no, only that he'd leave it up to us," Chow groused.

Takayama shook his head. "I know, that happens to me sometimes too. There's an American saying for that sort of response. It's called covering your ass."

They spoke of other things they might try for a few more minutes and then the doorbell rang. "That must be your pizza, Takayama said. "I'd better be going."

Late that evening Yukiko listened to the tape for the first time. She wasn't sure whether they were talking about breaking into the farmhouse or the lab but thought it sounded more like the computer lab.

Ames, Iowa

Dougherty had told Butterfield it was time she made a trip to Ames to learn more about the problem there and also to keep McGregor happy. Her flight out of DC was delayed at O'Hare for weather and didn't touch down in Des Moines until six o'clock. To top it off the drive up to Ames took twice the normal thirty or forty minutes due to the storm. By the time she finally checked into the Gateway Hotel and Conference Center a mile southwest of the university it was nearly eight o'clock. She gave up all thoughts of driving around town and the campus to get a feel for the place. Instead, she settled for a dinner of Chicken Normandy and a glass of chardonnay in the hotel's restaurant.

The next morning, as arranged, she met with Professor Evans and presented her credentials. He called Howland and asked him to assemble the team in the conference room so that everyone could hear what she had to say.

Dressed in a blue business suit, Butterfield introduced herself and shook hands. She began by briefly explaining that she worked for an agency in DC that that looked into cases of possible industrial espionage and that McGregor had requested they investigate what was happening here in Ames. She also mentioned that a group at another university in Boston was having a similar problem with a computer project. "That's what prompted this visit to Ames. Can you fill me in on what's been going on here?"

Ewen Howland began by recounting how Johnson had first been approached by Takayama and played along at Professor Evans' request. He also told how Takayama had spoken with various other university people in several departments but thus far hadn't appeared to have broken any laws. He then asked Hickman to run over how they happened to find the bugs.

Hickman told her finding them was purely an accident and went on to say they'd decided to leave them in place.

Butterfield grimaced. *These people are sure taking a hell of a chance.* "I'm surprised, but I'm also impressed. You certainly had guts to leave those devices in place," she said after a moment's reflection. "What prompted you to do that? Did you think you might catch whoever placed them if and when they returned to retrieve them?"

O'Leary broke in. "That's what we were hoping for. Right after we found them we installed a good security system. We also checked for similar bugs in all the professor's homes and will continue to do so on a regular basis."

Hickman went on to tell her about Takayama's two associates and how they were asking a lot of questions about Kate's project as well as the one in the computer building. He spent the next half-hour updating Butterfield on everything they'd learned so far and responded to her many questions. When Howland asked about the project at MIT, she told them that unfortunately it was privileged information and regretted she wasn't at liberty to talk about it.

Butterfield pressed them for anything else they might know before asking them how they planned to handle the problem.

"You'll need to catch them doing something grossly illegal. How do you figure to make them tip their hand?"

"We don't know yet, but fortunately the apartment next to Long and Chow's place was vacant so we rented it," Hickman replied. "Brian and I installed both an audio and visual monitoring system in their apartment. One of us reviews the tapes every day. We hope that'll give us some idea about what to do next."

At first Butterfield seemed surprised, but when Hickman described the equipment they'd used and how they accomplished the installation she was even more impressed and asked to see the apartment and the devices.

Hickman handed her photos of Takayama, Long, and Chow. He also gave her a set of notes recapitulating everything they knew about the trio.

By the time the meeting drew to an end Butterfield allowed that she felt more comfortable about their plans to deal with the problem than she had earlier. She turned to Professor Evans with a smile. "Sir, I appreciate you and your staff taking the time to share this with me, and I do hope this all can be resolved quickly." Then she turned serious. "But each of you must understand that these men could be, nay probably are, dangerous. I certainly don't want see anyone get hurt so don't take any unnecessary chances. I take it you've talked with campus security and the city police about your concerns?"

"I've spoken with a detective on the Ames police force," Hickman said. "I've known him for a few years and he's looking into it. He said we can count on him for backup."

After a little more give and take Butterfield announced she was supposed to return to DC the following day. "If you need me for anything I can be back here in a few hours. My boss has been in touch with Doctor McGregor. They're both very anxious to see this problem handled expediently."

The next morning the sun was out and by nine it had warmed up to the mid-twenties. Butterfield, now dressed like a student complete with a backpack and hat bearing the university logo, spent a couple of hours following Long, first to the microfabrication lab and later the physics building before checking out of her hotel. At eleven she headed back to the airport.

After wolfing down a sandwich and a coke while waiting for her flight, she pulled out her cell phone and hit the autodial for Dougherty. "The meeting with Professor Evans and his staff went well. They've been good about taking appropriate security measures. I tailed the one who calls himself Sam Long for a short time this morning but didn't notice anything suspicious. Did you get a chance to look at the pictures I e-mailed?"

Dougherty told her the staff had viewed them at the morning meeting. "We're sending the names and photos to Interpol and the other agencies asking for any information they have on these people."

Butterfield continued, telling him how the students had bugged the apartment the two Chinese men were renting and how Hickman had shown her around, recounting much of what she'd learned about the situation.

"This sounds hot, like things are coming to a head. You think you should stay out there for a while?" Dougherty asked.

"I don't see any reason to. They said they'd let me know if anything new came up. I told them I'd be perfectly willing to fly back out here at any time if they feel I might be of help."

Ames, Iowa

Hickman decided it was time for the group to meet to finally formulate a plan about how best to deal with Long and Chow. Cindy again volunteered her apartment for the occasion.

"Nice place you've got here, Cindy," Detective Bricker said. "Thanks for inviting me to join you."

"We're glad you came," Hickman said. "Brian and I talked it over earlier and figure we need to catch them doing something illegal like Butterfield said, but we already knew that. Brian had the idea of using a birthday party for Kate as bait. We'll talk about it some at the house and let on that we'll all be there. Kate can let it drop that she's doing some work on her thesis project at home in hopes they'll come looking..."

Bricker finished the sentence for him. "And they'll go to the house and snoop around while this party's going on and you'll catch them in the act. It's a long shot but it might work. It wouldn't hurt to try anyway, and you may get lucky."

"Right," Hickman replied with a tight smile. "Kate will let on that she doesn't dare leave things in her office anymore and mention a couple of places she might use to hide her papers. She really is afraid to leave them overnight in her office so she's keeping anything sensitive in the computer lab for the time being. I bring 'em over to her every morning. Mostly she does her work in the library now rather than her office."

"I'm thinking of using either the garage or one of the sheds unless someone has a better idea," Kate added.

Sheila had another idea. "How about inviting Jenkins to your place for dinner and have him mention something about you working on the thesis at the house because you're afraid to leave your stuff lying around that miserable little office you two share? That ought to whet their interest."

O'Leary said he thought that it would be better to keep Jenkins out of it. "When do we do it, the birthday dinner," he asked.

"How about the last weekend of the month? That gives us a week and a half to get ready," Yukiko said.

Sheila offered to make a reservation at the China Moon for that Saturday night.

"I think there's a good chance they'll take the bait and be at the Moon that evening to make sure we're all there," Hickman said. "Everyone will need to have their cell phones so we can communicate." He pointed at Bricker. "Don, can you position yourself out behind the house and call me right away if and when they show up out there. We'll leave one light on inside the house to make them think a bit before they try to get in. Brian and I will put back the old locks temporarily because they're easier to pick."

"Good idea," Bricker said. "It'll take you what, ten or fifteen minutes to get there?"

"Less than ten," Hickman replied.

"If they do show up at the Moon call me as soon as they leave. I'll have back-up ready to descend on the place as soon as we see 'em getting set to leave."

"Thanks. I also called Butterfield and she said she wants to be here. I told her it's on for the evening of the last Saturday in February, the twenty-sixth. She said she'd reserve a room at the Gateway Hotel again and would like to meet with all of us sometime on the twenty-fifth. I'll set that up and let you know the time and location. I also emailed her the address of the house and maps of the area so she can get an idea of the topography."

Ames, Iowa

Everyone grew increasingly anxious as the designated day grew closer. They all met at Cindy's apartment on Friday to go over the plan one last time. Kate had sketched out a rough map of the property and made copies for everyone.

Hickman began by introducing Butterfield to Bricker. "Detective Bricker will be watching the house while everyone else is partying at the Moon. He'll have two police units standing by out of sight but still fairly close by. He's brought along several pairs of night vision goggles. Dan and Brian and I will each have a pair."

Bricker passed out small police radios set to the C channel to each one and showed them how to use it. He pointed out where they'd station themselves when and if the time came. "We'll need to leave our cars far enough away that they won't see them or hear us. I put two blue marks on Kate's sketch to show each of you where you should park. Half of you will come in from the rear on the south side of the house and the rest from the rear on the north corner and wait behind that shed. Keep your cell phones on vibrate and no talking, nothing above a whisper, and even then use 'em only if absolutely necessary like if the radios don't work for some reason. Kate's false set of notes and her old laptop are in a trunk in the loft over the garage. The laptop contains nothing of consequence and requires a password. The folders hold a few old notes that she says are meaningless. My guess is they'll search the house first and when they don't find anything there we figure they'll try the other buildings.

We'll take them down when they come out of the garage. Any questions?"

"Do you think they'll be armed?" Butterfield asked.

"We don't know," Bricker replied, "but we should assume so. I'll have a weapon, of course, and so will Harry. He told me none of the rest of you carry but I hope things won't come to that."

"What happens after we catch them?" Sheila asked"

"I'll call in our backup when the time comes. They'll place them under arrest and transport them to the police station for booking. They'll be charged with breaking and entering and theft. What happens after that will be up to the DA. Hopefully they'll do time. At the minimum I'd guess they'd be deported and a formal note of protest sent to the Chinese authorities."

"What about Takayama? Has anyone seen him lately?" Yukiko asked.

No one recalled seeing him for a week or more.

Butterfield mentioned that her agency might be helpful at the federal level. "Every one of you should be sure to get a good night's sleep because tomorrow will likely be a very long day."

Chapter 11

Ames, Iowa

When Long had listened to the tapes, as one of them did each evening, he'd learned of the party. He and Chow made sure to arrive at the China Moon by five-thirty on Saturday, a good hour before the occupants of the farmhouse were due. They saw only one reserved sign placed on a large table in the back. "That's probably for them," he told Chow.

They found a table in the middle of the restaurant and each ordered a beer. A few minutes later Chow walked by the table with the sign and bent down as if he were tying his shoe. Instead, he taped a bug onto the undersurface and then rejoined Long to wait and see if Summers and O'Leary and the others showed up.

As planned, Hickman had also arrived early and spoken with Tommy Lee before stationing himself in the kitchen from where he had a view of most of the dining area. He figured they took the bait when he saw Chow go down on a knee next to the table Sheila had reserved and quickly snapped a photo of him in that position. He smiled as he called Bricker and told him it was game on.

The China Moon was hopping on this bitterly cold evening as it was still early in the semester and the students weren't feeling much pressure yet. Sheila and Kate were the first to arrive around six-fifteen followed by O'Leary and Cindy. Butterfield showed up a few minutes later. Soon everyone was talking simultaneously and sipping at their drinks, in this case sparkling water, while they waited for the food to arrive. Each was nevertheless acutely aware of the two Chinese men sitting not far away and seemingly not paying any attention to them.

At a moment when the noise level was even louder than usual, Oldenberg saw Long leaned over to Chow and point at Butterfield.

"I bet they're wondering who she is," he whispered to Hickman.

A half hour passed and Long and Chow showed no signs of leaving. O'Leary walked up to the bar and brought back a bottle of wine and a pitcher of beer. He whispered to Cindy, "Too bad this'll all go to waste if they take the bait."

Another few minutes passed and Hickman began to worry their targets may not have picked up on the hints they'd so carefully dropped after all. Ten minutes later they watched both men get up, pay their bill, and depart. As soon as he saw them leave, Hickman went out the back door and peeked around the corner. He spotted both men standing by their car smoking cigarettes, apparently watching the front entrance.

Another few minutes passed before he saw them get in their car and drive off. *Smart bastards. They're checking to be sure we're not following 'em.* Hickman called Bricker's cell phone again and told him the two targets had just left. "We're on our way, be there in ten." he said.

He hurried inside and used his handkerchief to pull the bug off the table leg and tucked it in a pocket. "

"They've gone. Let's move it everybody."

Hickman, O'Leary, and Oldenburg parked on a side road a quarter mile north and east of the property and walked the rest of the way. Hickman met up with Bricker in the clump of tress behind the garage. "You see 'em yet?" he asked.

"I saw a dark colored sedan drive by twice," Bricker whispered. "Maybe the light on in the house is spooking 'em. The others, they on their way?"

"They should be coming in from the back just about now. The ones on the south side are supposed to hold in the trees just over the fence until they're in the house."

Oldenberg positioned himself behind the shed he'd converted to a workout room. O'Leary waited behind the old hog barn that had seen better days and looked as if it was ready to fall apart. He reached in his coat pocket and pulled out a pair of hand-warmers which he slipped inside his gloves.

Kate and Sheila crossed through the field to the north and made their way behind the trees to the rear of the house. Celeste Butterfield along with Yukiko and Cindy came in from the south and held well back but still where they could see the rear of the house. Butterfield checked her weapon, blew on her hands, and quickly pulled her ski gloves back on before donning the pair of goggles that Bricker had loaned her.

Hickman saw a car stop on the road fifty yards or so past the driveway. When he saw its lights go out and he nudged Bricker. "That's probably our friends."

Bricker slipped his gloves off and shoved his hands in his jacket pockets. "Pretty dark out now, only a quarter-moon and a few clouds so that's in our favor," he replied. "You better move behind the garage to the east corner and hold there in case they approach that way."

A few minutes passed, and then they spotted two figures come into view at the head of the driveway. Hickman doubted that neither Oldenberg nor O'Leary could see them from their angles. He clicked his radio twice to alert the others and whispered, "They're in the driveway and approaching the house. Hold your positions."

Butterfield, dressed in dark ski pants and a camouflage jacket, had a good line of sight to the enclosed back porch. She could see both targets and watched one bend down and fiddle with the lock. A few seconds later she saw them go inside. She keyed the tiny microphone pinned to her collar and whispered, "They're both inside now." She turned to Cindy. "Is it always this freezing out here?" she whispered.

"This is nothing," Cindy mouthed back. "You should have been here a week ago."

Almost half an hour had passed before Butterfield spotted movement. She whispered into her mic, "They're coming out of the house now, heading toward the garage."

Bricker, crouching behind a barrel next to the garage with a fair view of the house and driveway, acknowledged. "Dan, move up behind the garage and join Harry. Brian, you move in and join me. Everyone else remain where you are for now."

Just as Long and Chow were about to enter the garage there was a sound. Bricker felt a tap on his shoulder that startled him. It was O'Leary.

"You hear that?" O'Leary whispered

"Yeah, sounded like someone coughed."

"Them or us?"

"Have to assume it's one of ours." Bricker drew his weapon and waited.

Cindy, trying desperately not to make any more noise, mumbled very softly in Celeste's ear, "Sorry."

Butterfield gave her a little smile and mouthed, "Don't worry; they probably didn't hear it."

Bricker saw that both suspects had come to an abrupt stop and appeared to listen for a few seconds. He worried they may have also heard it and decide to abort, but a few seconds later they moved toward the door on the right side that led both inside the garage and also to the stairs up to the loft. He pushed the button on his radio and whispered into the microphone, "Both targets are in the garage. Everyone move up a little but remain concealed until I tell you otherwise."

Shivering in the cold, Bricker waited as the minutes slowly ticked by. Finally he saw them exit and begin walking up the driveway. He pulled back behind the corner of the garage and dropped to a knee. The goggles gave him a pretty good view of Long who was glancing from side to side with Chow following a couple of steps behind him. He didn't think they'd spotted him. Bricker made three quick clicks with the button on his radio, the prearranged signal for everyone to move closer. He waited for a moment then stepped out from behind the garage and again crouched down, the .38 Police Special in his right hand. "Halt right there," he yelled. "Face down on the ground and hands out over your heads!"

Both men suddenly stopped abruptly. They appeared disoriented and apparently didn't spot Bricker right away or the weapon in his hand.

Long dropped the laptop and looked around frantically.

Bricker yelled again. "Police! On the ground now!" Then he saw Long start to reach in his coat pocket. Bricker fired a round into the ground. "Next one's for you! Flat on your face! Do it now!"

Long uttered something in Chinese as he dropped to his knees and then onto his stomach with his arms out in front of him.

Bricker tossed a pair of handcuffs to O'Leary. "I'll cover him. Stick his hands behind his back and put these on him."

Chow, seeing what was going on with Long, decided to make a run for it. He turned and began hurrying up the drive toward their car but slipped once or twice in the snow.

Oldenberg immediately took off after him. He'd nearly caught up near the head of the drive when Chow suddenly wheeled around and pulled out a knife. Oldenberg managed to stop just as Chow caught his balance and stepped toward him making stabbing motions.

Oldenberg jumped backwards, the blade missing by inches.

Chow made another lunge and stumbled.

As Chow tried to regain his balance Oldenberg kicked him hard in the right shoulder causing his assailant to drop the knife. He followed up with a vicious leg sweep to Chow's right knee and heard a snapping sound.

Chow fell clutching his leg and screamed something in Chinese.

Oldenberg picked up the knife and moved back a step or two.

Within seconds some of the others had caught up and surrounded them. Kate screamed, "Bastard! You finally got what you deserved you sorry piece of shit."

Seeing that Chow had been neutralized, Bricker called in their back-up. Soon two police cars raced into the driveway and the occupants jumped out with weapons drawn. Bricker held up a hand. "Everything's under control. The shot you heard was me firing a warning when it looked like he was reaching for something." He motioned toward Chow who was still on the ground and moaning. "That one pulled a knife on Oldenberg over there. Call in for an ambulance. Tell 'em the guy's leg may be busted." Then he nodded to one of the policemen and pointed at Long who was still prone and shivering in the snow. "That one needs to be searched for weapons Try his right jacket pocket first."

One of the cops knelt beside Long and began patting him down. "Found something," the officer said. A moment later he pulled out a pistol from Long's pocket. He wrapped the weapon with tissues and placed it in a plastic bag then affixed a tag with his name and the date and time. "You are now under arrest. Anything you say can and will be held against you." Then he read off the standard Miranda rights.

The officer who'd searched Long yanked him to his feet and herded him none too gently into the back seat of a police car. "Now we're gonna take you down to the station and book your sorry ass."

Once things settled down and both prisoners had been taken away everyone migrated into the kitchen to warm up. The officers began taking statements and instructed each of the participants they'd need to report to the police station at nine a.m. the next morning to sign their statements and go through a more detailed questioning.

While this was going on a reporter from the *Ames Tribune,* tipped off by one of the officers, showed up looking to interview anyone he could buttonhole. Bricker sighed and introduced him to Hickman. He requested that he leave the others alone at least until tomorrow.

"I'm Jerry Crawford with the *Tribune,*" the man said to Hickman, holding out his hand. "It's noisy in here. You think there's some place we can talk?"

Hickman nodded. He grabbed two cups of coffee, handed one to the reporter, and led him upstairs to Kate's room. "I'll give you a quick summary about what happened here tonight. You can come by the station tomorrow if you have more questions and maybe you can ask Detective Bricker if he'd like to add anything."

By the time Hickman was finished with the reporter Kate had simmered down. He pulled her aside and gave her a big hug and a kiss. "I've seen you pissed off before, sweetie-pie," he whispered in her ear, "but I've hardly ever heard you use language quite like that. You sure gave it to 'em. I'm really proud of you."

She planted a kiss on his lips and laughed. "I guess I blew my stack, huh? I'm proud of you too, honey. I wasn't sure they'd show up at all or that we'd catch 'em. The plan worked fine though. I'm glad I missed that part with the knife."

"Yeah, Dan and Brian and everybody came through fine. Guess all that Dan's taught us has paid off big time."

"Yeah, and for the second time," Kate added in a low voice.

Sheila made more coffee and brought cups over to the kitchen table where Cindy and Butterfield were sitting after most of the others had left. "Thanks for coming out and all your help, Celeste. You gave us a lot of good advice."

Butterfield smiled. "Thanks, but I didn't do all that much. Bricker is the one you should congratulate. He was the person who provided a lot of the gear and took charge. I hear you're finishing up in a few months and moving to the East Coast."

"That's right. My boyfriend is in grad school there."

"Are you two going to get married?"

"I'm pretty sure we will. It's been hard to make plans being so far apart these past years. How about you, are you married."

Butterfield smiled. "No, but I'm going with a fellow in the Navy. He's a pilot."

"'Where's he stationed?"

"Norfolk, but his ship recently deployed to the Med. He wants me to come over in the Spring when he gets leave."

Even though it was late, O'Leary took a moment to phone Sam Dalton to let him know what happened. Dalton promised he'd let the others know right away.

Chapter 12

Ames, Iowa

Despite the excitement of the previous evening and the late hour everyone showed up at the police station by nine the next morning. They all were interviewed for a second time but then had to wait until their statements were transcribed. Each was given a copy to review and sign and another for their own records. It was nearly noon before they were finished.

Crawford accompanied Butterfield and the students to the China Moon for lunch. He asked each to comment on the previous evening's raid. Yukiko admitted she'd been terrified something terrible might happen. Kate and Harry were exuberant about the way things turned out and relieved it was finally over.

"What about the third spy, Takayama?" Crawford asked.

It seemed strange but no one had an answer. "I haven't seen him around lately" O'Leary said. "Any of you seen him?"

"Not I," Kate said.

"Nor I," Sheila added.

It seemed no one had seen Takayama for at least a week or more.

"Don't know we missed that. I'll look up his recent travel records when I get back to the house," Hickman said. "We've been keeping close track of where he goes up until now."

Professor Evans called O'Leary and Hickman and asked them to stop by his home to give him a more detailed account of what happened the previous evening.

Butterfield arranged a conference call with Dougherty and Harrington to update them.

"How did it go?" Dougherty asked.

"Smooth up until the very end. Kate Summers hid a fake set of notes in the garage. When the two perps came out carrying some false folders and a laptop she'd placed in a trunk there, Bricker, the police detective who was with us and ran the operation, confronted them and ordered them to surrender. The one calling himself Long had a pistol. He started to reach for it but quickly thought the better of it when Bricker fired a warning shot."

Dougherty asked if there were any injuries.

"No, no one on our end got hurt. Chow, the other one, was carrying a knife and made a run for it. Oldenberg, who has a black belt in karate, had almost caught up with him when the guy turned and tried to stab him. Oldenberg took him down and got the knife away from him. The guy's knee got banged up pretty bad in the process, some ligament thing I was told. They took him away in an ambulance. You know, I was really impressed with the way these young people handled things."

"You're not that much older than they are, Celeste," Harrington chided.

Butterfield laughed. "Just seems that way sometimes."

Toward the end of the conversation Harrington questioned her about Takayama.

"Nobody here has seen him for two weeks or so. Hickman's checking travel records."

"Keep on it. We'll work on that end from here also. Shouldn't take long. When do you think you'll be back?"

"Probably Tuesday sometime."

Mashiko, Japan

Takayama had returned to Japan to bury his father who'd succumbed to a massive heart attack. He'd been busy trying to console his mother when he got the call from Matsuda-san.

"Takayama-san, I'm sorry to have to call you with more bad news. I just learned that those two men Chen sent to aid you were arrested." He went on to give Takayama the particulars. "Someone from the embassy called me and would like to speak with you. I think you should meet with him but do that here in the office. Don't go to the American Embassy under any circumstances. Obviously you cannot return to the United States so I will arrange a new position for you here. Again, I offer my condolences for the loss of your father. I hope your mother is taking it well."

It was almost more than he could bear. He felt crushed as thoughts of all the deaths, his child, his wife, and now his father flashed through his mind, and now this. It was some moments before he could force himself to reply. "Matsumoto-sama, thank you for all the kindness you have shown me and I am ashamed that I have failed you. I beg your forgiveness. Then he began to cry.

Ames, Iowa

Two days later Professor Evans hosted a party at Aunt Maude's for the participants. He made it a point to speak with each one individually and congratulate them.

Kate also made sure to thank everyone as she made the rounds with Hickman at her side while Hernandez sat down with Dan and Yukiko for a few minutes to get a first-hand account. "I'm sure I can speak for Ewen and Sam; we all believe you and the others did a great job and we're very proud of you." He stood up to shake Oldenberg's hand and gave Yukiko a hug.

O'Leary and Cindy huddled in the corner and talked about plans for the wedding.

Sheila, the only one whose beau was missing, felt a bit left out. She sat in a corner with Butterfield reminiscing. "Tomorrow we'll all have to go back to the grind, but this is a day I'll always remember."

Celeste smiled and patted her on the shoulder, "You and everyone else. If you're ever in Washington be sure to give me a ring. I'll take you to lunch and introduce you to the people I work with."

Sheila smiled, "And if you ever get up to Woods Hole Steve and I will invite you to go sailing with us, maybe out to Martha's Vineyard or Nantucket."

The End

www.ingramcontent.com/pod-product-compliance
Lightning Source LLC
Chambersburg PA
CBHW072051170626
46813CB00004B/1309